Let's Have
Coffee

Parul A. Mittal is the author of the national bestseller, *Heartbreaks & Dreams! The Girls @ IIT*. Her second book, *Arranged Love,* captured the hearts of Indian youth.

Born and brought up in Delhi, Parul did her schooling at Lady Irwin School, New Delhi, and Navrachna School, Baroda. She did her BTech in Electrical Engineering from IIT Delhi in 1995, followed by Masters in Computer Science from UMich, Ann Arbor. The author has worked for various corporates—Hughes, IBM Research, Nextag and Yatra—for over thirteen years. She co-founded an online parenting website called RivoKids. At present, Parul is running recreational Math camps for kids and trying to find her 'FLOW'.

She is married to Alok Mittal and has two amazing daughters, Smiti and Muskaan. Apart from reading and writing fiction, the author loves listening to old Hindi music, playing board games, painting, trekking, and lawn tennis. Parul is based in Gurugram and you can read more about her at www.parulmittal.com or join her Facebook fan page: www.facebook.com/parulmittalbooks or email her at parulmittal@gmail.com

Let's Have Coffee

PARUL A. MITTAL

RUPA

Published by
Rupa Publications India Pvt. Ltd 2017
7/16, Ansari Road, Daryaganj
New Delhi 110002

Sales centres:
Allahabad Bengaluru Chennai
Hyderabad Jaipur Kathmandu
Kolkata Mumbai

ISBN: 978-81-291-4866-7

First impression 2017

10 9 8 7 6 5 4 3 2 1

The moral right of the author has been asserted.

Printed at Repro Knowledgecast Limited, Thane

This book is dedicated to my teenage daughters,
Smiti and Muskaan, who mean the world to me.

Contents

Prologue

Hi, I am Meha. I am twenty-nine and weigh seventy-two kilos. I have recently won the award for the year's Best Wedding Planner. You may ask whether I am married or not. The answer is no, not yet. But I have a boyfriend, who is rather irresistible like this double-chocolate crème Frappuccino I am having at this moment.

If you are thinking that a single girl my weight ought to know better than to get carried away by the temptations of a calorie-loaded drink, then let me tell you something—I am a woman of this age and I don't worry that my boyfriend will stop loving me if I get any heavier. I exercise regularly, so that I don't crush the poor guy, as I prefer to be on the top. I won't deny that I used to be insecure once—about my looks, about not being as smart as my sister, and hell yes, even about why someone would love me. It has caused me a lot of grief and heartache. In fact, I was so consumed by my mind's chatter that not once but twice, I allowed love to slip away from me.

I was lost and confused. I was looking for a 'forever-wala' love, in a world where relationships can be as brief as the messages we send to each other on the inadequate devices—where we are spoiled for choices whether it's the screensaver on our phone or the flavours of condom—where we want our partner to look like a model from an advertisement—where everything we do is for short-term gains and instant gratification, without emotional connect or meaning—where we jump to quick assumptions driven by our insecurities that are built on the foundation of a desirable life sold to us—where reality and the virtual world are often confused—where quick fame and attraction often replace enduring appreciation and respect.

It's kind of befitting that in this fast-paced, inauthentic online world, it took me an online reality show to finally understand the true meaning of love and to get answers to some of the basic questions a girl asks herself, like I'm-still-trying-to-figure-out-this-whole-life. Beneath all this superficial flirting and drunken texts, what is love that all those movies and books talk about? How do you know when you have found it? Is a relationship nothing more than an intimate cup of coffee shared with an attractive stranger? People say that everything will be alright, but will it ever be? After all, life doesn't provide with an online exchange policy. You can't ask for a new one with different features or exchange a defective one. So how do you know life will work out for you? How do you know that you aren't one of those cheap Chinese toys? How do you know that you won't end up broken, even if you don't belong to one of those big, millionaire families? Life doesn't come with a manual. There is no repair shop, no way to order a new battery, no way to fix a broken screen. The question that I often ask to myself is how to get through all of this?

The Ex Connection

'Oh my God! Oh my God! A designer beach-wedding in Goa!'

Tanu Di's excitement spills over the phone and adds to my delight of sharing the good news with her.

'Finally, you get to rock Goa, huh?'

'I know! Unimaginable, right? Like a chocolate truffle cake with zero calories!'

'If it was Papa, he would have said, "*Goa choro, Har Ki Pauri chalte hain*",' Didi says and we both burst into laughter.

I often wanted to go to Goa, but Dad would always say, '*Paani mein jaana hai to Har Ki Pauri chalte hain.*' All our family vacations were to religious places. Hence, we used to end up at either Haridwar, which we had visited umpteen numbers of times, or at a beach in Odisha, near Jagannath Temple, or at a beach in Chennai, on the way to Meenakshi Temple—but never Goa. Dad only spent money on God.

Now, I have made it to Goa on my own and I am super thrilled. I look longingly at the ocean. I have been dying to go out and have some fun, but it's been so busy that I haven't even got a chance to dip my toes in the water. Some firang girls walk towards the golden sand from the hotel lawns in their sexy bikinis. I surely can't carry a bikini, but I do want to try out the new halter-neck top and beach shorts that I had bought online.

'I know it's a beach. But, please be careful. Don't go around exposing your boobs,' Didi warns me in her elder-sisterly voice, almost reading my mind. I don't know how she does this. That is read my mind. It got worse since she became a mother.

'There is a species called "sleazy men" that is widely found lurking on Indian beaches,' she says in a partly joking and partly warning tone.

'Didi, stop being a mom.'

I can hear three-year-old Rhea in the background, 'Mummy who are you talking to?'

'Okay, Rhea is here. I got to go. See you soon. Just be aware of your boobs,' she repeats as she disconnects the phone. But before she hangs up, I hear Rhea asking, 'Mummy, what are boobs?'

Perfect! Now Tanu Di will have to invent a story so that Rhea doesn't go around announcing, 'My masi has boobs,' to every person she meets in the park. I smile at the thought.

After disconnecting the call, I realize that I have been standing out in the sun for too long. I am feeling a bit dizzy and my throat is parched. I look around for a waiter to get me some water. Instead, I spot a creepy uncle, standing at a distance, staring wistfully at the bikini-clad girls on the beach. Ugh! Didi was right. I quickly pull my chunni over my breasts, and walk towards a shade. A waiter passes me, carrying six Sangria glasses. Topped with fresh orange slices, apple pieces and a lime slice on the rim, the cocktail looks divine. I know that I am not supposed to drink alcohol until the wedding, but I guess one glass of Sangria doesn't count.

As the cool, tingling taste of wine and fruit touches my

throat, I can feel happiness in the air. I love weddings. I have loved them ever since I was a little girl. I remember watching the baraat procession pass through the narrow lane, from the balcony of my two-room set house in south Delhi. The bridegroom is sitting like a king on a horse, grandly led by men in white and red uniform, playing popular, cheeky wedding songs on their golden trumpets. The bright lights and the general hubbub of the baraat added glitter to my plain 'school-home-playground-dinner-sleep' life. I knew that I wanted a huge wedding, since I was a ten year old. A wedding that is larger than life. A wedding like this—set in a luxurious hotel in Goa, on the sea-facing lawns. Truly, this is the way to get married.

My heart swells with pride as I look around the tastefully decorated venue. Fine cane chairs with white cushions are laid around circular tables, which are draped with lime-green linen. Vintage heart wreaths made with brown twigs and decorated with a delicate cluster of light pink roses and small white flowers hang behind every cane chair. The centrepiece of each table is a glass mason jar, holding a bouquet of pink roses. I, especially, love the freshly cut lime pieces that are used to fill the jars. They make me feel fresh and alive. I am sure that Deepak will love them.

I turn and steal a glance at Deepak's young, handsome face. In a pastel olive-green designer sherwani, he is talking to some relatives, a little distance away. My heart skips a beat as he catches me looking at him. He gives me a knowing smile. A smile that I had fallen in love with, on a bright Sunday morning, four years ago. My mind drifts back to the past.

It was a cool, crisp Sunday morning. Winter had just begun in Delhi and it was the perfect time to laze around and bask in the sun. I was sitting on a reclining cane chair, on the small balcony, deeply engrossed in a romantic novel. Deepak had entered the house, smartly dressed in foreign labels. He took out a pack of the finest chocolates and offered me some. On principle, I never refuse chocolates. On top of that, they looked divine. Without asking who he was, I took one, put it in my mouth and ate it a little quickly. He smiled and offered me another chocolate and I took it. It was sheer indulgence to eat a second piece of chocolate, when your weighing machine has been constantly complaining of an overload. In addition, it was totally criminal to gobble up an expensive chocolate, as if it was Dairy Milk. This time I was more patient and savoured it slowly. As the fine chocolate melted in my mouth filling my senses with its bittersweet taste, I closed my eyes and moaned in ecstasy. When I opened my eyes, I found him still standing there and smiling at me—a smile with which I instantly fell in love.

Deepak turned out to be the elder brother of my best friend's boyfriend. Freshly graduated from the University of Oxford, he had come to visit his brother, on whose balcony I was lounging. My childhood best friend, Anusha, and I both lived in the omnipresent, cream-coloured government flats near Sarojini Nagar market in Delhi. I was studying English Literature at Lady Shri Ram College and Anusha was studying Home Science at Kamala Nehru College. Her boyfriend was pursuing B.Com from a private coaching centre. He used to study with us at school. They had been in love ever since I learned to spell the word. He was from a rich, business family and lived in a beautiful, little house in Gulmohar Park, which we would visit quite often, especially during weekends. Since Anusha and I lived close by, our parents rarely questioned our absence from our flat. Anusha used to spend time with her boyfriend while I used to sit in his balcony, read a book and listen to the birds chirping on nearby trees. Also, there were occasional bribes from him to be mum about their secret affair—a romantic book, a movie ticket, or an imported, expensive pair of earrings. Of course, I used to tell my mother that the earrings were cheap, roadside purchases.

Deepak stayed with his brother for only a week. In that one week, he got to know me better than my Google search history. I told him things I hadn't told anyone else—like how I had broken up with my boyfriend because he had called me fat. Deepak helped me get over the heartbreak with his light banter and Oxford anecdotes. We discussed our favourite movies, our favourite books and our views on love, friendship and sex. He didn't try to flirt with me. Yet, I fell for him. I was merely eighteen. He was twenty-two. He had seemed to me like a handsome, rich graduate out of a romantic novel. Mature, aloof, and so much in control of his life.

After he left Delhi, we stayed in touch and after about three months, he came back especially to meet me. He took me out on a romantic, candlelit dinner at the Grand Hyatt. He told me that he really liked me but he had to go back to London to set up an extension of his family business. He said that he didn't know what his future held, so he didn't want to keep me hanging. I was touched by his honesty. He had flown to Delhi and had taken me to the new, exquisite five-star hotel, just to tell me that we should part ways. I had been more thrilled than hurt. I loved the attention and importance he was giving to our little, fleeting affair. We kissed passionately. I knew he was breaking up with me, but the setting was perfect and so was he.

I hadn't been in touch with him ever since. Imagine my surprise when last night I discovered that Deepak was the groom of this wedding. This was the first wedding I was planning while interning with the Dream Wedding Planners Inc. That too at the Grand Hyatt in Goa. I found this to be an amusing coincidence.

Wait a minute!

Did you think I was the one getting married?

Hello! My Dad does grow money plants, but only in our little veranda and not in a Swiss bank. Besides, I am only twenty-two.

Standing inside a quaint, romantic hut, decorated with green satin ribbons, brown vintage laces and bunches of fragrant flowers, I am feeling content that our décor experiment has turned out perfectly. Technically, I am just a trainee who is meant to execute designs created by the design head, but I am also exercising my creative talent by adding my own special touch.

'Whose idea was to put slices of lemon in the flower vases?' I get an SMS from my boss. I confess it's mine. She texts that the groom likes them. I am thrilled that my boss likes my innovative ideas. There is no need for my boss to know that I had insider information on what the groom may like. I just thank her.

I vaguely look at Deepak's direction and find him staring at me with a quizzical expression. As I didn't get a chance to talk to him, I have no idea whether he knows that I am present here as his wedding planner. When our eyes meet briefly, I vividly remember our parting kiss at the lobby of Grand Hyatt in Delhi. Perhaps, he too was thinking of that at the moment. He gives me that same old knowing smile. I sheepishly smile back and then look away. I have no feelings for him. No regrets either. Just happy memories of some beautiful moments spent together.

I look at the devastatingly beautiful, tall and slim bride

dressed in a light fuchsia lehenga with a deep-neck blouse. Her smile is so captivating that it is hard to look away. You know, how some people have this strong magnetic pull? Like Deepika Padukone. I am certain that every guy in this wedding is secretly ogling at her.

'Isn't she looking gorgeous?'

Lost in my own thoughts, I don't notice when this good-looking stranger comes and stands next to me. As he speaks to me, he is looking at the bride through the lens of his camera and clicking pictures. I assume that he is speaking to me, as there isn't anyone around, though he could be using hands-free and talking to someone on the phone. I can't see his face as it is hidden behind his camera. He is in the perfectly casual attire for a pre-wedding ceremony, at a private beach resort in Goa—khaki pants and a slim-fit, button-down, white, linen shirt with sleeves half-rolled up. I notice these things.

'Believe me, she looks even sexier in a bikini,' he says, somewhat smugly, still focused on the bride.

Sexier in a bikini! Wouldn't anyone with her kind of body... Wait a second! How does he know that and say it with such certainty? Did he see the bride in a bikini at the beach? Oops, I hope he doesn't go around zooming in on girls in bikinis through his lens. It would be such a waste of a handsome face. While he is glued to his camera, I tilt my head backward to get a better look of him. He doesn't look like the cheapo type. He seems like a professional photographer, just more elegantly dressed than the usual boy from a photo studio. Perhaps, the bride did a bikini photo shoot as part of her wedding album. Who knows what these rich designer types do? Alternatively, he may just have a good imagination. You've got to give a smart bloke like him the benefit of doubt.

Intrigued, I stare at him for a few minutes expecting some answers to pop up. He totally ignores me, as he adjusts his camera lens and clicks different shots. Since he seems disinterested in letting me know further juicy details, I conclude it to be none of my business about how this cool dude knows what the bride looks like in her smalls. If anyone is to worry about this, it should be Deepak. 'Who cares,' I shrug and head towards the grand ballroom, where the stage for the sangeet ceremony has to be set up for the evening.

A couple of hours later, I am totally exhausted but immensely satisfied with the results. The ballroom looks straight out of the set of a period movie. We have worked with a Bollywood theme. Brightly coloured georgette panels are hung from the ceiling along the periphery of the hall. At one side of the stage, a lavish two-seater swing made of Gujarati bronze and metal engraving hangs for the bride and groom. Although it was not in the design plan, but I have added a canopy of matching golden and bronze coloured fabric on the sides, to give them some privacy. My boss seems impressed by my work, so I think it's a good time to ask her for a favour.

'Sarika, can I please attend the sangeet ceremony?' I ask in my most pleasing voice.

She just shakes her head in negation, without even bothering to look up at me. 'Why don't you go around and explore Goa? You are free for the evening.'

'Please, pretty please. It's not every day that I can get to meet Ranbir Kapoor.' I plead her retreating back. I don't think that she even heard me. She is usually nice but can suddenly get all cranky and rude. Maybe it's because of PMS. I don't know. I mean, I like that she is strong and has a vision, but why is she such a stickler for rules?

Just then Didi messages me.

'WTF! Ranbir Kapoor is coming to the wedding? Get an autograph. No flirting. He is dating Katrina right now. Besides, I spotted him before you.'

I had told Didi that Ranbir was performing at the sangeet but I had forgotten to mention that it was a private, family only affair. It is okay. I tell myself. I will find a way to meet Ranbir and get his autograph.

'And hey! Do check out the Saturday night flea market, it's the best place to get junk jewellery.'

'How do I go anywhere? This grand resort is in the middle of nowhere.'

'My dear little sis, why did I teach you to ride a bike? Hire one. You can't go to Goa and not *go-aaut*.'

I laugh at her word play. She is my smart, brainy, IITian-sister Tanu. She always has answers to all my problems. Already, I am feeling confident. I will first somehow meet Ranbir and then will somehow go out on a bike. For now, I want to head to my room and soak myself in a relaxing, bubble bath.

I walk with a light step towards the lobby door, softly crooning the latest catchy chartbuster from Ranbir's movie *Ajab Prem Ki Ghazab Kahani.*

'Shining in the sand and sun like a pearl upon the ocean, come and feel me, oh feel me.'

My room is located outside the main hotel building, beyond the lawns. I barely step on the grass, when I accidentally bump into our crisp-linen-shirt photographer. Without prior warning, the wild-rose fragrance of his deodorant invades my entire being. You know how they say that each smell has an association with a memory in our mind. Magically, this wild-rose smell transports me back to my childhood. I am running around and playing 'catch' with Didi in the rose garden, near our house in Delhi. My parents are sitting on a bench, watching us and laughing. I am very happy. This is my favourite family outing. I smell the same rose fragrance. It is so refreshing. As I relive the snippets from my childhood days, I revive with vitality and joy.

'Sorry, I hope you are not hurt,' he apologizes and brings me back into the present. I realize that we are standing very close to each other, facing each other like two slices of a sandwich. I feel his hand lightly holding my waist to prevent me from falling back. I know I was singing 'come and feel me', but I wasn't literally asking someone to come and feel me. I look up to excuse myself from his grip and find his mischievous eyes smiling at me. Did he bump into me purposely? Is he trying to flirt with me? What kind of a guy wears a wild-rose deodorant? Was he gay? No way! If he would have been gay, he wouldn't have noticed the bride in a bikini.

'I am fine, thanks,' I say, a plastic smile plastered on my face. My peanut of a brain still confused with too many awkward questions popping up. Questions that I want to be answered without asking out aloud.

He gently lifts his hand from my waist and steps back, before extending that same hand to shake mine. 'Let me introduce myself. I am Samir and I am an amateur photographer.'

As he speaks, I can feel the warmth of his hand gingerly holding mine. Not sleazy. He smiles confidently while I stand captivated. I know my eyes are dilating and giving away my excitement. Oh God, no!

'Capturing beauty on camera is my passion and I am here to shoot the wedding,' he continues.

Wait! Am I dreaming or did he just give me a look that says he is interested, as he paused and then stressed on the word 'beauty'? I don't know what game he is playing at. Whatever it is, it is working like alcohol on me—boosting my confidence and lowering my inhibitions.

'I am Meha. Making dreams come true is my passion,' I pause for effect and taking pride in my work I say, 'I am in charge of the wedding decor here.'

He glances around to check the decorations in the lawn. I can tell by his raised eyebrows and approving nod that he is impressed by my work.

Then turning his attention back to me, he says, 'I am sorry if I scandalized you back there with my bikini confession.'

'You definitely got my attention!' I smile back, flushing a little as I visualize him clicking pictures of the bride in a bikini.

'Let me tell you a little secret,' he says, bending forward to literally whisper in my ear. 'Radhika, the bride, is my ex-girlfriend.'

Fuck. The hot and rich bride is his ex-girlfriend. I mean this guy is good but nothing compared to the bride. He is like Filmfare awards while she is like the Oscars. 'She is hot.' That is all I can bring myself to say.

'Yeah, she is amazing,' he admits with a sigh and then letting go of my hand, he steps back. Looking at the ocean, he adds, 'We dated for a while last year. She always thought that my pictures brought out the real woman in her. So she invited me to shoot her wedding.'

Boy! I try to read his face. What I see looks like a forlorn gaze. Maybe he is heartbroken. I was never that deeply involved with Deepak, but if Samir had been intimate with the bride, then who knows what he must be feeling right now. Although, going by his flirtatious smile, it's hard to believe that he is grieving.

'I am sorry that she is marrying someone else,' I try to

sympathize.

'No, you needn't be. Radhika and I, we were just…you know, like friends with benefits. It's no big deal.' He's rather nonchalant.

Seeing the confusion in my eyes, he explains that he and Radhika started out as friends. 'At some point, we both felt attracted to each other so we decided to have sex. But after that it got complicated because she had a thing going on with Deepak and I also had a thing or two running in parallel. So we decided to get back to being friends. Except it's never that simple, is it?'

'Friends with benefits' (FWB) isn't even an idea yet—the movie will not release for another two years. This is 2009. I do not belong to Tanu Didi's generation, who still think that the mere idea of pre-marital sex with your own fiancé is a taboo, but I have to admit that even I am a bit startled by this. Virginity is not a wedding gift anymore and I am up for beta testing in relationships, but parallel processing like this is a little forward for me.

He explains further. 'We've had that story for ages—Radha and Shyam—our very own FWBs icons of Hindu mythology.'

I stand there stunned, my mouth agape, wondering if Dad has ever thought like this about his Radha-Shyam.

'Did I shock you even more?' He asks relishing the WTF expression on my face.

I would be lying if I said no. I simply shut my open mouth.

'Shocking an intelligent girl is the best way to impress her.'

I think he is making a pass at me, yet there is something honest about him for which I can't tell him to shut up or get lost.

'Where do you get these ideas from?' I find my voice.

'Copyright Sam, 2009. Absolutely original. Hey, were you

and the groom also... I think I saw you two share an intimate "we-go-far-back-in-time" look.'

His remark throws me off guard. I didn't know anyone had seen me share a smile with Deepak. Not that it mattered.

'Deepak was my boyfriend. I mean ex-boyfriend. I mean we were not really a couple. It was just a very short-lived friendship.' I am trying to sound as casual as a girl can be, while talking about her affairs. 'Without any benefits!' I add, just to be absolutely clear. I deduce that one time doesn't really count, does it?

'What a coincidence! Isn't it amazing that we meet at our exes wedding like this? As if we were meant to meet each other—but we met the wrong people first! Would you care for some coffee or beer so we can further explore our connection?'

Okay. He is clearly flirting with me and I am enjoying it.

'Umm...I actually have to go.'

What? I am not playing hard to get. Remember, I have to take a bubble bath and get ready to meet Ranbir and after that rent a bike and go out.

'Really? Is someone waiting for you? Just to let you know, I am the most handsome bachelor at this wedding. You couldn't get better company.'

Okay. So he is clearly conceited, flirtatious and damn cute. I know I ought to go back to my own room, but it's not like Ranbir Kapoor is waiting in the bathtub for me. For me, this wedding is not a celebration but work. I don't know anyone here personally, except Deepak of course, but again this is not the best time to engage in casual talk with the groom. There are folks from work, but folks from work are...well... from work. In a nutshell, I am in Goa and craving for some fun company. Moreover, he is witty. Besides, it is bizarre that we are both 'exes' of the bride and the groom respectively.

Surely, that must mean something. Like a mathematics equation, $x + x$ is always equal to something.

Before I can accept his offer for coffee, he looks at his watch and suddenly remembers that he has to be somewhere else. 'Hey, Senorita! I would really like to spend more time with you, but Radhika is calling me. Duty calls. Catch you later.' He winks and goes away.

When opportunity knocks, answer the door. If you delay too much, it will go to the girl next door. This message has never hit me like this before. Feeling disappointed, I trudge back to my room. I guess I will have to settle for a chance sighting of Ranbir Kapoor.

Love Is Overrated

An hour later, clean and freshly scrubbed, I decide to wear my most expensive salwar kameez, which befits the occasion but is not very heavy. It is a look inspired from Sonam Kapoor in Delhi 6—short kurti, tight pyjama, an embroidered net dupatta coupled with a pair of dangling jhumkis. I was saving it for the wedding function that is on the next day, but I feel Ranbir deserves it. OK, a teeny-weeny part of me also wants to impress the studio boy, in case I meet him again.

I confidently walk up to the ballroom, as if I am a member of one of the families, except that there is a guard with a guest list at the entrance. I try to think of the names of women from the wedding family. I don't know any. I haven't been associated with this project for long. Should I use Anusha? She was in love with the younger brother of the groom. However, I don't even know if they are still together. Last year Anusha and her family suddenly vanished overnight like a beautiful dream, without giving an address or a number. In addition, I haven't even seen the younger brother at the wedding. Will the guard allow me if I tell him that I am the groom's ex-girlfriend? While I am debating on what approach I should use, a couple walks in wearing Tarun Tahiliani design. The guy just whispers his name to the guard and without even waiting to be verified, they stride in.

Their ease boosts my confidence. I decide to try my luck with probabilities. Now, I am not a huge fan of maths, but according to Didi there is a 99% chance that someone in a gathering has the same birthday as mine. So I think that there should be a decent chance of someone on guest list being named Meha. I say my name confidently at the entrance. Then we both go through the names on the guest list. I see an Isha Somani, a Sneha Kukreja, a Mrs Shakuntla Devi, a Mrs Punam Gupta and a hundred other names, but no fucking Meha. I can see Samir's name on the list too. I am so desperate and so very envious of all these names. Why couldn't my parents pick one of these names for me? How much can it hurt anyone here, if I get to see Ranbir Kapoor?

I am figuring what to tell the guard, who is giving me a look as if I am some *kamwali bai*, when Samir comes out from the ballroom. He seems pally with the guy. He conveys by the flick of his hand that I should be allowed inside. Feeling vindicated like Julia Roberts in *Pretty Woman*, I gather my respect, which has fallen around me like autumn leaves and proudly walk inside.

'Thanks.'

'Cool. I'll be with you in a minute. By the way, teal blue suits you.'

I can feel myself blushing, but he is gone before I can return the compliment.

I look around. The place looks like a designer showroom. I'm sure that even the undergarments of the guests are either Calvin Klein or Victoria's Secret. I feel out of place in my local, padded and underwired bra. Just when I am thinking I should probably head back, I notice Samir winking at me. He gestures me to stay still, then raises his camera and clicks. He smiles and signals a thumbs-up to say that the shot was good. I smile back. He then gets busy as the dance performances start. I love movie songs—so I am having fun watching the bride's and the groom's family and friends dance. Ranbir makes an appearance but his performance gets over faster than the free SMS packs. He's out of the ballroom before I can even think of a way to get an autograph. After Ranbir leaves, I look around for Samir.

I can see that Samir is having a gala time. He is surrounded by hot, pretty girls, all dressed in latest designer outfits. They all want to pose for him and then hang over his shoulder to see their shots in his camera. I suddenly don't feel so good and decide to leave.

I go and change into my Goa outfit—denim shorts and a Madhubani-painted holy-cow tee, which are far different from the expensive wedding clothes. As I walk to the beach, someone grabs my hand from behind. It's Samir.

'Senorita, I need you to come with me,' he says, looking straight into my eyes—his freshly shaven face inches above mine. I notice that he has showered and has also changed into casual shorts and tee.

'Aah! Sorry, but I am very busy,' I say dismissively, still a little irked that he didn't pay enough attention to me at the sangeet.

'Why don't you ask one of the chicks who were hovering around you, as if you are a Prada handbag on display?' I tease.

'Because none of them can ride a motorcycle,' he chuckles and hands me a helmet to wear. 'And as one of them dug the heel of her stilettos into my foot, in her excitement to get too close to me, now I need someone to give me a ride.'

I am thrilled when I realize that we are going somewhere on a rented bike. The receptionist had just told me that the hotel could only arrange for cabs, not rented bikes. A stroll on the beach had seemed like the last resort.

Wait, but how did Samir know that I love riding? I draw my eyebrows together and look sceptically at him.

'I FB-spied on you,' he admits with a cute, naughty, little-boy smile—picking up on exactly what I am thinking. 'I don't habitually stalk pretty girls on Facebook. I was just curious about you. The fact that you are a member of the Delhi Bike Riders was purely a chance discovery.'

I look at him. He is standing with his head down, as if he is in front of a teacher, owning up a prank. I can't stay angry with him if he's going to look so cute. Besides, he just called me a pretty girl. I didn't admit that I have also checked his profile on Facebook. I give a forgiving smile, and he promptly takes my hand in his and starts to run.

'The bike ride is just a pretext. Actually, you are being abducted for the night,' he says as we reach the parking, playfulness dancing in his eyes.

'Hmm…That should be fun,' I laugh, feeling light-hearted and happy.

One look at the bike and I can feel adrenaline coursing through my blood.

'Hurry! We are already late,' he says as he sits behind me.

I turn back and give him a don't-mess-with-the-driver look. A girl needs to get ready before she can ride. I remove the scarf from my neck and tie my hair in a low ponytail. I put on my helmet, and then quickly apply a fresh coat of lip gloss. With a last glance at myself in the side mirror, I am ready to hit the road. Except, I don't know where we are headed, which makes it even more adventurous and fun.

I love the feeling of freedom, whenever I start a bike and

press the accelerator. For me, riding is like being in a wind tunnel, with gushes of wind blowing on your face. Samir is navigating from a printed map. I can't believe my luck when half an hour later, we arrive at a bustling flea market in north Goa.

'How did you know that I wanted to come here?'

'You did?'

'Thank you so much for bringing me here'. I give him a friendly hug in excitement and get a fresh waft of his wild-rose scent.

'Actually you got us here, but I don't mind the thank you hug,' he chuckles.

We park the bike and walk to the marketplace. There is a group of people with cameras hanging down their necks. A young, bearded firang, who is sporting a *Hare Rama Hare Krishna* tee, is at the centre of the group giving instructions. Samir tells me that the man is Francisco, an award-winning travel photographer. He goes and joins the group. I figured that we are here for a walking photo tour of the marketplace. Francisco leads the tour through the flea market talking about the camera's capabilities and explaining techniques of capturing real people on the road. While the others are busy capturing the earthy chaos in their camera, I pick up a few inexpensive knick-knacks. The whole charm of the flea market is in the serendipitous discovery of random stuff and buying junk.

I notice Samir turning around now and then to see if I am fine. Sometimes, he is just clicking his camera in my direction. I am smiling, frowning and making faces. It's fun. Once the tour is over, we sit down at a bench and gorge on falafel sandwiches and cool lemonade. I browse through some of the pictures on his camera. I see one of mine. I am standing at the stall of the German jewellery seller. He has caught me unaware—trying on a pair of butterfly earrings. The shot is really nice. No kidding. My dark-brown eyes are sparkling with the desire to possess those earrings. The loose ends of my orange scarf are hanging on either side of my neck and are complementing my warm skin tone. He definitely knows how to make anyone look beautiful, without using an editing software.

It's about 10 at night. He asks me if I want to go back to the hotel. To be honest, I don't. But I don't know what he wants. Moreover, a girl can't be too available.

'Do you have work back at the hotel?' I ask playing the subtle card and trying to gauge his interest.

'Only a dozen girls are waiting to step on my toes,' he jokes.

'Then I would rather not get your feet injured anymore,' I say playfully.

He looks at me with a touch of amusement in his eyes. 'That's rather considerate of you Senorita. If you are not tired of driving, how about we go to a local shack by the beach?'

I really like the way he keeps calling me Senorita. He must be using this on every girl, but it still makes me feel special. I smile at him and get ready to drive. Our next halt is at the Andrews shack on the lively Baga beach. The peak tourist season is yet to start, but Samir tells me that Baga beach is always alive with music and action.

We sit down on one of the many plastic chairs and tables that are laid in front of the shack. He orders a couple of chilled beers and a plate of Manchurian-corn starter. I am rather tired after standing all day long. I sit back, put my legs up on a chair in the front and watch the vast, awe-inspiring ocean stretch out before us. Samir raises his camera every now and then to capture a bird in flight or click the kids making a sandcastle nearby. I am surprised at how comfortable I am in his presence.

In fact, I was shocked when I had seen his Facebook profile and discovered that he was an engineer. I am usually self-conscious around engineers. I once met an IITian boyfriend of my sister. He asked me the probability of picking a random person in a gathering and finding a girl who had casual sex before marriage. At first, I thought he was flirting with me, but then he started explaining it to me in Venn diagrams and probabilities. I had to literally excuse myself saying that I have to use the loo. It's not that I don't like maths. I actually used to love it during my school days. Just that I didn't want everyone to compare me with Didi and expect me to ace IIT. So, I pretended to hate it.

But Samir seems different. He has a calm aura around him. No pretence—not trying to prove that he was better than the other person. Just comfortable the way he is.

Curious to know more about him, I ask him what he does.

'I sell soaps,' he says and smiles. 'Olay—love the skin you're in.'

Wow. Really? I had assumed he'd be doing something more exciting.

'Is that fun?'

'Not sure about fun but it pays my bills. Did you know that P&G coined the term "soap opera" by being the first in the 1880s to run ads on TV for women?'

Soap opera sounds more interesting than soaps. 'Then why did you do engineering?' I ask without thinking—my curiosity getting the better of me.

I see a caught-you smile cross his lips. Oops! Now he knows that I have also checked his FB profile, but he doesn't pull my leg. I like it.

'You know our education system is like a factory producing soaps. All soaps have to smell the same. No soap can have its own special fragrance.'

I know what he means. Our society doesn't encourage uniqueness. I remember being forced to use my right hand instead of my left hand by my dogmatic aunt, whom I still dislike. I wonder if that aunt realizes that a left-handed misfit called Steve Jobs created the iPhone that she proudly flaunts.

'How come you didn't become a journalist after doing English Literature?'

For a minute, I am surprised how he knows what I studied. Hmm… Our common friend FB. I tell him that I found mainstream journalism too depressing—our daily reality is so much about rape and riots, while I would do anything to help change that reality, but for my own life, I would like to do something that is optimistic. I tried corporate events, but found it regimental. The grey in the logo can't be changed to any other shade of grey. No scope for creativity. Therefore, I landed up with a wedding-design firm. So far, I love it.

'Good for you. You can now experiment with different shades of grey.' He smiles and we both laugh.

For a few minutes, we just sip our beer and silently watch the world around us, like two old friends. I have barely known Samir for less than twenty-four hours, but I am beginning to feel like I have known him my entire life. My mind wanders off in all directions but comes back to one thing. How many girls has he hung out with like this before?

'Are you seeing someone?' I finally ask after two bottles of beer.

'Only you!' He says, looking into my eyes.

I blush at his flattering response.

'You? In love with anyone?'

I shake my head.

'See, this is where you are mistaken. Of course you are in love, at this moment, with me.'

'What do you mean?' I giggle.

'You know what, we overrate this love thing. We think love is a sort of bond that can never break,' he says. 'You know what I believe. I believe that each of the positive moments that we share with others is love.'

Ok, he is beginning to being philosophical, but I am listening.

'Like the common interest in photography that I shared with the photo tour group today. That was love. The pride for your work that you share with your team is love. The gratitude I feel for you for giving me a bike ride is love.'

I smile at this one.

'It is when you co-experience these tiny moments of positive emotions with someone and you feel connected to that person, that is love,' he concludes.

I am at a loss of words—although beaming with love. He has just described love so beautifully and yet so simply. He has told me that he loves me and yet he has told me he loves everyone else too. I want to ask him if he thinks that having sex with Radhika was love. I want to know how he will ever know whom to marry if he loves so many people. I want to ask him if he thinks kissing is love. I want to ask so many things, but as I am getting high, I keep my thoughts to myself.

We order some food and while we are eating, he calls for a cab. I insist that I can ride but he says that we can come back and pick up the bike later. I let him be in charge. Everything becomes a blur after that. We do some crazy things, but there is no touching, no intent to get to bed—only pure repartee, fun, and friendship. At some point, he drops me off in front of my room. I want him to stay but he says he has to go click some pictures. I think I curse Radhika and we both laugh. Then he leaves and I promptly doze off.

Coffee or Wine

The next morning, the buzz in my head could be because of a hangover, but I think a lot of it has to do with Samir. I want to call him but I don't even have his number. I get ready quickly and rush to the hotel lobby humming 'Tera hone laga hoon...' from the movie *Ajab Prem Ki Ghazab Kahani*. I don't know why I am humming this song. Maybe it was playing at the shack yesterday. I don't remember. I don't remember most of the things that happened after he started describing love. Fuck! I can't even recollect if we kissed. I don't think we did, but I am not absolutely sure.

I can't see him anywhere. Maybe he is still asleep. Should I go to his room? I don't even know his room number. Can I ask at the reception? I am trying to sort my own thoughts when I hear my boss, Sarika, call out from somewhere behind me.

'It's the big day today, Meha. I want you to do your best. Shall we go over the plans once more?' She has a brisk, business-like tone.

I finally wake up. Today is the wedding. Indeed a big day for us. A little disoriented, but definitely motivated to do my best, I follow my boss to a conference room where the rest of the team is already gathered.

In middle of the meeting, when we are deep in discussion, my phone beeps. I sneak a glance. It's a message from him. I can tell it is from him by the few words I can read 'Thanks for saving my...' I am desperate to read further, but Sarika is in the middle of giving us instructions. I somehow manage to check the message holding the phone with my left hand under the table.

'Thanks for saving my toes from the hot babes yesterday. I had a LOVE-ly time ;)'

My heart begins to beat very fast. I wonder what the wink and that LOVE in capitals mean. I can barely hear Sarika anymore. She is talking about someone adding blackberries in champagne glasses last night. I vaguely hear that it's a good idea but we need to stick to the original plans and not to innovate on the spot. Wedding planning is as much about creativity as it is about following processes.

'Meha.'

I hear my name being called.

'Yes, Sarika.'

'If you have any ideas then please share with me.'

'Sarika, I was thinking we should shift the pheras from the mandap on the beach to a cemented patio. Sand can be a bit annoying in sarees and high heels.'

She glares at me as if I have suggested shifting the venue to the moon.

I realize that by 'share with me', she didn't mean to say share with her right now. What she meant is to inform her before implementing any changes. Too late! I have already told the chefs to add rose petals to the green ice candy to match the lunch theme, which is green and pink. Big deal. No one will notice.

Thankfully, she ends the meeting soon and I am free. I go

back to the hotel lobby but still can't spot Samir anywhere. At least I have his number now. What should I message him? I can't ask him if we kissed because if we didn't, he will think I want to kiss him and if we did, he will think how stupid I am that I can't even remember kissing him.

'Where are you?' I keep it plain and simple.

'In my room. Just woke up.'

Wow, he just woke up and the first thing he did is to message me. It feels good to know that I am on his mind.

'What's the plan for today?' I message back.

'Love, sex and dhoka!'

'???'

'I am doing a photo story on Deepak and Radhika's affair :)'

'Good title. See you around.' I slide the phone back in my sling bag.

Half an hour later, it beeps again. I am sitting on a sofa in the lobby. Mansi, the associate production manager, is discussing alternatives to the Banarasi border drapes for the backdrop of varmala. Apparently, the truck carrying the drapes met with an accident and we need to redesign.

I excuse myself to read the message.

'You should leave your hair open more often. You look nice.' It's him.

'How do you know?'

'I am standing on the balcony above the stairs.'

I look up, smile and wave at him. He waves back.

Mansi is surprised that I know anyone else here. I like Mansi. She is friendly and open to suggestions. She also has a perfect figure to carry an off-shoulder, body-hugging dress. I tell her that I met this guy yesterday, at the wedding. She gives me an understanding smile.

There is another message from him a few minutes later.

'I just realized who you look like. Drew Barrymore, except prettier.'

My heart stops beating. I look up, but he is gone. I reread his message multiple times. Every time I read it, I find it even lovelier than the last time.

'Flirting is just foreplay to get a girl into bed. Women need a reason to have sex, men just need a place,' warns Mansi. 'Take my advice, get a dildo.' I simply smile. I like to be serious about my relationships. But to write a story, you have to start with a chapter first.

The whole morning passes in a blur. Both Samir and I have been very busy, but we have been texting each other. The decorations of the lunch hall are done. Mansi and I are now sitting with Sarika, going over the revised plans for the backdrop of the varmala. She is still furious. Even if that poor truck driver escaped alive from the accident, by now he must have died from her curses.

My phone beeps yet again. Surprised at the number of messages I am getting today, Sarika asks me if it is my birthday or something. I tell her it's my sister at a shopping mall asking for advice. Mansi knows I am lying but Sarika seems to understand. I guess there are some advantages of having a female boss.

I read the message as soon as Sarika is not looking at my phone over my shoulder.

'Do you like the Sunday crossword?'

'It's my favourite pastime.'

'Solve this: Midday meal (5).'

It's too simple. I immediately type back 'LUNCH'.

'Something unexpected (8).'

Again an easy one. I type back 'SURPRISE'.

'You are good at this. How about this: Dried-petal mixture (9).'

This is taking me a while, but finally I am able to decode the clue. After two minutes, I type back 'POTPOURRI'.

'You are amazing. You deserve a prize. Go get your SURPRISE from the POTPOURRI in the LUNCH hall.'

I am lost at this one. This doesn't make any sense. But a bunch of hungry frogs have been triggered at the mention of the word 'lunch'. Since we can't eat before the guests, I decide to take a quick bite of the desserts for the time being. I also want to see how the rose petals are looking in the green popsicles. The hall is relatively empty now, but the food is laid out. I head straight to the dessert counter. The pink petals in green ice are looking unique and rather beautiful beside the pink *chamcham* and green *pista burfi*. Next to the desserts is a beautiful array of vases with green and pink potpourri. My brain begins to work and I figure out the last clue. It's obvious once you know the answer. I had arranged these potpourri vases myself a while ago, but I didn't link them to Samir's clue. I examine the vases carefully and see a small pink, cloth bag in one of them. I carefully take it out and open it. Inside the little pink bag is the pair of vintage wire butterfly earrings that I had tried at the German stall yesterday and then left as they were beyond my budget. There is a small note with it. It says, 'Love is like a butterfly. The butterfly counts not months but moments, and has time enough.'

How beautiful. I feel a bit gooey inside. It's like the fluttering of butterfly wings just before a flight. A flight to an unknown place. I try calling Samir but his number is busy. I don't want to send a simple thank you message. I want it to be more personal. I send him a message, 'Call when free'.

It's around 5 p.m. I am setting the mandap for pheras on the sand. It's very stressful. Nothing is going as per the plan; loose sand is hurting my feet, and Sarika is calling after every ten minutes for updates. I haven't heard from Samir since lunch and though I have been busy, I am feeling a bit ignored. I want to thank him for the earrings which I have promptly worn. I am about to check my phone again, when I hear Samir's deep laughter coming from somewhere behind me. I turn around and there he is with his back towards me—clicking pictures of the bride and her friends. I can see them trying to compete with each other to catch Samir's attention. I turn away and focus on the bamboo pole, which is refusing to stay straight.

A minute later, my phone beeps.

'Do you think the blue bikini wants to have sex with me?'

'Why are you asking me? Ask her!' Of course, I am irritated. He sends such loving messages and a most romantic surprise gift in the morning. Then he doesn't text for three hours and now this?

'C'mon, you are a girl. You know how girls think. Won't you help a friend?'

'Ask Radhika. Blue-bikini is her friend after all. Surely she will help.'

I then see blue-bikini walk up to Samir and whisper something in his ears. Something bubbles inside me like molten, red lava.

'I think she wants to eat your ear lobes.' I type on my phone. If only there was a way to bite through a message, I would have bitten him myself.

'Ouch. That hurt!'

'What?' I gesture with my hands, wondering if she actually bit him.

'The arrow you just shot with your eyes. It pierced straight through my heart.'

'Serves you right.' I message back and pretend to get busy.

'Are you trying to do a pole dance for me?' I hear him speak softly. I realize that he is standing very close to me. The girls seemed to have finally gone inside to get ready for the wedding.

I give him an angry stare and leave the bamboo pole I am trying to stabilize. It falls straight on him.

'What is my crime, Senorita?' He asks, ducking just in time to save his head.

Senorita softens me a little, but how dare he ask me if another girl wants to have sex with him.

'How can I help it if girls think I am honey and flock to me like bees?' He is now looking straight into my eyes.

I see that he has managed to dig the pole deep enough in the sand so that it can stand on its own. Looking at him, I can somehow tell that he was just pulling my leg—that the blue-bikini meant nothing.

'Are you always this obnoxious?' I ask him cynically.

'Only on weekends when I am flirting with a beautiful girl outside office. Weekdays I stay within official limits.'

I don't know what he does or how he does it, but he has done it again. He just makes me feel special in his own funny way. I can't help but smile. Besides, he has managed to fix all the bamboo poles for me. So I am feeling relaxed.

'So, do you like them?' He asks looking at the butterflies on my ears.

'Blew me away!' I admit.

'Well, I am Samir—the wind. You are Meha—the clouds. It is in my nature to blow you away.'

Gosh! He is truly full of himself with his nose in the air (just like his name), but I like the way he has connected our names.

'By the way, when are you decorating the honeymoon suite?' He asks.

'Why? You want to go there with that blue-bikini?' I snap immediately.

'*Arey baba nahin. Photoshoot karna hai.* How about you take me to the honeymoon suite later?'

I feel a fluttering in my stomach again. It's no big deal, I assure myself. 'Okay. See you at 11 p.m. in the lobby,' I say.

He gives me a friendly peck on the cheek and then dashes off inside.

It's almost 11 p.m. Thankfully, the work is all done. Everyone, including the boss is busy getting drunk at the bar. I meet Samir in the lobby. I am wearing a turquoise-blue, georgette saree with a halter-neck blouse. He is in a maroon, khadi-silk kurta from FabIndia with denim jeans. We smile at each other and then take the elevator up to the honeymoon suite on the fifth floor. I unlock the door and walk inside. Its dark, but I can smell the light fragrance of jasmine. As my eyes adjust, I can see the four-poster decorated with strings of jasmine flower. On the pillows, there are hearts made with red, rose petals. It had looked beautiful during the day, but it looks ethereal in moonlight. I walk over to the window. I can see the crescent moon through it. As I open it, cool breeze gushes in. I can feel a tingling sensation on the soft, naked skin of my hands. It's not just the wind. It's him. I see Samir watch me intently from across the room. He walks across with a steady stride, his eyes glued to mine. I can hear my heartbeat loud and clear, like the drums at the party downstairs. I feel strangely drawn to him, both physically and emotionally. There is a strong connection; a chemistry—the only subject that I could never understand.

He is now standing very close to me. A lock of my hair is flapping against my cheek in the wind. I feel his fingers graze my lips, gingerly move across my cheek and tuck the lock behind my ear. He pauses to admire the butterfly-earrings dangling down my neck, while caressing my soft skin. The wind throws the hair back again on my face.

'Here. I have your scarf,' he says as he hands me the scarf I was wearing yesterday.

I don't remember when I lost it.

'Last night, when your head was resting on my shoulder in the taxi, it came loose and fell down.'

'I don't remember anything,' I say, feeling weird.

'I hope you remember our kiss. Although I have to admit you are not the best.'

I am turning red now. How can I not remember anything?

'It's okay. Practice makes one perfect. We can try again now,' he teases.

How dare he tell me I don't kiss well? I am about to show him how I kiss, when suddenly I hear the door open with a loud thud. I feel Samir move away with a jerk. I try to open my eyes, but I am blinded by an array of shining bulbs. Their bright, ochre-yellow light overpowering the moon's soft, whitish-yellow luminescence.

'*Kya ho raha hai yahan?*' I hear a stern, accusing voice. I still can't see her in the flood of light, but I recognize it as the voice of the groom's mother.

'Just clicking the pictures of the honeymoon suite, Aunty,' replies Samir smoothly.

'In the dark?' Aunty challenges. I see her gaze turn towards the beautifully decorated, king-size, mahogany, poster bed.

I feel a pang of shame and excitement as I read the thought

passing through her mind. The scorn on her face eases a little when she sees the undisturbed sheets. Two sex-hungry youngsters had not maligned her son's wedding bed.

'I was trying to get the moonlight shots first, Aunty,' lies Samir convincingly. 'Can I click a picture of you in the moonlight too? You are looking like Madhubala!'

Aunty immediately softens at this praise from a young, handsome boy. She adjusts her *pallu*, letting it fall just below her cleavage. Samir clicks multiple shots, advising Aunty to pose differently each time. I am amazed at the ease with which he is able to connect even with an older woman. I step behind the curtains and watch him in action and admire his lean body as he captures his current object of attention with his SLR camera. His fingers adjust the light aperture. I remember the softness of those fingers on my lips. My cheeks begin to burn.

After he has captured Madhubala, Meena Kumari and Nargis poses, he quickly takes a few shots of the honeymoon suite from varied angles with professional ease, while Aunty pretends to look around for something in the room. She doesn't trust our raging hormones. She wants to make sure she locks the room after we leave.

'Thanks, Aunty. We are done here,' I hear Samir say. I quickly follow him out of the room. The moment we are out of Aunty's sight, he grabs my hand and we break into a run. I don't know where we are going. I don't care. We climb down two flights of stairs. I am holding the folds of my saree above my heels with my right hand, to avoid stepping on them. My left hand is secure in Samir's firm grasp. We stop in front of a room on the third floor. We hear voices of some elderly people coming from the end of the corridor. He pushes the door of the room with his left hand. It opens without any hindrance.

We slip inside the room and wait for the noises to subside.

A few minutes later, when all is quiet, he tells me that this is his room.

'No one will disturb us here,' he says and starts walking to the bed, still holding my hand. He sits down on the bed, pulling me along with him. I can feel the tension beginning to grow in my chest. Suddenly he leaves my hand, which became sticky from our sweat, and starts laughing.

'Did you see the look in Aunty's eyes as she scanned the bed in the honeymoon suite?' He says chuckling.

I watch his eyes sparkle with childlike amusement at our little adventure. I find myself join his laughter as I first recall the look of horror and then the relief on her face.

As the thrill of the escapade subsides, his eyes rest intensely on my face. A different thrill begins to build between us. My body tenses as his finger slides down the side of my face resting just above my shoulder. He is aware of my pulse rising and falling. He doesn't wait any more this time. His lips are on mine, lingering softly in the beginning, then possessing me with the intensity of a storm. It's too soon, a voice in my head warns. It's okay. Just go with the flow, contradicts my heart. Soon, I can't hear any voices. My mind goes blank. I am lost in a cyclone of cloud and wind spinning together, which is fed by the heat of our passion.

I wake up at the crack of the dawn as the rising sun peeks through the curtains at our intertwined bodies. I slowly lift my leg lying on top of his, extricate my arm from under him and then gather my clothes, which were thrown across the floor in haste last night.

I look at the clock above the bed. Shucks! My flight back to Delhi is in three hours. I need to pack my stuff and leave now, if I want to get to the airport in time. I don't want to leave, but I have to. I want to wake up Samir and kiss him goodbye. I wonder when we will meet. He had said he keeps coming to Delhi. I hope he comes soon. Okay, this is definitely crazy. I haven't even left him yet and I am already desperate to meet him again.

I pick up his phone to edit my contact name to 'Butterfly'. I decide to call him from the airport and surprise him.

I am swiping the screen on his phone when I see a yellow post-it app with some notes. It reads, 'book ideas, thoughts, feelings'. I am tempted to see his inner-most thoughts. I double click to read the complete note. I realize these are Samir's notes on anything he wants to record as ideas for his stories. I am surprised that he didn't tell me anything about writing a story or a book. Another engineer who wants to be a writer—how clichéd! I smile and go through the notes.

Love is like an umbrella. Share it with everyone.

My favourite flowers are Tulips—two lips.

I saw two birds today on a branch of a tree outside my room.

They seemed to be in perfect harmony. No binding of marriage and yet together, forever.

The notes are so sweet, so touching, so vulnerable and so romantic. I know I ought to be leaving right now, yet I scroll further down.

Let's Have Coffee *is a funny take on our generation's casual attitude towards sex. Having sex with a friend or a stranger is like meeting for coffee. With no responsibilities and disposable incomes. My twenty-something friends believe in trying new partners like we so often order new products online. We are used to free returns within thirty days, no questions asked, whether it is shoes, dress or a date. If his feet start smelling after a month or she farts too much, we go back to being friends with benefits like nothing happened.*

My hands are shaking and I am sure I will miss my flight, but I can't leave now without reading it all.

They first meet at a wedding. She is from the groom's side and he's from the bride's. They feel an immediate connect. They end up having sex in the bridegroom's honeymoon suite in the hotel.

I gulp down the lump in my throat but it is hard to control the tears brimming in my eyes. Is this what he thinks of me? An idea of a story? Was he planning to sleep with me in the honeymoon suite so he could add realistic experience to his story? Am I just a cup of coffee to be had at a designer wedding? All these questions are hammering in my mind and are demanding to be answered.

Just a minute ago, I wanted to say how much I had enjoyed our time together. I wanted to tell him how I felt a connection with him. I wanted to get to know him more. I wanted to develop a taste for our togetherness, as one develops a taste for wine. Slowly, beautifully forever. But after reading this, I can't. I can't tell him any of it. It will mean nothing to him. What I want to savour as wine is just coffee for him. A mere act of sex at a random wedding. A spicy, saucy chapter in his story.

Sitting in the plane on the way back home, my mind goes back to the two beautiful days I had with Samir. I feel horrible. I feel used. I feel I have been wronged. I feel angry with Samir. The logical side of my mind argues that he didn't do anything wrong. It's not like he forced himself upon me or confessed his love for me. It was my mistake too. How could I sleep with someone I knew only for forty-eight hours? It was like blowing away one's caution in the wind. In this case, literally.

Nevertheless, I felt a connection—my romantic side cries in its defence. I felt like I had known him for years. I felt safe and secure with him.

Well, there is nothing that can be changed now—both sides of my mind agree. It is best to forget and move on. That chapter is over. End of story.

Samir wakes up from the most beautiful dream he has ever had and tries to feel Meha next to him in the bed. She is gone. Everything was so perfect; why did she leave without even a goodbye kiss. He rubs his eyes and looks at the clock. She must have left for the airport, he realizes. Confident that she must have left a message for him at the reception, he runs out in his boxers to the reception and inquires about her.

Madam checked out an hour ago. No. She didn't leave any message for anyone. The girl at the reception stares disapprovingly at his under-dressed state.

He instinctively reaches for his phone to call Meha. It's in his room. He rushes back to his room and finds his phone lying on the table. He tries to call her but the number is switched off. She is already on the flight. He is thrilled to see a note lying under his phone. It is scribbled on the complimentary hotel stationary. He quickly reads it, once, and then once again.

'Thanks for sharing your lovely umbrella with me. Sorry, but I peeked into your private notes. Just to let you know, I don't believe in friends with benefits. I prefer to forget a random hookup like an unknown cafe in a narrow lane, where you enjoy a nice coffee on a vacation, but you wouldn't care to remember its name or street. Don't try to find me. I won't remember you.'

He crumples the paper into a ball and throws it away. He walks out of the hotel to the beach. How stupid of him to think that she was the one!

A Public Proposal

Five years later

I am nervous as I go through the Cyber Hub security. After all, it's not every day that a girl proposes to a guy. That too in front of a crowd! C'mon, don't tell me you think that proposing is not a big deal. Did you ever have to get a poor mark sheet signed by your parents? How about being caught the only time you lied to your best friend? How about going to a party without makeup? See, you're getting it. Proposing is like baring your inner self to the one who can hurt you the most. If that is not vulnerable enough, imagine being watched by hundreds of spectators as you propose—like in the one in Oprah Winfrey show. Only this is not a staged show—it's real life. Moreover, I want this to go well—more than anything else.

I am patiently waiting as the female guard is counting the number of lipsticks in my purse. She then opens my handbag and takes her own sweet time confirming the expiry date on the pack of glucose biscuits. Then, she is touching me everywhere. I respect her dedication to duty, but squirm at this invasion of privacy.

I can hear my heart as I walk hurriedly past the Wine

Country, the California Pizza Kitchen and Nandos. I tie my sweaty hair up in a loose knot with the help of a clutch. It's almost five in the evening, but the scorching June sun is unrelenting in its mission to prove the ineffectiveness of my sunscreen.

About to faint with the potent mixture of anxiety and heat, I smell from a distance, the bittersweet aroma of fresh coffee beans. My legs take me to Starbucks. I am tempted to go in, get some cool air and my regular Frappuccino. Just as I unlock my phone to see if I have time, it begins to ring. It's the dance troupe. I promise myself to visit Starbucks later. For now, I head straight to the open-air theatre. The place is bustling with crowd of young people from the nearby office buildings. Had it been any other time, I would have loved the energy. Today, I am just hoping to not make a fool of myself in front of all these people. I talk to the dance troupe and go over the sequence of events for the flash-mob proposal. I check the sound system and the life-size display screen. Everything seems to be in order. I have been working on this proposal for the last two weeks. There is no reason for me to worry—but my mind warns that if everything is going well, it can never be a good sign.

Just then I get a message on WhatsApp that he has arrived. I realize that it's not the preparation that I am worried about. It's his answer. What if he rejects my proposal? No! Don't even think about it. Bad things happen if you think negative. Your blood group is 'B positive'—be optimistic! I try to think about the delicious Frappuccino waiting for me at Starbucks. The trip to Maldives that is due. The new pair of silver earrings I saw at Anokhi. Those earrings are gorgeous. I smile. I am already feeling better.

'He is in front of Donut Factory.'

'Now he is at the Pita Pit.'

I am getting real-time updates on his movements from the team. The video guy has started recording his walk from the Cyber Hub entry to the open-air theatre.

'He has stopped to buy a kulfi at King's Kulfi.'

It's okay! No need to panic. I tell the team to keep recording. I had kept a buffer of thirty minutes for such unexpected deviations. As he approaches the open-stage area, the music comes on. The song 'Lat lag gayi' is one of his favourites. And mine too. The lead dancer goes to the floor and breaks into some supercool steps. As predicted, he gets tempted and walks towards the stage to check out the dance performance. The heat does not bother him. The mist-sprinklers stationed around the stage was a good idea. I move closer to one. Two more guys join the dance and the song changes to another one of his favourites. He looks happy, unaware that he is soon going to be the star bakra of a live show. There are eight dancers on the floor now. All the dancers are moving in amazing synchrony. A large crowd has gathered around to enjoy the free show. People are cheering and grooving to the latest chartbuster tunes.

A minute later, right on my cue, she joins the dancers on the floor. Wearing a cotton palazzo with a sleeveless, lace top, she grooves to the tune of 'Tumhi ho bandhu sakha tumhi'. I can't believe she is the same girl who couldn't dance a few weeks ago. Here she is—perfectly coordinated with the experts from the dance troupe.

Who is she? Hello! She is the heroine of our show. The brave girl who is risking it all for a guy. I am only the proposal-designer and I am tense because my business survives on the success of this proposal. Wait! Did you, by any chance, think

I was proposing? I agree that it's not an impossible thought. I mean I am twenty-seven now. I should be getting married. In fact, my mom desperately wants me to get married. It's just that I am yet to find someone who loves me for who I am—one in a million!

As she continues to rock the floor, I keenly observe his expression for a clue. First, he is surprised to see her dancing. Then, he is confused. Then the worst happens. His face becomes expressionless, like a blank television screen.

'What does this mean?' I anxiously ask the team on my mike. 'Is he feeling trapped or is he blown over?'

No one responds. Then Pyare Mohan, my production guy, who is managing the music, whispers, 'He is in an empty box. Only men go there—never a woman.'

'Obviously a lady would never want to visit an empty box. But what the fuck is he thinking right now?' I am tense now, fiddling with my earring.

'Nothing,' comes the reply.

The love of your life is wooing you and you are thinking of nothing. You see, it is only possible for guys to think of nothing, because God messed up while creating them. He used up all his boxes, full of creativity, moods, and feelings, while designing a woman's mind. When he got to creating a man's mind, he ran out of stuff. A woman has these boxes in her brain, which are meaningful and connected with high-speed, fibre-optic cable, which allows her to jump topics and moods at astounding speed. On the other hand, men can at their best be looking at the box right in front, with no ability to multitask. Often that box in front turns out to be empty. Like what just happened to our star-hero.

As I am trying my best to make something out of his

nothingness, I see him touch his throat. This is definitely not good. He is having doubts. Oh, please God, make him say yes. I need the money badly. It's only a proposal and not a full wedding. But it will help my start-up to survive another month. I feel bad worrying about material gains when someone's love is at stake. Yet you have to help yourself first, isn't it?

The song ends and she walks with slow, confident steps towards him. I am very impressed by her poise. The crowd is going mad—shouting and cheering. They have never seen a girl propose in public at Cyber Hub. She reaches him, stretches out her hand and ask him to join her. She knows he loves to dance. He is an expert ballroom dancer. That was one of the reasons we had settled for the flash-mob idea. He hesitates for a second. My heart drops. Then he takes her hand in his and they move into their own world—eyes locked, dancing only for each other. The world fades away. Just the way it happens in the movies. The music stops. I can hear her as she speaks, loud and clear, on my earphone.

'Last year, I met you right here on this date. I remember that day very well. Meeting you was the best thing that has happened to me. We clicked like strawberries and chocolate dip, didn't we? I never thought that I would ever say this to anyone and that too in front of so many people. But, you always tell me to flow like a river and ignore all boundaries—so here it goes. Will you be my partner in crime on a journey full of arguments that you can never win? It will require sharing your bedroom, bathroom, sometimes a towel, and in emergencies even your toothbrush with me. And you also have to give up your single, no-strings-attached FB status.'

Ooh. It was so romantic and witty and so beautifully said. I would have said yes without thinking twice. I wait for the crowd to cheer, but everyone is quiet now. They are eagerly waiting for his answer, as he holds her hands and looks into her eyes.

'Before I met you, I never knew how someone could spend hours buying a pair of shoes or even know that the colours on the shade card of Asian Paints actually exist. It's been a steep, learning curve for me. I have to say you have changed since we met.' He pauses. 'For the better,' he winks and continues. 'I have changed from a late riser to a 6 a.m. alarm. Every day has been worth waking up early, just to hear your voice but...'

There is pin-drop silence. The roar of the traffic fades away. '...er...marriage is a huge commitment.'

She maintains a steady eye contact. He is silent now. He drops his gaze. He lets go of her hands. He is looking at his phone. Fuck! He is going to reject her in front of hundreds of strangers. I wipe the sweat off my palms on the sides of my dark, olive green, linen trousers.

'I am willing to share my entire life and all my assets, barring my toothbrush. If that works for you, then I promise to always be the convict, even if you do the crime.' He smiles at her.

'How about a bold selfie on Facebook as our first crime?'

The smile couldn't be brighter on her face.

He raises his phone, clicks a selfie while kissing her, and then posts it on FB, while a huge sigh of relief emerges from the crowd.

I realize I had been holding my breath too. Dad would have been happier, had I worried this much for my IIT exams. I shed a few tears of relief at the happy conclusion of this romantic chick flick I had co-scripted. People start to disperse. Show is over. It's time to get back to work. I congratulate the couple, tell my team to wind up and head for a well-earned, double chocolate chip, crème Frappuccino.

Savouring every sip of my coffee, I open another button of my summer-thin, floral, chiffon shirt. I feel a pleasurable shiver as the cool air caresses my bare skin underneath. I notice the guy sitting across the table. He is blatantly staring at the hint of bare cleavage, peeking over my top shirt button. Aaarrrgh! A girl can't even dry her sweat in public!

I turn away and bury my face in the phone, purely out of habit. Reading messages and responding to FB posts and tweets gives me a sense of accomplishment and safety. I could definitely do with more people changing their FB status from 'Single' to 'Married'. I scroll down my contact list to a prospective client whose office is in Cyber Hub. I pause for a brief second as my eyes scan a defunct contact, 'Samsung Do Not Call'. Even after all these years, my breathing stops at the mere sight of Samir Singhal's name. I have no idea where he is or what he is doing. Is there a wine he likes? Is he still having coffee in different cups? It's too dangerous to ponder. I quickly move down to Sandeep Rathi, who had contacted me last month to understand the expenses of a wedding consultant.

'She called me an ignorant, workaholic idiot in front of all her friends,' I hear Sandeep's voice, hurt and shocked. 'After three years of gifting her roses on every Valentine's Day, an "I love you" card for Friendship Day, a box of Ferrero Rocher on every single going-out-anniversary and her favourite perfume for each birthday, she leaves me just because I didn't get her a gift for just this one occasion. I told her I was very busy and she said it was fine. She didn't care for gifts. I even asked her that if there was something she wanted, then she could send me the link and I could order it for her. What more can a man do?'

I don't have the heart to tell his poor soul that he is indeed a dunce. How could he give her the same gifts year after year?

Obviously, his fiancé doesn't care for his gifts. She wants something special. Sandeep blabbers on, but if he doesn't have a fiancé, he is of no use to me anymore. I just apologize for this unexpected sad demise of his engagement and disconnect.

I have nothing more to do. I could leave now, but its peak traffic hour. The sun is still blaring and no hugs and kisses are waiting at home for me. I look around. There is a bunch of people from nearby offices, either taking a break or doing business meetings. Girlfriends are catching up on last-minute gossip before heading back home. I reach out to my pacifier and find a missed call from Tanu Di. She was supposed to join me at Cyber Hub for a beer. Her treat, of course, but she cancelled because her maid wasn't feeling well. I tell you, her priorities are really screwed. I decide to call Di.

'Hi, Proposal Queen!' Tanu Di sounds ebullient.

Couple of days back when I had called her, she was sounding very low and cynical. She said she was envious of her maid who had a well-defined paying job. Peculiar IITian! Although, soon if I don't find more people willing to upgrade to a lifetime of sleepovers with one person, I might be envious of her maid's steady job too.

'You sound happy today?'

'Yeah.' she says, almost dreamily. 'Rohan and I tried this amazing thing last night. It's like a...'

'Stop Di!' I interrupt not interested in knowing the details about her sex life. I can talk sex stuff with my friends and even Di, but it becomes awkward when Rohan *jijaji* is involved.

'Ok,' she sighs. 'So how is work? You must be very busy.'

'Pff, not really, I could do with some more.' I didn't tell her I am working on exactly zero projects right now.

'Never thought I will hear you say that, little sis,' she chuckles.

'I know. I am the fat, lazy bum of the family, while you are the smart, slim one.'

I think she can smell the younger-sister envy. She goes quiet. I hear the two-year-old Diya, over the phone, shouting *'Mummaaaaa, pottee ho gayeeee.'*

Ignoring Diya's calls for mumma, which are becoming louder and more insistent by the second, she speaks, each word coming from her heart. 'You know Meha, I truly admire your clarity on what you want and your courage to go out and get it. I am so very proud of you.'

Oh my God! Compliment coming from Tanu Di. This is BIG. I can't bring myself to say anything but I feel a halo of happiness shining all around me.

'By the way, I know you want to make it big on your own and I already said I am very proud of you, but let me know if you need money,' she says, sounding worried and uncomfortable.

'Why do you ask?' I am quite stunned. She knows this start-up means everything to me. I grew up being compared to Di, clad in her hand-me-downs. This is the first meaningful thing I have done in my life. Why is she offering to ruin it?

'Well...er...Chugh uncle...um...told Papa that you may be in...er...financial crisis,' says Didi softly, knowing well how I hate this uncle.

'That fucking Chu—always foretelling my misfortune,' I curse under my breath. I mean, he has dictated my life more than God has. On my naming ceremony, he prophesized that water will bring me ill luck. Didi and I discovered this only after my return from the not-to-be-remembered trip to Goa. Papa went berserk when I returned from Goa. First, he hugged me like never before and then he forbade any future ocean trips for me, unless they were holy waters. I even discovered that my parents had named me Meha because clouds control water. Not that I have a problem with my name. I like it. But all my beachwear has been rotting ever since—all because of a stupid prophecy. Like I am some Harry Potter and prophecies really come true.

'Chugh uncle also said…'

'You can't believe him Di,' I cut her short. 'Remember he said that you will have a daughter, followed by a son, and then a daughter. But you didn't right? You have only two daughters.' Not only do I want Di to see reason, I want her moral support for the Maldives trip that some of my friends are planning. Although, I doubt moral support will be enough. I will also need money. Moreover, how much I may hate Uncle Chugh, he is sort of right about my financial crisis.

Didi is silent. I can hear the water running in background. I think she has put my phone on speaker as she washes Diya's potty.

Moments later Di speaks, her voice accusatory. 'Papa worries for you Meha, and it's not good for his weak heart. Chugh uncle said…'

Irritated, I hang up before Di can finish her sentence. If I had let her complete, then things might have turned out differently. Apparently, Chugh Uncle had composed an entire verse to predict my future.

The dark sins of the seas loom,
Within the waves lies her doom,
Only the wind may change her fate,
For it can make water evaporate,
Have patience and wait,
Wind and water must mate.

Had I heard the verses and understood their meaning, I might have clicked on 'Samsung Do Not Call' and called Samir Singhal—the free-spirited wind, to mate with Meha—the watery clouds. But I didn't and hence my story continues to unfold differently.

Tying a Knot

It's only 7 a.m. and I am already counting money at the office of 'Tying a Knot'. Counting money is part of my morning ritual. It's the first thing I do every day on reaching office, to ensure that my shopaholic self hasn't been squandering away all my hard-earned money on shopping or worse, a calorie-rich mixture of chocolate, milk, and sugar, which is sold under the code name 'Frappuccino'.

Always an optimist, I quickly added the earnings from yesterday's Cyber Hub proposal. Hmmm. The numbers are refusing to look rosy, even when I highlight them in bright pink. The uncoloured reality is that, I have very little money. I can pay office rent, salaries and other fixed expenses for a maximum of two more months. I desperately need a big, fat wedding to carry on my business. Never the one to worry about troubles, I immediately pull out the list of all the leads that had come in last month. I have leads on twenty wedding, all within a two-week period in November. But, there are only two leads in the entire twenty weeks—starting from now till November. Rather unfair, don't you think, that just because some pandit ji has declared a few selected dates auspicious for weddings, my business should suffer? Grrr...

To be fair, pandits are not the only ones to be blamed. I mean no one in the Indian wedding industry likes summer. Not the bride who wants to dress up, nor the relatives who want to show off, least of all the gods. C'mon! Don't tell me you thought it was a coincidence that most Indian festivals fall in the winter months! Gods take a summer break from their duties on Earth and go off to different mountain ranges.

I know all about gods because Dad and his gods have ruled my childhood, which includes the days of the week when I could wash my hair or cut my nails. But, I will not have them govern the success of my venture. 'Tying a Knot' has done some great weddings in last nine months, since it has started out. I am confident there is someone out there who wants to get married in the next sixty days and is looking for me. I mean looking for my company. I mean my services. Gosh, why do you guys always find double meanings into everything! Anyway, I just need to find an exception. And the beauty is that in India, even exceptions run in millions.

Recharged, I dial Amit's number. I really need him to get his business-development sense together. The sweet, coy voice of his newlywed bride reminds me that he is on his honeymoon. Fuck! I try calling a few of my previous clients for references. I get to hear the caller tunes ranging from 'Payoji maine ram ratan dhan payo' to 'Ye duniya peetal di, baby doll main sone ki', but they all go unanswered. I guess it's too early to call anyone up in the real world, so I go online.

I send an updated finance sheet to my accountant for review. I am hoping he can suggest me some ways to make our savings last longer. I hesitantly delete 'Flat 50% off' and 'exclusive sale preview' messages from my phone. Then, I ask my travel buddies on WhatsApp group the last day to pay for the Maldives trip. I really want to be able to make it. It's one of the items on my bucket list. Except, I don't have the money right now. Hopefully something will click. I check the likes on my FB page. Five more people have liked 'Tying a Knot' in the last two hours. I only need 30,167 more Likes to get to the 50,000 milestone. Yippee!

No one hears me, because there is no one around.

Usually, I like the quiet and peace of the office at this hour of the day. No good looking, long-haired, creative assistant to distract me. No tempting aroma of Maggi wafting from the kitchen to resist. With only the relaxing sound of birds chirping in the office backyard, I can concentrate on my work. Except, I don't have any work today.

So, I check my mail again for any new leads that might have come in the last ten minutes. There is indeed a new mail but it's from my accountant and the subject is 'Bed Noose'. Eww! It sounds like a masochist sex position. He has written that my '*bijnes*' can only last for '*thurty-won*' days and not '*sexty*' because I had forgotten to include his tax-filing fee, my outstanding credit-card bill and I have counted twice the income from yesterday's proposal. He has attached the updated excel sheet, highlighting my mistakes in red. I open the excel sheet. It looks like my math exam paper covered with red marks all over. This is really bad news. And when did I shop for ₹50,000 on my credit card? I wish I had saved it for the Maldives trip. I don't know what to do now. '*Thurty-won*' days only to save my start-up from extinction! I can literally feel a noose strangulating my neck.

That frigging Chugh uncle. How could he have known that I will be in such a financial crisis?

I try to tell myself that thirty-one is better than thirteen, but I know that only optimism will not work. I urgently need a wedding project. I really can't let my business fail. It's the only thing I have ever done different from Tanu Di. It's my identity, my baby. It means everything to me. I will do whatever it takes to save it. I click Mansi's number from the speed dial. FYI, Mansi is my apartment mate and BFF. She is also the hottest and the best production manager I have known. Sadly, she is still working with my previous company, Dreams Wedding Planner Inc., but only until I can afford her.

'*Bachhon ke naam pe kuch de de Mansi.* My *bechare* employees, my babies, are sitting *bekaar*,' I plead, in my best filmy voice.

'*Dramebaaz*, you know I will pass on any leads Sarika rejects, but she is bloody not refusing any project.'

I know that egoist Sarika, the owner of Dreams Wedding Planner Inc. She wants me to starve.

'These days, kids think a start-up is as easy as blowing soap bubbles,' Sarika had said dismissing me when I had submitted my resignation. 'But bubbles burst as easily as they blow. Creativity and innovation is not enough. You need systems and processes to keep a bubble afloat.'

She never did like me. Not five years ago. Not now. I never thought I would have to live off Sarika's leftovers, but start-ups teach you humility. I so can't let my start-up story end with four weddings and my funeral.

'What if you make a mistake?' I suggest to Mansi casually. 'Like accidentally just forward me the next lead instead of sending it to Sarika. It's just an email after all.'

Start-ups also teach you manipulation skills.

'Meg honey, that's convenient for you, but not right for me.' Mansi refuses sweetly.

'Arey, but you don't always have to be right!' I insist, almost nagging.

'Of course, I do. I am a woman.'

I don't find Mansi's joke funny. My usually good sense of humour has gone into hiding, like a sulky, wet cat.

'Hey, do you want any kiddo parties? I think I can arrange for those,' Mansi says, with a soft, partly suppressed laugh.

'Hello Ms. Right, I am a wedding planner not a bouncy *wallah*,' I say with a hurt pride.

'Can you wait a sec, hon,' Mansi says, her voice drowned by the sound of engines. I can hear a chopper landing at a distance. I know Mansi is busy with the wedding of some big-shot political leader's son, with an insane budget. Why does no one with a wedding budget the size of annual GDP of Lakshadweep, want to share his or her *shaadi ka laddoo* with me? At this point even the budget of a Tata Nano will do.

'My skirt just got lifted up by the helicopter's wind,' Mansi says, coming back on line. I can hear a man's teasing laughter in the background. I am about to ask her if she can at least treat me for dinner when she says, 'Bf calling. Gotta go. Bye. See you tomorrow.' And she disconnects the call.

I can't believe Mansi Luthra, aka manslaughter, whose favourite pass-time is verbally slaughtering men, hung up on me for a boyfriend. It's the same Mansi who warned me five years ago that men only need a place to have sex. Boy, had she been right! She must be serious about the guy she is dating. I mean, she even got curtains put in her bedroom window so that the neighbours won't peep into her bedroom to get a free show. She has been telling me to get curtains too but I like the openness and the unhindered view from my huge glass window. The sprawling suburb, which is under construction, high-rise apartments in Gurgaon, cars honking on roads, a huge patch of uneven, dry land with pigs roaming around freely and rickshaw drivers bathing from an open tank. I know it's not the Manhattan skyline, but you've got to agree it's unique. Besides, I like it when my friend *Surya,* the glorious sun, barges unannounced into my room every morning and wakes me up. Okay! I admit that the real reason for not putting the curtains up is that I don't have a boyfriend or the money to buy curtains. To be fair, I had chosen the material for the curtains but then I spent all the money in the Global Online Shopping Festival. Shucks! That's the outstanding ₹50,000 on my card. At least, now I know it was well used.

I check my phone again. Its 8.17 a.m. I have the whole day in front of me but no money or boyfriend to spend it with. It's really not fair.

When I had a regular job, I used to envy people with their own start-ups. I thought entrepreneurs could have breakfast in bed and reach office post lunch or work the mornings and go shopping after lunch. They had to report to no one. I learnt the hard way that running your own business is not easy. You have to go around begging for work. Plus, you get no salary. You can't enjoy no-work days. And, there isn't any time for a relationship. Or sex for that matter. I have been on off-sex diet for the past ten months, the longest I have stuck to any kind of diet ever. Obviously, this isn't deliberate. It's just that in the beginning the start-up needed me all the time, leaving little time for any other sustained relationship. Then came the babies, my three hires, and I got even more busy. At this rate I am going to be heading for a year-without-sex record. Just between you and me—I don't care for the record. So, if you know of a really nice guy, like the kind who understands Venusian silence and brings presents, please give him my number. It's TYING A KNOT (8946425668).

'I knew of one such guy, who understood your silence. He even gifted you those beautiful, butterfly earrings,' a dim voice from the deep recesses of my mind speaks up. 'You left him and you even left behind those earrings!'

I am surprised to hear this voice. I haven't heard it in a while. It must be the lack of Vitamin S. Everyone knows lack of sex can affect your mental health. I need to fix this deficiency soon. How about now? I am free. It might actually be the most productive use of my time.

As my mind whirrs, Neeta walks out from the bathroom wiping her face with a tissue. Her hair is a mess, her eyes are puffed up and she looks tired. Wait, she is wearing the same *kurti* she wore yesterday and it is rather crumpled.

'Did you do an all-nighter?' I ask, surprised. It's not like we are loaded with work.

'Well, I stayed back last night to finish an article for my food blog. Then I met this hot guy from Sydney who asked me out on an online date. After that I had to play Ticket to Ride to maintain my daily score. But it wasn't a busy night. I actually slept for four hours,' she replies, while ordering breakfast from one of the many food apps on her phone.

Her name is Neeta Jain, but NetGen suits her better. She is one of my employees—our food expert, menu designer and digital marketing in-charge.

Minutes later, during which I receive, read and delete twenty-one online shopping offers, NetGen comes back with fresh, delicious bagels and cream cheese. She opens the pack and starts eating. I pick a multi-grain bagel and break a piece. The inside pulls apart gently. As I relish the first bite, doughy, yeasty, and not too sweet, NetGen tells me about a wedding photography start-up called KISS featured by Yourstory.com.

'We should also get featured by Yourstory,' she suggests and then takes another bite of her bagel, scattering black sesame seeds all around her keyboard.

'Aren't we too small to be featured on Yourstory?' I ask, my confidence a bit dented by all the grim forecast.

'You have the advantage of being a woman. The online world loves young women entrepreneurs,' NetGen informs me, quite passionately. I can see admiration and ambition sparkling in her young eyes, behind her specs. Having done a pass-course B.Com from an unknown college and being a twenty-year-old, she is happy to have a job that pays her to surf and use her passion for food.

I feel good that women are finally getting their well-deserved and long-due share of glory. But, I am not sure what the story will be like. I ask her, still slightly sceptical of my own success.

'It can be about the unique challenges of our business. Not many start-ups have a pandit asking for a *neem ki jadi* in Austria to break *toran* or have to import flowers, worth twenty lakhs for a wedding, only to burn them later because the Mauritius sugarcane industry can't risk infection.'

'Or have to clear an old, run-down palace in Jaisalmer and deal with snakes littering all over,' I add, recalling another incident. Each wedding is a unique project, with its own set of challenges. That's what I love the most about my work.

'I think it will be a nice piece,' assures NetGen. Leaving me to carry on the conversation, she turns to her laptop to start framing the email to Yourstory about our story.

I really like her. She can't ever be idle—definitely an asset for a start-up. Never mind that her friends are all Twitter handles or Facebook profiles. I turn to my laptop to check the link she has sent about today's start-up which is featured. I click on it and am directed to a page titled, 'Capture your love in a story with a KISS'.

'*KnotsInShotS* or KISS started out three years ago from a small office in Mumbai out of passion and love.'

Interesting name, I think.

'Now they are a team of twenty-five people across three cities, including Hyderabad and Pune. They believe that photography and the Indian wedding film market, valued at over 2 billion USD has a huge potential and they have barely scratched the surface.'

Two billion USD. Fuck me! I am sitting on a gold mine. I speak to myself, already feeling better.

KISS has won many awards for wedding photography and cinematography. Many wedding magazines and dailies have also featured them. A huge chunk of their clientele are the NRIs.

How come I didn't read about them before? It would be a good thing to collaborate with them, especially on NRI projects. I can do with more money and less pandits controlling my business.

I scroll down to see a few samples of their photography work. There is a picture of a couple amidst yellow mustard fields, *Dilwale Dulhaniya Le Jayenge* style. There is a photograph of another couple dancing at an Udaipur fort in black and white. The ebullience mingled with surprise on the bride's face at having matched the dance step with the groom who is looking at her with an I-told-you-I-am-good expression, is simply superb. The photographer has managed to capture the hints of emotions expressed at the right moments.

Looking at the photograph, my heart reminds me of someone I knew a long time ago. Someone who brought out intimate expressions just like this. I can't believe this is the second time today my heart has reminded me of the same person.

'Hello? Exercise some restraint! We are in the middle of an end-of-the-road crisis here,' my mind warns me.

'But what if it is him?' My heart begins to thump wildly at the possibility.

'Don't be stupid,' my brain chides. 'He used to sell soaps, remember.'

'But he did shoot a wedding,' my heart persists.

'Yes, but that was for his ex-girlfriend. Besides, he wanted to become a writer not a photographer.'

I look at the headline staring at me. KISS.

'It's definitely him,' my heart declares. 'This is exactly the kind of flirtatious name he would use for his business.'

'I think you are overreacting. Just scroll down and see. In any case, he can't jump out of a webpage.'

'But, I am really scared of a face-off with him,' my heart whimpers, '...even if it is only digital.'

I feel goosebumps on my skin. Hands shaking, I press the down arrow to read further about the founders and am immensely relieved to see the picture of a non- impressive guy named Abhinav Rathore, in a grey sweatshirt.

Abhinav left his well-paying, multi-national job to follow his passion for photography. He describes how his engineering and MBA degrees had shackled him to a safe job. Then, one day he met his friend Sam, from an engineering college. Sam had already left his job and had been working on a novel for two years without success. Sam seemed to have lost his inspiration. Sam didn't comment when we asked him if it was a girl. He was looking to do something else. Their shared passion for photography and their need to do something for themselves led to KISS.

The co-founder, Samir Singhal, says, 'There were some dark clouds in my past, but every cloud does have a silver lining. Mine did too. I decided to pursue photography and it seems to have worked for me. Three years since the evening I met Abhinav, I haven't regretted a single KISS. Maybe it was all meant to be.'

No fucking way. Did my thoughts conjure him up on my laptop? Because it is him. The same treat-sex-as-coffee Samir. The Senorita Samir. The wild-rose fragrance Samir. Haven't regretted a single kiss, he says. Bloody must be kissing each bride during their shoots. My mind knows he's talking about *KnotsInShotS* and not real kisses, but I am not thinking coherently and my heart is freely blabbering.

I stare at Samir's picture in the article. He looks just the same. A fucking handsome opportunist. *Dark clouds in my past!* I wonder if he is referring to me as a dark cloud who led him astray from his story writing. I am happy if I made it difficult for him. If I was dark clouds for him, he had been an ill wind for me.

For five years, I had kept him away. I had his number but didn't call him. Neither had he. I had not googled him or checked his Facebook page. Now suddenly, my heart is humming, 'Behati hawa sa tha woh, udati patang sa tha woh, kahaan gaya use dhundon'.

I am finding it hard to control the tide of repressed feelings—hurt, anger, frustration, desire and, I have to admit, a deep longing to be loved. That too at a time when my business is in the doldrums. I wouldn't be surprised if Murphy has a role to play here.

A New Boyfriend

There isn't a problem that retail therapy, junk food, and a dose of laughter can't fix. Unable to deal with the sudden resurgence of feelings for Samir and impending financial doom, I leave the office immediately and go to the nearest mall. It is too early for any shops to be open, so I buy the last row ticket of the latest blockbuster and purchase an extra-large tub of butter popcorn. Two hours later, having laughed my guts out, I leave the mall feeling much lighter. I have read online that laughing intensely for an hour can actually burn as many calories as lifting weights for thirty minutes. Awesome, isn't it? Who knew that reading all those funny, forwarded messages on WhatsApp can help you slim down?

Happy with my mini-aerobic workout, I walk out of the cinema hall into the mall and find viciously tempting sale signs all around. I might be happy, but I still don't have money. I check my phone to see if any new business leads have come in, so I can consider buying a few things. I scroll through each one of the hundred messages patiently. I finally find one useful message from Mansi apologizing for having cut me off earlier. I immediately message back saying she can compensate by passing on a lead and going out pubbing with me.

'Pubbing? Isn't that a big no, given your financial crisis?' Mansi messages back.

Oopsie! She is right. I mean, even spending on movie is a BIG NO. While I am justifying my unwarranted expenses to myself, Mansi texts, 'Let me treat you. In mood to celebrate. Can't go pubbing. Let's watch *Tanu Weds Manu Returns* tomorrow in the afternoon.'

Shucks! I can't tell Mansi that I have just watched *Tanu Weds Manu Returns*. She and I had planned to watch it together over the weekend. I know she will understand my dire circumstances, but I can't give her the entire context over the phone—without which she will not see my point. And, I desperately want someone to see my point—to understand my need to prove myself, my need for sex, and the strange stirrings in my heart at the mere sight of Samir in the virtual, online world. I can think of lots of friends to go to pubs, movies and shopping with, but not many with whom I can share the secrets that even I am afraid to face. I wish my childhood friend Anusha was here right now. She would have listened to me without passing any judgement. I really miss her. If you have ever lost a bff, you will know that losing a friend is like losing an earring. You can never find a substitute. I know I have Mansi and I am thankful to God for her friendship. But she is older and she is very anti-men. Even cute, sweet men. Even wild-rose-fragrant men. She always manages to find flaws in the men I try to date. And she is right every single time. But being right is not always fun. Like now, it's often lonely. Anyway, since Anusha is still missing, it's only Mansi whom I have. She is also so busy these days with work and her damn boyfriend that I need to book a date to be able to talk with her. I settle for a tea date, in our humble drawing room, for tomorrow evening. Really, what has this world come to?

Keeping my head down, so that I don't end up stretching my already-bursting-at-the-seams credit card balance, I step out. The earthy smell of raindrops mixed with Gurgaon's construction dirt welcomes me. The air seems fresher, less smoky and clearer, so I decide to walk back and ignore the honking auto-wallahs' shouts, 'Madum, madum, cum hare, pleeeze'.

Playing hopscotch on the side-curb, to avoid stepping onto dog poop, I remember how Mansi and I had gotten close five years ago after the disastrous wedding in Goa. I recall, how I had reached the airport extremely late and completely heartbroken. My team members had kept the plane waiting for me. The moment I stepped in, Sarika had given me a stern look and started muttering about how the new generation has no sense of time or respect for processes. I, of course, was clueless that she was angry because it had started raining the night before and a pit viper had crawled up a bamboo-pole of the mandap. Can you imagine a real venomous viper in a mandap? I could have been killed while digging those poles, but Sarika didn't care a damn about me. The team had called me many times during the night, as they had needed my help to shift the mandap for the pheras from the beach side. But, I had been lost in a passionate cyclone of cloud and wind spinning together. Oddly, Samir had turned out to be the real viper in my bosom. I remember rivulets of tears flowing down my eyes, in the flight, in front of all the passengers. Sarika had been embarrassed, but it was Mansi who had stood up for me and consoled me. She had helped me get over Samir. Since then our friendship had grown like Jack's giant Beanstalk. We share an apartment now.

I barely enter the office, after having absconded for over four hours and feeling guilty about it, when my phone rings. It's Mom. Well, I am so not in the mood to listen to her now, but

I know if I ignore her too much, she will fly down tomorrow to check on me. Don't get me wrong. I love my mom and she is very loving too, but sometimes she can be a little clingy. And at this moment, I need my space.

'Have you found a boyfriend?' Mom asks the moment I say hello.

'*Ma, ladke ped pe nahin lagte,*' I whisper, turning to face the window, looking out at the lovely trees in the backyard. I don't want anyone in the office to hear this conversation.

'You don't worry about that, beta. *Ladka main dating app pe select kardoongi.*'

My mom, I tell you. She has become super savvy since Didi gifted her an iPad on her sixtieth birthday.

'You have to start somewhere, beta. If you don't start a chapter, how will the story get written?' She insists, while I say nothing.

Mom's remark reminds me of Samir's Yourstory title, 'Capture your love in a story with KISS'. For a moment, I feel tempted to contact Samir and go on a date with him. Purely for my mother's mental peace. I quickly drop the idea before it can gather support from my heart and do an illegal *dharna* in my mind.

'Do you know how old you are?'

'Yes Ma, I know I am twenty-seven,' I say in a hushed tone, as I remove my strappy, khaki wedges and stretch my toes under the desk. Ahh!

'When I was your age, I was already a mother of a five-year-old. Even Tanu was on her way to motherhood by this age. I understand that you are from a different generation. I am not even asking you to get married or to have kids. *Par ek boyfriend to health ke liye zaroori hota hai na, beta,*' she says very softly, sensibly and lovingly.

You can't argue with this one. I know that I can do with some love, pampering, and gifts. I would love to have a boyfriend. It's the boyfriend without love that I dislike. Although, someone once told me that love is rather over-rated.

'Why do you hate this someone so much?' My heart argues. 'It's possible that he has changed his *dheela*-character, especially now that he is making money from capturing love stories. I think you should meet and check him out.'

'Hello, you love-struck girl! He can also contact you. After all, he knows he was wrong. No more thinking about this someone,' my mind rebukes my fickle heart sternly.

'Beta, your Papa is also not keeping well,' Ma says in a soft, concerned voice.

Now, this is not fair. First, it was Di and now Ma. Both are telling me that Papa is not well because of me. This is so not done. I am already in so much tension.

'Ma, what exactly did Chugh uncle say to scare you all?' I ask getting annoyed.

'*Kuch nahin…bas* some danger is there…so Chugh ji said ki ek *ladke ke saath sambhog* will solve *bitiya's* problems.'

I am so tense that I can cry at the slightest provocation, but I burst out laughing at this. Chugh uncle has, perhaps, told my Dad that marriage will keep me out of danger, but Ma has literally translated it and is urging me to go on a date, so that I will end up having sambhog (sex) with a boy, which will keep me safe. For all you know, the prediction might even be fucking right. I do need a marriage, although not mine, to get through my current financial crisis.

'*Chal beta,* time for me to get ready for my tea date. Your Papa must be coming back from office soon,' I hear my mom say.

It's so sweet how she changes her *saree* every day, puts on fresh *bindi*, and excitedly waits to have a tea date with my dad, sharp at 4 p.m. My mom is as romantic as I am.

'Okay Ma. Love you. Bye,' I say after assuring her that I will try to find a guy soon. Anyway, I need some Vitamin S to keep my sanity.

How simple her life is and how complex is mine? Work and boyfriend—I have neither. Bhagvad Gita says *kaam karo* and here I want to do *kaam*, but I can't find a wedding to design or a boyfriend to love? God, a little help here please, I say, looking up at the ceiling. Promise, I will take your idol and give you a dip in the Maldives Ocean.

Running out of ideas on how to save my 'biz-n-ass', I look around. The office is buzzing with activity now. Most of the employees of the boutique marketing firm, the one with whom we share office space with, are gathered around a round table to my left holding and examining a bunch of bras. They are discussing the ad campaign for the popular 'body line' of Veronica Secret bras. I know because the creative assistant had given me few free samples, earlier this week, for consumer feedback. I try to catch the cute assistant's attention, but he seems busy.

'Bas ek sanam chahiye, aashiqui ke liye...aur ek pandit chahiye, muhrat nikalne ke liye.'

Humming to myself, I sit back with my legs outstretched on the table and my neck resting against my hands in a power pose. Feeling more relaxed, I swirl my office chair slightly to the right and look out at the flamboyant red Gulmohar flowers flirting with the streaming gold clusters of Amaltas in the backyard. Monsoon is the perfect season for romance. If only there were more monsoon weddings! I would love to design a '*haldi*' ceremony in rain. Like a natural Holi, where everyone applies the traditional Indian paste of turmeric, sandalwood, rose water and milk on the bride and the rain washes it away. The sangeet ceremony could have a rain dance. It would be so much fun. There is nothing sexier than a girl in a saree, drenched in rain, and saying I love you. I am sure the groom would love it.

'Do you think that girl in a transparent, wet saree wants to have sex with me?' I hear Samir's voice whisper in my ears.

Whoa! Where did that come from? I shake my head vigorously to dispel any Samir-related thoughts still lurking around in my subconscious. My mind is shocked at how anyone can survive five years of deep freeze. My heart, like a teenager is dancing to its own tune.

'Ispe bhoot koi chadha hai, theharna jaane naa…Badtameez dil, battameez dil badtameez dil…maane naa.'

I open the window a bit, and splash a few handfuls of chilled water from my water bottle on my face. I look around for my team.

I find NetGen watching a video of a course on Digital Marketing. I like the way she keeps herself gainfully occupied, even when there is no work. I also know Amit is on a six nights and seven days honeymoon package to Manali, but I can't see Pyare Mohan anywhere. His chair, which is adjacent to NetGen is empty. I hadn't seen him in the morning as well. I call out to NetGen but she doesn't hear me. Thirty seconds later, she shifts her focus from the computer screen to her phone to check if anyone in her digital world has tweeted, WhatsApped or updated their FB status. I manage to catch her attention in the split second that she takes in switching back from her phone to the computer. I ask her about Pyare Mohan, our production and logistics manager.

'Pyare is working on the monsoon-wedding special you have

assigned to him,' she informs. 'He mentioned some vague song from *Shree 420* with the bride and the groom walking under an umbrella. Also something about a *kagaz-ki-kashti* corner, where each family can make a paper boat and sail it in a mini pond. He was going to email you the details but he got an emergency call from his home town.'

'What emergency?' I ask, worried.

'I think it is a baby's delivery.'

'What the fuck! I didn't know he is married.' And I can't pay any paternity allowance. I am alarmed.

'No, it is his cow Noori. She wouldn't let anyone else touch her during the delivery. He said he will be back in office on Monday.'

I imagine Pyare, clad in his faded kurta and frayed jeans, lying in a shed, with a new born calf next to him, all covered in whatever gooey stuff a new-born calf is covered in. Yikes! Pyare and his unique rustic ways, but they help us in dealing with the local people, as they are able to connect to him. Guess it's best if he can deliver all his farm babies over this weekend. To be honest, there is no concrete project to engage him—so I have assigned a hypothetical wedding to plan. But he better come in on Monday, else I will have to cut his salary.

Determined to succeed, I call a few hotels and offer to collaborate with them for any upcoming events. I register on some online wedding portals as well. I join an NRI group on Facebook to tap into any wedding opportunities. I add some of our wedding decor images to Pinterest. Making all the efforts to spread my digital presence makes me feel better, albeit misguidedly. At this opportune moment, the office boy brings a tray of steaming-hot cutting chai and mouth-watering Maggi. NetGen takes the Maggi while I take the tea. I know none of my problems is solved, but for now I allow the *bagano ki taazgi* to replenish my soul.

'So she wants you to marry?' NetGen asks out of the blue, with a string of noodle hanging out of her mouth like a worm.

What? I burn my tongue as I swallow too much of the tea. Many people want me to get married, including myself, but I have no idea who NetGen is referring to. I look at her, but she is focussing on curling the noodles around her fork.

'Your mom,' she clarifies a few seconds later putting a mouthful inside her mouth.

Oh! So she can hear even when she is glued to her computer.

'Which mom doesn't?' I joke, as I enjoy my tea. 'Moms are always standing in the queue, with their daughter's matrimonial application, outside every eligible bachelor's door that has a sign that reads looking-for-fair-virginal-bride. I think their daughter's marriage gets them a huge star in their mommy journal by the UN Council of Parenting.' I didn't tell her the lame forecast that predicted my demise unless I marry, which is behind my mom's urgency.

'Mine has been threatening me with a "groom wanted" ad since I turned eighteen,' NetGen reveals. 'And, I don't think she cares a shit for some stars. I think she married a useless dork and wants to make sure I find a suitable boy before they are all taken.'

I am shocked to hear this. My poor mom only wants me to get a boyfriend and hopefully have sex with him to save my life. I feel truly blessed now.

'Do you have a boyfriend?' I ask. I don't know if this an important aspect in NetGen's life.

'A couple actually, but nothing serious. There is this one guy whom I call Tinderfish because he has a fish on his Tinder profile. I regularly chat with him online. Then there is Woody whom I met on Woo and he follows me all over the net. Then I go on random online dates like the one I did last night with this guy from Sydney.'

'Wow. I didn't realize you have a happening social life,' I say, almost admiring her candidness and capability to manage multiple relationships simultaneously. I might not believe in it myself, but why should only men have all the fun? After all, women are known to be better at multi-tasking.

'How about you? Do you have a boyfriend?' she asks.

'Nah. But I need to get one for my mom's sanity and also for mine.'

'Well, then get one,' she says shrugging her shoulders with a no-big-deal air.

'Now, you are speaking like my mom. I don't want to pick up a new candle stand or crockery set. I need to find a guy, like a real human with an XY chromosome, whom I like. And he has to like me too. Then we have to cross the five rungs of relationship together before we become boyfriend-girlfriend. Do you think I have time for all that?'

'Five rungs?'

Clearly, NetGen is unaware of real-world dating mechanisms. So I start to educate her. 'First, you start with a booty call to check out if he is hot in bed. Then, if he is intelligent enough to make conversation, you promote him to FWB. Then, if he shows deeper interest and starts picking the dinner tab and buy presents, you can start dating him. Next stage is exclusivity. This is when you meet each other's best friends, talk daily and meet regularly. Finally, it becomes FBO when you announce the relationship officially on Facebook. You have pet names for each other and you officially become boyfriend-girlfriend.'

'Whew! Is that how your generation does it? That's a lot of work. No wonder they start so early but are still unmarried at thirty.'

She is talking to me as if I am from another generation, although she is only seven years younger. But again, I think of Tanu Di as someone from a different generation and she is also eight years older to me.

'So what do you guys do?' I ask, curious.

'We just go to the app store and download one or visit a website for a customized version.'

I look at her confused, wondering if she has switched tracks and gone to one of her digital worlds, because whatever she is saying makes no sense to me.

'See, there is this invisible, virtual boyfriend app,' she starts to explain. 'You just need to download it on your phone and then you specify what you would like in your virtual guy. You chose the name, age, looks and even his personality. Once you've settled on your dream guy, that's when the real fun begins!'

'But if he is virtual and invisible, how does my mom meet him? After all, I really need a boyfriend for my mom to get a star in her mommy journal.' I don't point out that the side perks like sex and gifts are also missing in this relationship.

She looks at me like I am from the pre-Internet era. 'Your mom meets him through voice mails, SMS and his Facebook activity. How many friends do you really meet these days?'

She is fucking right. My eyes shine at this opportunity to create a guy and decide his traits. I can be God for once. And get Ma off my back for a while. One whole fun-filled hour later, I am actually excited about Vir Chawla, my virtual boyfriend. I met him through an ex-colleague on my wedding project at Jaisalmer. He is thirty-one years old. He is five feet ten inches tall, wheatish complexion and handsome. He is clean and organized but not a neat freak. He wears his shirt fully tucked in. He is a bit of a workaholic, since he is a highly placed consultant, but he never misses my FB posts and promptly RTs my tweets. He has Ranbir's innocence, Saif's naughtiness and Farhan's seriousness. I know—unbelievable right? In addition, he has an amazing sense of humour. Like I have barely known him and he's already sent me a message, 'Meha, you make Me-ha-ppy!'

Smiling to myself, I sit back and relax. Now I just have to wait for my mom to discover Vir, which I am sure she soon will. With the boyfriend-problem taken care of, I open my laptop to check for any new mails. I find a mail congratulating me on my new boyfriend. It says, 'If you find any issues with your order, please feel free to get in touch with our customer support. We are always open to feedback and suggestions.'

How APPtastic? A customized boyfriend that has a reference manual and is open to feedback. Martians couldn't get any better.

There is also a mail from NetGen informing me that she has already heard back from Yourstory and they are ready to highlight us. Woohoo! This is the best news I have heard in the whole day. I am positive we can get some leads from a Yourstory article. NetGen rocks! It's weird though that she didn't inform me verbally about it while we were talking. I turn around to praise her efforts but find her listening to something with headphones plugged in her ears. I wait thirty seconds for her to shift between her screens. But she doesn't. I send her an email commending her efforts. Next instant, I get her mail saying that she needs to send them my picture for the story. I turn to look at her, but I still can't make eye contact with her. She seems as occupied as she looked a minute earlier. Sometimes I feel like she is lost in the fast-pace of the digital world, which demands constant attention. *Congrats, your friend has endorsed you on LinkedIn, click here to build your reputation and identity. Follow fascinating people on Twitter and watch events unfold, in real time, from every angle. Buy now—slimming panty—up to 70% off.*

The irony is that in the online world, you do a whole lot of actions, all very quick, but you don't really do anything. It's like the movie *Click* where Adam Sandler puts his whole life, even having sex, on a 32X speed. You end up becoming a robot. The regular beeps of your devices keep your heart beating, but you lose the ability to deal with the imperfections of real world. There is a tiny bit of problem in this, especially if you live in Gurgaon. One hour into the interiors and there is no internet connectivity. Boom! Your source of subsistence is wiped out. And, God forbid, if it is a bigger issue like the network repairing broken cables without any connectivity for days, then you can go crazy like Tom Hanks in *Cast Away*—alone on an island, with only a dead piece of metal for a friend.

I shall get NetGen to go on a digital detox camp soon, but for now she needs my picture for the article. Quicker the article goes out, sooner I can get some respite. I put on some fresh makeup, undo the hair clutch and comb my hair, so that I can look my best. No, it has nothing to do with Samir looking as attractive as Keanu Reaves in his story. I don't care what he thinks of me. I mean he might not even see the article or my picture. I just need to look good because looks matter in my business. Technically, it's the look of the decor and designs, but you know, I can only create beauty if I feel it within and whatever is within shows in your picture.

I turn on my phone camera, smile, and click a selfie. There I am in a short, puffed-sleeve, yellow-printed Anokhi top. I like the way my lustrous dark brown hair bounces around my face and cascades down my shoulders with reckless abandon. But my earring is not visible. I try again, raising my hand this time for the perfect angle. I can see the wooden fish-shaped earring dangling down to my shoulders against my shiny locks, but my smile is forced. I am aiming for another, my hand hurting now, when I hear a sound from the window. I look outside and find myself eye to eye with a squirrel. She is standing on her hind legs, leaning against the window, holding a purple, squashed jamun in her paws for me.

I click a picture of the squirrel instead and post it on my FB with a caption, 'You never know who you may meet around the corner, holding a bittersweet treat for you.'

Nibbling on the juicy jamun, I decide I will ask the dimpled, creative assistant to click a nice photograph for me tomorrow. I have accomplished enough for a day. I have saved on Uber cost (by walking back from the movie), I skipped lunch (and avoided unnecessary calories), I am about to be featured in Yourstory, and I got a designer boyfriend (so what if he is virtual!). I smile at how imperfectly perfect my real world is. Glad that I can still handle whatever noose real life throws at me, I am about to leave for home when NetGen gets off the call and turns to me.

'We may get an international project,' she announces enthusiastically.

I am completely alert, with my eyes wide open. This is going to be one of those lousy days that eventually turn lucky. I wonder whose face I saw this morning. Before my heart can say someone's name, my mind crushes its voice ridiculing baseless superstitions.

'I messaged the founders of KISS on Facebook with a link to our FB page,' NetGen reveals her reason for hope.

'You what? No way! They wouldn't even bother to respond. You are wasting your time,' I tell her confidently, my balloon of excitement suddenly going *phuss*.

'Actually one of them already accepted my FB friend request.'

'Really?' I am surprised at how fake friendships can work in digital world. *Na naam pata na kaam, par teri post pe meri like aur meri post pe teri like.* 'It probably means nothing,' I tell NetGen.

'Ya, I thought so too, but then he called me up. I was talking to him just now.'

Now I am literally holding my breath. Relax! It must be the digital marketing manager of KISS. Why would someone as big as him bother to check a link in a random FB friend request?

'He called and said he sees potential in our work. He liked the wedding pictures showcased on our FB page, especially the one with rose petals in green popsicles on the dessert counter, decorated with matching potpourri.'

This can't be happening to me. It is Samir. That's where he hid the butterfly-earrings. I can't allow Samir to gatecrash like this into my life again. Maybe all is not lost, says my glass-is-half-full spirit.

'Did he…er…by any chance ask about…er…our team?' I inquire trying to figure if he knows this is my company. After all I did that potpourri design while I was working with Sarika.

'Of course I am not stupid. I informed Mr Samir Singhal to talk to you for any further discussions. I gave him your number. I hope that's fine. He promised to give you a call.' She looks eagerly at my face and expects an appreciation.

I know what she has done is indeed commendable. A project with KISS may save my company from dying. If I can survive the shock and the aftermath.

'Awesome (as in like OhSam),' is all I can bring myself to say weakly. I already feel like I am sinking.

I seek refuge in the impersonal, online world, but it seems Samir is now leaving traces in my online world too. He has already liked my FB page and the squirrel-post, which has gone viral. The post's title stares back mockingly at me. Samir Singhal is definitely the most unexpected bittersweet treat I could have run into.

I can hear the warning bells of impending doom, but my heart is stupidly humming, 'Tune mari entryan, dil mein baji ghantiyan'. It's amazing how my mind-jockey, MJ, always finds the song that suits my situation! For once, I wish I was living in a digital world. I could have just closed the browser window, erased the entire day and gotten Samir out of my life.

Of course, I have no clue that my stroke of luck has just begun!

Stroke of Luck – Part 1

Good luck or bad luck—I surely have a stroke of luck the next day.

My daily money-counting exercise reminds me that my ticket to the start-up island expires in thirty days. So much for safety in numbers! I always knew it was a farce. Weighing machines, report cards, credit card bills—numbers have often betrayed me. For your information, good numbers like good guys are rare.

After 2020 days of waiting, I finally get a message from Samsung Do Not Call.

'Lkng fwd to catching up soon.'

Hello? Please explain! Do you want to catch up for the lost time? If yes, how? What exactly are you looking forward to? Coffee? Will you call? How soon is this soon? If only guys can be more to the point, they won't have to produce a truck load of sperms to fertilize one egg.

A nasty argument breaks out between my mind and my heart on whether or not to call Samsung Do Not Call. The heart is still sulking in a corner singing, 'Love is a bhaste of time, karna hai bhaste of time'. This internal bickering results in calling names. My thoughtful self-calls my spontaneous self a shopaholic, frappoholic fatso. Just for a measly ₹3,000 that I didn't even spend. I only added some items to an online cart and wondered if we could do a quick stop at Starbucks on the way back home.

So I am trapped in *moh-maya-ka-jaal* with neither moh (love) nor maya (money), while I get my lucky break. A phone call from a business family planning their only son's wedding. I rush for the meeting, where I am greeted by a pot-bellied gentleman, an adraki mom in salwar-kameez-dupatta and an elegantly dressed grandmother.

'Is there a manager we can talk to, someone senior (like a guy, not a girl)?' Asks the uncomfortable father.

'But your costs are double that of colony's Raj tent-wallah. And he did such good arrangements for *mata ki chowki!*' That's the grandmother.

'How can your parents allow you to be out so late at night organizing marriages? Give me your mother's number. I will help her find you a nice guy. You are a *soni kudi. Rang kitta chokha hai, thoda weight dickreez kaar le vas,*' advises the mom.

I know entrepreneurship is not a first-class journey, so I patiently go through the social niceties. Two hours into the discussion and the deal is confirmed. The grandmother applies a *tilak* on my forehead to mark the auspicious occasion. Eating the celebratory *boondi ka ladoo,* I ask for some advance. The father takes me to a corner and tells in hushed voice that he is a law-abiding citizen and his money is all white. No murder or rape charge also. He will pay me handsomely, but there is one little *sick-ret.* '*Bas ladki abhi kachi umar ki hai.* We are very modern in our thoughts. Our son loves her so we agreed. You see, all is fair in love and war. The police is our friend, so no problem.'

Huh? No rape charge, police is friend and child marriage.

I smile my best smile, promise to work on the wedding plans and scoot as soon as possible.

Looks like it's one of those days where the 'L' in my luck has changed to 'F', so I decide to leave office early. It's 5 p.m. sharp; time for my tea date with Mansi. I get out of the lift and walk to our apartment. Sharma uncle, our neighbour, opens his door as he sees me walk by in the corridor. He hands me the newspaper bill, revised with deductions for the days when the newspaper wasn't delivered and a courier. I smile and thank him for his help, unlock the door and go in.

Mansi is sitting at the coffee table, dressed in a sleeveless, body-hugging, red dress. A diamond pendant dangles down the front of her sexy scoop-neck. Her stylish short hair adds to the look. I whistle as she stands up to welcome me. The dress stops slightly above her knees and the thin straps of her black stilettos climb up her slim, shapely legs. Behind her, on the table, is my favourite Frappuccino and mouth-watering cinnamon-streusel coffee cake, fresh from the bakery. OMG! Mansi is better than a boyfriend is. I open my arms and give her a huge hug.

'Whom are you planning to kill?' I ask teasingly, my stress melting away as fast as the cake and the coffee in my mouth.

'Just Aseem,' she says casually, her dimples accentuating the warmth of her smile.

'You mean you are in this explosive bomb of an outfit just to be diffused by your six-month-stale boyfriend, who is a bag of shit.'

'His name is Aseem Bagchi.'

'That's what I said,' I snigger. I can feel my mood elevating with my sugar levels.

'You're still angry because he didn't let you go on the wedding team to Venice? Grow up Meg! That was two years ago.'

I didn't tell her how Aseem had wanted to ride me in exchange for a free gondola ride. I mean I had warned her when she had started seeing Aseem that he had the reputation of a playboy, but Mansi had said he has changed. Besides, Mansi is an expert when it comes to judging guys. She knows their psyche in and out. And she has been happier in the last six months than ever before. Therefore, I really hope and pray for her sake that the asshole has changed, because Mansi really deserves to be happy. And I also hope Samir has changed because I deserve to be happy too.

'Aseem is taking me out for dinner tonight to the Leela hotel. I think he is going to propose,' Mansi squeals excitedly.

'Wow!' I say, although that's not quite how I feel.

'You sound like I am stepping into a pile of poop.'

'You mean like a BAG of CHHI!' I shrug my shoulders and raise my eyebrows in a smirk and we both end up laughing.

I really want to be thrilled for Mansi. If there is one person who deserves true love, it's her. She has had a string of stories of bad luck with scumbags. She almost got married six years ago to one. Even the wedding cards were printed. At the last moment, she realized that he had a history of alcohol addiction and drug abuse. After that, she had met one dickhead after another. I am all for marriage. I mean, I am a wedding planner after all. I know there are jokes about marriages but I think marriages are beautiful. I think marriage is the only way to make love last. And a life without love is functional but meaningless—just like soap without fragrance, a rose without colour and a cloud without rain. A life like mine!

'Ok, now tell me what's bothering you besides your start-up's frail health?' Mansi asks, looking straight into my eyes.

She knows me too well. She can sense the storm brewing

in my soul.

'Samir Singhal. I had a sort-of encounter with him.'

'The same treating-sex-as-coffee Samir? The Senorita Samir? The wild-rose fragrance Samir?'

I nod to all.

'Where? How? Did you kiss him?'

'No, I didn't kiss him,' I say in my defence and then update her. 'But, what makes you think I will kiss him even if I met him in person?'

'C'mon Hon! Whom are you kidding?' She shakes her head knowingly at me. 'You haven't been able to get over Samir in all these years. Every guy you have dated in the last five years has fallen short in comparison to him.'

I sullenly take another sip of my Frappuccino, but say nothing. The truth is that every guy I have dated has been interested only in sex under the pretext of love. And its Mansi who has helped me see through their intentions. Although Samir was no different, Mansi knows I have not been able to forget him. Mansi is supposed to make me feel better and not be honest.

'Listen, I am sorry but I've got to run,' she says, ruffling my hair affectionately as she picks up her handbag. Before she is out of the door, she turns back. 'I seriously think you need to get closure with Samir. Just go and meet him. Sometimes the best way to move forward is to go back.'

The door shuts with a bang, as there is strong cross-ventilation on high floors in our building. I take the last sip of Frappuccino and close my eyes. I know Mansi is right. I still have feelings for Samir. I don't know what else he had, but he had a knack of making me feel special. He could touch me with his words and do magic with his eyes like no one could. I can see him smiling at me from the balcony. I smile back.

He comes closer and moves aside a strand of hair falling on my cheek. He holds the hair behind my ear and looks at me questioningly. His eyes are sad. I can see he has missed me. 'I have missed you too,' I say as he comes closer and then lean forward to kiss him. I come back from my reverie with a start as my phone beeps for my attention. Shucks, I kissed him in my thoughts. Mansi is absolutely right. I need to move ahead, but no way am I going to meet Samir Singhal. What I really need is a dose of Vitamin S—just like my mom suggested.

I log on to Facebook and send lets-meet-up messages to guys who had approached me in the last few months but I had been too busy to explore. I am excited to see a comment on my FB squirrel post from Vir, my new virtual boyfriend.

'I wonder who you met around the corner? ;);)'

That's amusing. I like his comment. Realizing that I am online, the next minute, he sends me a message asking what I am wearing. Three naughty smiles trail behind the text. I am about to tell him that I am wearing a brown skirt with a loose, yellow top to hide my bulges, when I realize he is not real. I don't need to be real either. I need to get back in the dating game. What can be a better opportunity to practice?

I type back, 'Nothing. I am in the bathroom getting ready for a shower.'

'Can I join you?'

Wow, this software is good.

'What are you doing right now?' I ask to see how far the programmed mind can go.

'I am driving back home. I can be with you in half an hour.'

C'mon, he is digital. Why can't he be here now?

'But I need you here with me right now,' I say flirting with him in my imagination.

'Oh babes! This Cyber Hub road is all broken and blocked with traffic jam.'

Wow, the app can customize his location to mine.

'How about we talk naughty over the phone?' he suggests.

Fucking awesome, I think. Even if he was here with me, we would be talking over the phone. But him, stuck in traffic and talking naughty makes it more exciting. The best part is that the social-interactivity feature costs thousand bucks a month, but NetGen had enough referral points to get me a free three month full-service pack including FB posts, SMS, WhatsApp, calls, one hand-written note every month and even a small gift.

'Why don't you wear a smile? You'll look pretty with it,' I hear him say.

I smile.

'So you are in the shower?'

'Mm-hmm,' I say and walk over to my bathroom to make it a real experience.

'Does your soap have a fragrance?'

'Yes, it's the wild-rose fragrance from FabIndia.'

'I love that smell. Ok, Give me the soap and hold my hand and I will rub it all over you.'

Wow. He actually has a bathroom-sex module. I wonder what he will say next.

'I like the touch of your skin. Its soft and silky, like Cadbury.'

I close my eyes let my imagination run wild.

This is too good. Why can't this chip be implanted into real guys?

'Just hold on. I can see a traffic police coming towards me. I will have to keep the phone down for a minute.'

Shit man! This is good. The romance, the sensitivity, the tension.

Half an hour later, showered, satisfied and smiling, I pick up my phone again. There is a message from Vir saying that he is sorry that the phone got disconnected. He will make up for it next time. I don't bother to reply. What gets me jumping on my bed is the picture of Mansi with a diamond on her finger. I can't believe that the asshole actually proposed. I message her back that she has to let me plan her wedding. I am elated. I play the latest catchy number, *Banno, tera swagger laage sexy,* on my phone and start dancing.

In the kitchen, I chop some tomatoes, cucumber, onions and toss them with feta cheese, vinegar, lemon, salt and pepper. My Greek salad ready. I sit back on my favourite orange beanbag with a Sophie Kinsella and get lost in meaningless romance.

I don't hear Samir's call because of the loud music. I only check my phone an hour later. My heart starts waltzing at the sight of the missed caller's name. Without seeking neurological consultation, I press the call back button. It rings and rings and rings, but no one answers. I resist the temptation to throw away my phone. Instead, I open Facebook. I am stupefied to see that while I was lost in a book, a whole war of words has transpired between Samir and Vir on my squirrel post.

Samir: I also got a bittersweet treat today.

Vir: Is the treat more important or the person holding the treat?

Samir: Depends on the treat :)

Vir: It's definitely the person for me!

Samir: People leave, treats stay.

Vir: Then you need a course in the 'Art of Loving'.

Samir: Still looking for the right person to teach me.

Vir: Good luck.

Something in Samir's comments tells me that the fire is

burning on the other side too. My mind knows I am wrong, but my heart wants to meet him now. To be his treat. To educate him in the 'Art of Loving'. To make him fall in love with me!

Eagerly, I try his number once again. It's switched off now. I leave it dejected. I have already called twice. I already look so needy.

I reply to his comment on FB, 'What if the person is sweet but the treat is bitter?' I wait impatiently for the sweet Samir to answer back and offer me a better treat than last time.

Stroke of Luck – Part 2

I must have fallen asleep while reading, as I didn't hear Mansi walk in. I wake up to her movement, then she cuddled up to me by the beanbag and then her stilettos crash into my empty salad bowl.

'Hey, congraaaats,' I say, yawning widely. 'Where is the ring? Show me.'

She gets herself together to sit straight, but falls back on the floor with a thud. I laugh loudly. It looks like she's had a little too much wine. Usually, she knows when to stop, because she hates hangovers. But I guess it's not every day that you get proposed. Thinking of which, I ask why she is not with assho…er…Aseem tonight. I can hear some incoherent sounds coming from her, almost like a rhythmic yoga chant. Seconds later, it's a full-fledged, convulsive wailing. Shocked, I turn her body sideways so I can look at her. She looks like she is at a Halloween party; her eyes are ghastly with the makeup all smudged by her tears.

In the last five years, I have seen Mansi drunk and pass out many times—even down and low when her dad was diagnosed with cancer few years back, but this is the worst condition I have ever seen her. I just stare at her helplessly. She continues to sob silently. I try and get her to drink a glass of cold water. She manages to get herself upright, her back leaning against the beanbag.

'I must be looking scary,' she mumbles as she takes a sip of water, her voice hoarse from crying.

'Ya,' I admit glumly. 'Like Kareena Kapoor in that movie *Heroine*.'

'Ick! I much prefer how Deepika looks when she cries in *Cocktail*.'

'Maybe you should try not to wear eyeliner next time,' I offer my advice with all sincerity.

She goes silent. It looks like she is going to burst into another round of tears and nose blowing, so I try and be flippant. 'But you sure sound sexy with a deep, melancholy voice—totally Catherine Zeta Jones types.'

The compliment brings a hint of a smile on her kajal and tear-streaked face. I smile back. I don't ask her what happened, although I am dying of curiosity. Perhaps some lovers' tiff. I know she will tell me anyway, so I wait for her to compose herself.

'It was all very well planned,' she starts to narrate a few moments later. 'I reached the hotel lobby at ten minutes to eight. Aseem was there to meet me. Light pink shirt and black trousers—he was looking quite imposing. He held out his elbow and I wrapped my hand around his arm. Our table was set at a corner, with the most beautiful roses in the centre and two pretty, scented candles. He ordered the finest wine and we talked about our ambitions, future plans and families over an elaborate, sumptuous meal. The band was playing romantic numbers softly in the distance. It was almost time for dessert and he hadn't bought up the topic, so I thought he might be getting cold feet. I didn't mind. The evening was perfect in all ways. I was happy. Then came the dessert plate with the words "Will you marry me" inscribed on it in chocolate. I was zapped. And then, he took out this most exquisite diamond solitaire ring and went down on his knees. Meha, I was absolutely swept off my feet. The joy I felt is indescribable. Immediate I said "yes" and he put the ring on my finger and the waiters clicked some pictures of us together.'

'You look divine in the picture you sent,' I say with real heartfelt happiness. At this, she bursts into a long, whining whimper.

'Mansi, what happened? Did your engagement ring fall off in the commode?' She shakes her head.

'You didn't...er...fart in his face, right?' I mean that's the worst I can imagine. At this, she completely stops crying and looks at me, disgusted. 'Eeww, no way.'

She takes another sip of water and continues her story. 'Feeling all bubbly, like the champagne we had quaffed, we were about to go to his place, when he excused himself to go the men's room. A minute later, I heard his phone ringing from under the table—having fallen from his shirt pocket when he had bent down to propose. I picked it up to see that it was Sarika calling. It was rather late for her to call, but you know how she is. When she gets an idea, she has to announce it to the world instantly. I ignored it and let it go unanswered. I didn't want any business discussion to spoil our special evening. The phone stopped after a while, but seconds later a message flashed on its screen. It was from her saying, 'The million-dollar-Spain wedding is...' Eager to know more, I swiped his phone to read the full message. She had written, 'The million-dollar-Spain wedding is yours, provided you can make me happy tonight. I am waiting for you in my bedroom, wearing only your favourite

Jasmine perfume.'

'No way! That bitch! Isn't she married or something?' Startled, I speak my thoughts out loud. I am too sober for this shit. I knew Sarika was a mean, conniving and a manipulative boss, but I didn't know that her employee's performance appraisal sheet included the number of successfully delivered orgasms. No wonder, I could never satisfy her.

Mansi is back to crying, but it's a drizzle. An occasional tear drop falling from her eyes, without the rumbling of a thunder.

'What if it's one-sided? Maybe she is forcing herself on Aseem?' I try to console her. There is very little conviction in my voice.

'I hoped for that too, so I left the phone back under the table and pretended not to have read the message. When Aseem got back I helped him search for the phone and we found it. He then checked the notifications and saw Sarika's message. I saw his eyes gleam with joy as he read her message. Seconds later, he clutched his stomach and grimaced with pain. Then he had the gall to tell me to go home because with the way he was feeling, it wouldn't be the night he had planned.'

Surprisingly, I find that I am not at all surprised. I can see that asshole changing colours at the sight of money. I strongly resist the temptation to say 'I told you so' to Mansi. She is not crying any more, but the pain is going to transform into a bruise, which will hurt for a long time. I can see that she is already blaming herself for having fallen for his charm.

'Why is it always me, Meha? Why does it always happen to me? Why can't I find one decent guy to get married? You know, even after he read the bitch's message he said he loves me. Why?' She looks almost childlike.

I want to comfort her. I want to tell her that she will find a decent guy who will love her with all his heart, just like I want to tell myself that Samir loves me. But I can't bring myself to give her false hope. I just hold her tight and hug her. She hugs me back and then after a while, she falls asleep on the floor, her head in my lap. I lift her head, set it on a pillow and lie down next to her. We both fall asleep.

Next morning, I wake up to the sound of loud music playing on Mansi's phone through an external speaker. She is standing in our balcony, drinking straight from an open bottle of vodka, singing loudly, and dancing wildly to her own tune.

'Char botal vodka,
Ass-fucked-up Sarika
Na use koi roke
Na Mansi ne roka
Saari raat Sarika, subah Mansi honey
He asked me to marry, but he only loves money

kyunki kyunki kyunki...'

I rush to the balcony. Mansi is now standing on a chair and yelling her version of the song. She is still wearing the red dress from last night, crumpled and tear-stained, but seductive nonetheless. I try to pull her down, as I see the uncle next door in white kurta and pyjama trying to locate the source of this wake up call in the morning. A couple of other guys are also staring up from the floors below. I put on a 'he-he-she-is-a-little-high' smile as I drag an inebriated Mansi inside the house. I take away the half-empty bottle from her hand and drain it down the sink. What a waste of Absolut! The sacrifices one has to do for one's friends!

I then sort of push her inside the bathroom. I am glad

that she is rather light and much thinner than I am. Imagine someone having to drag a drunken seal like me. I open the shower and let the water pour over her. As the cold water hits her system, she sobers a bit.

'Don't sleep off in there!' I warn her and go to the kitchen to fix some breakfast for us. It's 8 a.m. on a Friday morning and I have to get to work. But there really isn't a lot of work and Mansi needs me. Half an hour later, Mansi walks out to our small round breakfast table looking sorted. Wearing a blue, cotton palazzo and white spaghetti, her hair freshly washed and last night's make-up all gone, she looks as attractive as ever. I wonder why any guy would leave someone like her for another woman.

She gives me a grateful smile when she sees the food and attacks the sandwiches with the ferocity of a hungry pauper. I check my phone to see if Samir has messaged yet. No response. He has gone silent. What is it with Martians running up the hills when a woman shows interest? And they say women are complicated. At least we are consistently complicated.

With the hangover washed down by carbohydrates and two cups of hot ginger tea, Mansi looks totally fresh and alert.

'I am leaving Dream Wedding Planners,' she says, her eyes focussed on the bird-feeder in the balcony. Her fingers toying with the empty cup in her hand.

I smile at this awesome news. I have been telling her to work with me for months. She is well networked.

'You don't have to be an employee of course. You can come in as co-founder.'

'I am going for the Everest Base Camp trek,' she says, ignoring my suggestion.

'What?'

'Yes, I am flying to Kathmandu tomorrow afternoon. I just confirmed with the trekking group. They have a vacant spot. The EBC trek starts the day after.'

'Are you mad? Don't you need training for this kind of stuff? What if you die there? Have you told your parents?' I bombard her with all random fears.

'Meg, I have wanted to do EBC for a very long time, but the bitch would never give me a three-weeks off. EBC is an easy trek. It doesn't require any specific training, only basic fitness. And no, hopefully I won't die there. About my parents, there is connectivity all the way up to the base camp. I will keep talking to them. They won't know a thing.'

I stare at her determined self, totally dumb-founded. I am scared for her. And, I am scared for myself too—of being alone, without her. Girls can survive without a boyfriend, but not without a best friend.

'Oh! You will be fine, honey,' she says reading the fear my eyes. 'In fact, you will be more than fine. I am going to make you happy and rich. Very, very rich.'

I cannot fathom anything she is saying anymore. Either she has gone crazy with shock or I used vodka instead of water while making tea and we are both drunk.

She picks up her phone and calls someone. 'Hi Sonia,' she says warmly. I see a very pretty face appear on her screen. It is a video call.

'I hope you were not busy,' she asks, still warm but formal.

I see Sonia is sitting and smoking in a luxurious hotel room.

'I am always free for my proposal designer,' Sonia says in a sweet, Kat-like anglicised voice—dressed in a short, spaghetti-strap dress, she looks model-hot.

'Sonia, I am leaving Dream Wedding.'

Sonia's eyes grow wide with alarm at this unexpected news. She takes small, quick puffs of her cigarette.

'Don't worry. Your proposal will be in safe hands.' Mansi assures her.

'You know how comfortable I am with you,' Sonia sort of complains. 'Can't you stay on for two weeks more?'

'I really can't,' Mansi says earnestly. 'But I have Meha here, who can do your proposal better than me.'

I totally understand the discomfort on Sonia's face. I still don't know what game Mansi is playing.

'Sonia, Aseem has been sending you all the ideas from Meha's blog. The presentation he had me mail you was designed based on a wedding Meha planned in Thailand last year.'

Both Sonia and I look aghast at this revelation. Mansi had used pictures from my blog for her company.

'Honey, its competition!' she informs me, putting the call on hold for a moment. 'Aseem got a junior to do it. Besides, to be fair, not that I want to be fair to the asshole, it's out on the net. Anyone can use and copy it.'

I have no idea what to feel right now. Flattered like Picasso at being plagiarized or angry like the HarvardConnection.com whose FB idea Mark Zuckerberg had stolen.

'And she can do it at much lower price,' I hear Mansi say, as she continues to give the spiel about my services to Sonia.

Sonia's eyes sparkle at this latest information. 'I am not the one to compromise quality for money, but I am always interested in encouraging upcoming talent. If no one had encouraged me when I was a newcomer, how would I be a top model today?'

'So Meha, can you design a surprise proposal for my boyfriend, in about two weeks from now, at Phi Phi island?' Sonia asks, this time looking at me directly.

I will deal with Mansi later on plagiarism. Right now, it's time for business. I get down to understanding the details from Sonia. She tells me her mom is planning her dad's sixtieth birthday in eighteen days from now. It's a two-day-long event, which her mom is organizing. She expects her boyfriend to join her. With all her family around, she wants to propose to him on the second day, before dinner. She needs me to do only the proposal design, a post-proposal dance and a photo story the morning after. She asks me how much I can do it for.

I calculate the expenses roughly for a twelve-member crew, flights and an extra day for shopping at Bangkok. I won't go so far and not shop at Bangkok. All costs included, the project should be doable in about twenty lacs. I am about to say thirty lacs adding a fifty percent service fee, when Mansi shushes me.

'Sonia, Meha can do it for a crore, with a twenty-five percent advance,' says Mansi in a business like tone. 'You've got to agree that it's a steal. And you will get work of better quality.' That's my personal guarantee to you.'

Sonia walks around the room, considering the price, while I hit Mansi's feet under the table for overpricing. I am about to reduce the price when Sonia says, 'It's a really great deal Mansi, but what about ethics? You know I have verbally committed to Aseem. Only the paper work is left, which is to be signed today.'

'Sonia,' Mansi is personal and intimate now. 'I am the first to honour a commitment. You know that "I" in my dictionary stands for integrity. But, I realized that some people don't know decency from dick-sense. Not only did Aseem steal Meha's ideas and present them as his team's work to you, which is in itself unscrupulous, he also proposed to me last evening and then went and obliged Sarika later in the night.'

Mansi Luthra is in full a 'Man-ass-i-Lootera' (I will rob the guy's ass) mood, while Sonia looks horrified.

'I hate cheaters,' Sonia is vehement. 'Meha, you are on. I will have the paper work sent to your email in an hour and the advance wired within the next twenty-four hours.'

There is a knock on Sonia's door and a vaguely familiar voice calling her name. 'My boyfriend is here. We will discuss the rest later,' Sonia whispers and immediately disconnects.

'Ooh Mansi. I love you!' I jump in delight and kiss her. I have suddenly gone from brooding like a bounced cheque to glowing like a million bucks.

An hour later, as promised, I get an email from Sonia with all the paper work. She has also sent her personal details like her favourite colours, songs and brands, her family background and other necessary information. The deal is signed and confirmed.

I still can't believe that my luck has turned. I feel like I have stepped into *The Land of Take-What-You-Want* from the Faraway tree in the novel *Enchanted Woods*. I am drinking from a Frappuccino fountain. Sonia is like Silky, the Fairy.

Few hours later, I get more good news. Samir has replied. He is busy travelling for the next couple of weeks and then guess what? He is also going to be in Phi Phi Island on the same dates as me, shooting a sixtieth birthday celebration.

There is just a slight hitch. Samir has got changed to a hot-bod model Sonia for a girlfriend and I am their official proposal designer.

Dear bad luck, let's break up!

The Surprisee and To-Be-Surprised

Right now, I am on a ferry to Koh Phi Phi, trying to fall in love with my new boyfriend. I can't believe I finally got Samsung. To tell you the truth, it's not been a great experience so far. I mean I like my guys to be grounded, simple and open source, but I am having trouble adjusting with this new phone.

I hope you didn't confuse Samsung for Samir Singhal. Did you? Haven't you heard jokes about the phone being the other girl in a guy's life? Tell you what. We are a generation of equal rights. For a girl, this smart piece of hardware has become very much like a phoney boyfriend. I realized this only a few days back, when I broke the screen of my really cool, but a bit too sensitive Xiomi for the third time. Do you think it's normal for a person to break their phone's screen thrice in three weeks? But then, not a lot has been normal since Sonia got added to my client list.

So, for last few days I am trying to get familiar with my new boyfriend. It's not been easy. I have to admit I miss my old one and wonder why it had to break. The new one doesn't know any of my previous conversations. No context, no understanding, no auto-correct. Communication is so hard and I end up pressing the wrong buttons. I also don't like the boring clothes it wears.

I must get it a flowery, colourful cover from Bangkok, on my way back.

The only plus point is the show-your-palm-to-click-selfie feature in-built in the camera. Sitting on the open deck of the ferry, I can see endless vast, deep, blue ocean all around me through the phone's camera lens. It's an amazing photo opp. Mesmerized by the scenic beauty, my mind wants to hum 'Aaj blue hai paani...aur din bhi sunny...aa jao on the beach yaar, photo meri kheench', but my heart is not cooperating. The mind can't understand why the heart is being so moody when everything is so perfect. Our FB page has seen unprecedented action with the Yourstory article coming out last week. My latest FB post titled, 'If you want to know how committed your girlfriend is in a relationship, see how often she changes her phone', has also been doing rather well. My beachwear is sneaked out of its hibernation and is looking forward for some action, while my parents believe I am in Ooty for work. I got a tight grip on my new phoney boyfriend. Vir is only a touch away. Even Surya is being friendly despite the rainy season.

I ought to feel exhilarated. Yet, I am a bit gloomy. I know it's not sea-sickness. It's not even the fear of losing the insanely expensive, most exquisite, heart-shaped engagement ring that has taken the outstanding balance on my credit card up by twenty-five lakhs. I wish it was mine, but it's Sonia's. I am only a-Frappuccino-a-day rich. But I am not miserable because she is sixteen-warehouses-full-of-chocolate rich. It's something else. I can smell its dampness. I can feel its lingering presence, like a shadow lurking in a corner. I think I recognize its blue, sulking outline. It's sadness. Sadness that a story is going to end soon. The story of a young girl and a handsome boy. The story that started out with a hot and steamy affair on the beaches of Goa, but got lost in the haste of youthfulness. I should be glad I am getting to write the final act. And I have done an excellent job of the same.

But I don't feel good. I wanted to be the girl who gets the guy in the end. I wanted the lead role. I even resisted being sidelined as a supporting cast.

The night before Mansi left for the EBC trek, she, Tanu Di and I went to a pub. I told Mansi that I don't want to do this project and she said I was being stupid.

She said, 'Sonia is going to propose any way. The only variable is who gets richer in the process, Sarika or you?'

When she put it that way, there really was no choice. What else was I supposed to do? Call up Sonia and tell her that I can't design her proposal, because I love your boyfriend. In fact, I think he might love me too, although we haven't spoken in the last five years. But he mentioned something about a bittersweet treat on FB, which can only be me, because you are all so sweet and can't possibly be bitter. Well, I almost did. In my thoughts at least. And every single time I tried to imagine the scenario, it never ended with Samir saying he loves me.

So, I am just doing my work and taking the people out of the picture—don't even articulate their names. They shall be the Surprisee and the To-Be-Surprised. It's the healthy and cheaper option to maintain my sanity and it lends a whole secretive flavour to the project. It works most of the time. Except when Sonia starts to rave about the charm bracelet with stiletto, purse and dress charms that Samir gifted her. Or how he made a photo puzzle with her pictures and although she hates puzzles, she loved it because her pictures were amazing. Or how he calls her baby doll and told her that this is the longest he has been with any girl. She thinks he was hinting they should get married and so she has decided to propose.

It is at these times that my heart takes refuge in the land of 'Take-What-You-Want with seventy-five lakh rupees' in the Enchanted Woods, while my mind continues to pencil in details of the Surprisee and To-Be-Surprised. I am so often wandering in this dream land that even my virtual boyfriend is feeling neglected, my weighing machine is feeling lighter and I have no idea that a certain rat is wrecking havoc in the office, having already chewed and gnawed the butts of over six dozen HB pencils. I am stuck with Blue Cloud as a constant partner.

The boat reins in sharply and I am summoned from my wool-gathering expedition. I see these giant black rocks looming ominously over us and our ferry heading for a fatal collision into the rocks. Oh God! I lied to my parents and ventured into the dangerous waters. Now I will die unmarried and my mom will never get a big star in her mommy journal. I am just about to call my mom and tell her I love her when it suddenly appears, almost like a mirage, concealed behind the high rocks. The popular, picturesque paradise of Phi Phi islands with its famous white-sand beaches and turquoise blue water.

I sigh as I take in the beautiful view. I look around for my team. They are all happily scattered. The seasick ones are holding their stomachs in the cabin below. Amit is clicking his selfie and WhatsApping his newly wed wife. Pyare is holding NetGen's hand so her slight frame doesn't get carried away by the strong wind, while she shoots a video of the approaching island for our FB post.

'It's OK, you will have fun,' I assure myself. 'Just avoid a five feet ten inch tall, extremely handsome guy, with a wild-rose fragrance that can set you back by seventy-five lakh rupees.' I turn around, smile and click a picture-postcard selfie.

As I get up to disembark the ferry, I sneak one last look at the ring, inside my purse, to make sure it's there. It is designed as two diamond-studded S's, facing each other. The two S's, representing the Surprisee and To-Be-Surprised (TBS), which are joined at the top and the bottom to form a heart. Ever since I got it, the ring has been weighing me down like the Hobbit. I really didn't want to shoulder this responsibility, but I couldn't refuse. The Surprisee told me to buy the ring on my card, as she didn't want her dad to be alert by the expense and foil her surprise proposal. I shall be glad to soon unburden my purse. Acting confident, but feeling nothing like it, I walk out of the ferry to meet the Surprisee.

Thirty hours later, I am stationed in a snug, tree house, about ten feet above ground, on a strong sturdy tree. I take a swig of beer, munch on some cheesy chips and look through binoculars. I can see the partially covered patio of the bar and lounge, minimally decked up for the evening cocktail party. The lounge is mostly empty right now. An SMS from NetGen informs me that we are all set for lights, camera and action. She sends me pictures of all the ten crossword clues of Sonia's treasure hunt proposal, hidden around the newly built, boutique Zeavola resort. Clues that will lead TBS to the precious ring. Good job!

I love this unusual work place. A rope ladder leading up to a small, open porch and little shed with two windows. It's straight out of a *Magic Tree House* book. I had chosen this hidey-hole to hide well. But now, I can feel a childish excitement of running a covert operation, from a secret hideout. I suddenly feel a strong desire to talk to my childhood friend Anusha. This magic tree house has brought back memories of our secret hideouts. I have been missing her more than ever in last few weeks. Ever since

I got her email saying, she is alive and is soon coming to visit her parents in Gurgaon. But I have had no way to reach out to her. I have only an email address, which simply takes my mail in and returns nothing.

I grab another big gulp of beer as I wait for the treasure hunt to begin, with only tear-shaped sadness in his blue PJs for company. I can't resist another look at the message that I had been waiting for in the last two weeks. TBS finally SMSed this afternoon, after he landed in Phi Phi, apologizing for being busy and in no network areas. He wants to meet me next week for coffee, only it will be too late to have anything other than coffee. I am wondering if things would have been different had we met for coffee before I took on Sonia's proposal, when an 'F' icon materializes on my phone.

It's from him. He has just replied to my bittersweet comment on FB. No way! He is supposed to be with Sonia, in their villa, at this very moment. Why is he FB-ing me from his girlfriend's bedroom?

'If the first treat is bitter, ask the sweet person for another treat.'

Ask for another treat? He got to be kidding? I am tempted to jump off the tree house and go running into his arms, but I guess I am a little high—topographically, as well as alcoholically. So I just lie down, my heart humming 'Chadhi mujhe yaari teri aisi, jaise daaru desi'.

Luckily, although I am wary of using this word these days, whether I smile or cry—this chapter ends in an hour. So I might as well enjoy my stay in this offbeat, heaven on Earth. I grab hold of the gloomy figure in blue garb tailing behind me and put it in a box marked 'Sadness. Do Not Open'. Beerily buoyant, I start dancing as the music that comes on in the lounge. It's 7 p.m. The older people have all left on a private yatch for a celebratory dinner cruise. Young adrenalin and ecstasy are beginning to pulsate on the dance floor.

I visualize Sonia in a provocative beach kaftan seducing TBS. She is about to challenge him to solve a treasure hunt. She will promise to fulfil each one of his fantasies and more if he can crack the clues within ten minutes.

Hunt started. I get an update as TBS is seen heading out of Sonia's villa. As I had predicted, he has taken on the challenge.

Clue 1 solved. TBS moving to Clue 2...Clue 5 solved. Updates. He is solving them faster than I had calculated, obviously eager to get his prize. When it comes to guys, happiness is finding a solution, more so if it involves having sex.

Sonia makes a grand entry on the porch. Having changed into a short, off-shoulder dress. She looks more stunning in real life than on the computer screen. It's obvious why anyone would fall for her. She pretends to enjoy the party and chatters excitedly with the guests. I know she is waiting anxiously for TBS to make an appearance.

'#9 deciphered. Final countdown begins,' NetGen's voice booms in my ears. I am getting non-stop live commentary on the phone.

I hold my breath as I wait for him to appear on the patio any moment now. I can see the hiding place of the last and final clue from my binoculars. The entire proposal is a series of crossword clues leading him finally to a potpourri vase, which contains the ring. This should be easy for him. The potpourri container holds the ring in a pouch, exactly the way he hid the butterfly-earrings for me. I can't hear his voice or smell his fragrance, but I can feel the colour rising to my cheeks as he enters the porch. In denim shorts and a pale-blue shirt, he looks dashing even at a distance in the dim light. He glances at the potpourri vase and then looks around. Sonia is standing real close to him, giggling and whispering something in his ears, but he seems distracted. 'Why is he not reaching for the vase?' I ask but no one in the team answers. I know they are all waiting in their positions, to capture the finale.

After what seems like eternity, he finally fishes out the pouch from the vase. Sonia is bubbling with excitement like a shaken cola. I don't want to see or hear the drama any more. I stumble over the pile of empty beer cans and step out on the open wooden platform. Two orange and white butterflies follow each other around the tree house. They seem to be in perfect harmony. *No binding of marriage and yet they are together forever.* Involuntarily, I smile as I recall these lines from Samir's notes. Sweet memories seem to be my refuge right now. I don't want to focus on the present and it doesn't even register when it starts to rain crazily. The lounge porch is covered so there is no need to panic, but the tree house porch is not exactly waterproof.

Suddenly I hear his voice calling my name over the din of the rain. It sounds clear and up close. It's coming over the phone connection I have on with NetGen. Standing on the ledge of the platform, I try to focus on the lounge porch, which is roughly twenty-feet away. I can see Samir holding the ring in his hand. But instead of looking at Sonia, why is he looking towards the tree house? I can't help but melt into a smile when I figure he is looking at me with his mischievous eyes. I feel something glowing within.

'What is Meha doing here?' he asks.

'I hired her,' explains Sonia. 'She is our proposal designer. Isn't she terrific?'

'Yeah…she is terrific.'

'This whole treasure hunt proposal is her brainchild,' Sonia is being kind to me. Why is she so nice? It would have been easier to hate her if she was nasty, mean and rude.

'What? The treasure hunt...' He looks from Sonia to the ring, utterly confused. 'You're...er...proposing to me, right now?' It seems like he was so involved in solving the puzzle that he has missed the whole point of the exercise.

With an angelic smile, Sonia tilts her head to a side, extends her left hand, waiting for him to slide the ring on her finger.

'Can you wait? I need to talk to Meha,' says Samir.

'I am sure it can wait until after our engagement dance,' Sonia asserts, slightly irritated, but Samir is moving forward.

'You are ruining it, Sam. Let's dance,' Sonia is exasperated, but he is long gone. 'Why do you care for Meha?' Sonia shouts aloud after him.

He is coming towards me, ignoring the rain. I can hear the engagement song playing in the background. 'Tera hone laga hoon...jabse mila hoon...come and feel me...'

I walk forward too, wet hair on my face, water dripping on my nose, crooning 'come and feel me'. Except I slip and fall over the ledge of the tree house, in my inebriated state. But I don't land with a thud on the ground. I land softly in his warm arms, just like I had bumped into the crisp-linen-shirt photographer five years ago, crooning this very song. Without any warning, the wild-rose fragrance of his deodorant invades my personal space and magically transports me into a blissful, dreamy state.

Tsunami

My head is resting in someone's lap. I breathe in the wildly sweet fragrance. I know whose lap it is. I feel his fingers running through my hair. It slows down the merry-go-round spinning in my head. I know this dream. I have had it before.

As if on cue, my favourite song starts to play in the background. 'Nahi jeena tere baaju...main tenu samjhawan ki...na tere bina lagda jee...tu ki jaane pyaar mera...main karoon intezar tera... tu dil tui-yon jaan meri'. I don't want to live without you. How do I make you understand that my heart feels lonely without you? You don't know my love or that I wait for you, but you are my heart—my life!

It takes me a minute to register that it's actually my phone ringing. Only yesterday, while I was waiting for Samir in the tree house, I had set this song as my caller tune. I reach out for my phone, but I can't find it. It goes unanswered. I try to open my eyes but it's too bright. Argh! Surya has again barged into my room. Through half-closed eyes, I lazily watch cotton candy clouds float above me. Wait a sec. I don't remember putting cloudy-sky wallpaper on my ceiling. Something is amiss. I am not at home, at least not mine. Where am I? It can't be a dream because I definitely heard the phone ring and I can still see the white castles sailing in the blue sky. Focus, Meha,

*focus. Okay, yeah. Last I remember, I was in a quaint tree house.
Samir called out my name. I started walking towards him and...
and I fell. Oh my God, No! Really? There is no other explanation
for the clouds and Samir's presence. I am dead! I hope its heaven.
It sure feels heavenly lying in Samir's lap, being caressed by him.
Did he die too or is he a figment of my imagination?*

I wish he would kiss me.

*He pushes a lock of hair from my face, looks into my eyes, and
smiles. 'If you are waiting for a kiss to wake up from your beauty
sleep Senorita, it's not happening.'*

*I am in heaven and Samir is with me. He can even hear my
thoughts. I smile. I suddenly wonder where Sonia is. Did she and
Samir get engaged?*

*As if in response, he hands me my phone and there is a message
from Sonia. I get up and sit straight. I am still groggy so I rest
my head against the bench and read the message.*

*'You backstabbing bitch. You stole my Sam. I won't pay you
a dime now. I will see to it that you suffer, like the way I am
suffering. You selfish, dark-hearted...'*

*I don't read the complete message, but it's obvious that Sonia
is livid. And she is talking about money so she has no idea that
we are dead, which means she isn't! I feel jubilant.*

*There is also a missed call from Ma. I am happy to see that
heaven now allows free incoming calls and SMSes from earthlings.
I would really like to let Ma know that I have reached heaven
safely. And that I am sorry I didn't listen to her. I try to call her
but there is no signal. I guess Ma will have to wait.*

*I look around and see vast ocean all around. I wonder aloud
where exactly in heaven we are and how did Samir die? Samir
doesn't answer. He is distracted by a commotion. I hear familiar
voices. A group of people wearing what seem like orange life jackets*

are rushing towards us. Are they here to save us? Am I in a transient stage between life and death? Meanwhile, people are helping us wear life jackets. I shut my eyes and resist as much as I can.

'I would rather be dead if it means I get to be with Samir,' pines my heart.

My mind is shocked at this candid admission. 'I also feel at peace here,' it admits.

I can't believe that my heart finally got my mind to agree with it. Hmm, deathly influence, I reckon!

'You look muddled. Here, drink some water,' Sam says handing me a bottle.

I guzzle down the whole bottle. I hadn't realized how parched I was. I devour the chocolate chip cookies Samir gives me. I crave for some ginger tea to clear my head. Which food delivery app works in heaven? I turn to ask Samir. He seems anxious. Why is he talking to these people? I want him to be just with me. I hold his hand and try to comfort him.

'Samir ji, you saved us all. Thank you varry much sir ji.'

My eyes are shut in an attempt to continue my stay in heaven, but I am certain that it is Pyare's voice.

'We're still not out of danger,' I hear Samir say. He sounds worried. 'The ferry has been instructed to stay in the middle of the ocean. Captain tells me that both the shores are completely washed out.'

'Whatever happens is for the best. If you had gotten engaged, we would have stayed back for the morning photo shoot and gotten drowned.' This is Amit's voice.

'Straight talk is this ji, ki proposal chaupat so we salamat. Nahin to hamara bhi photo tang jaata ji,' Pyare concludes.

'Any news of Sonia or her parents?' Samir asks. I can sense guilt mixed with concern in Samir's voice.

'Sonia ma'am is like a demi-goddess. God rest her soul. But why did you refuse such an apsara?' Amit inquires sounding genuinely curious.

'Guys please. Can we stop this nonsense? I really hope Sonia and her family are safe.' Samir shouts angrily.

I feel tears stinging my eyes. He still cares for Sonia. And he doesn't sound dead. Somehow, I am getting the feeling that my time in heaven is over. I am trying to negotiate some more time with God when someone splashes water on my face forcing me to return to senses.

I open my eyes and see NetGen's wan face staring right back at me. I hear Pyare informing me in his broken English, 'Tsunami again...all over news...so many dead.'

Tsunami? Didn't that happen back in 2004? I remember we did a charity sale in school to raise money for the victims. Hundred feet high-waves swept away homes, cars and trees. Still confused but more awake, I look around. We seem to be on a ferry, heading away from the Phi Phi Islands. Apparently, a Tsunami has struck the island minutes after we boarded the ferry. I find it hard to believe that killer waves could be swallowing people right now on the shore, while the ferry rocks no more than a baby's swing in the heart of the ocean.

I haven't the foggiest idea about why we took the ferry today instead of tomorrow, but it looks like that has saved our lives. I also don't know how I got into my teddy bear print night suit. I look at Samir. He is standing at the far corner of the ferry looking out at the sea with forlorn eyes. He is worried for Sonia. I really hope for Samir's sake that she is not dead, although she just sent me a venomous SMS.

'Wait, what time did Tsunami strike?' I ask abruptly, the gears suddenly churning in my brain. This is the first time I have actually spoken in all this while. My voice is still hoarse from all the drinking last night.

'About thirty minutes back,' says NetGen.

'Then she is alive,' I announce, walking towards Samir. 'Sonia sent me a SMS...er...about five minutes ago,' I add, checking the exact timestamp on her message.

Samir leaps towards me at this joyful news. All I can think of is that he looks damn hot in a white shirt with three buttons open. He is standing so close that I feel tempted to accidentally bump into him.

'I can kiss you Senorita for giving this good news,' he says softly so that only I can hear.

A bubble of hope rises in my heart and a ripple of excitement runs through my body.

'Although you perhaps deserve a mega bouquet of kisses for saving all our lives,' he says and winks at me.

'I do?'

'Except, I haven't brushed and neither have you. And you even puked last night.' He smiles cockily, his voice full of amusement.

'I did?'

'Ya, all over my favourite shirt,' he sounds disgusted, but his eyes are sparkling.

'And then we had to get you changed!'

Huh? I don't know whether to be excited or embarrassed, but now I know why I am draped in a teddy print.

I look around. Most people have gone to the lower deck, possibly for food and water. We are almost alone barring a few strangers holding their phone up in the air to recieve the signal. I also lift my hand up and try calling home, but the ferry swings violently, throwing me literally into his arms. Once again, his fragrance invades me—sweet, luscious, and inviting. Ahh...this is dream come true. If only I could ignore the loud drumming inside my head. I press my fingers against my temples as the throbbing pain blinds me. He gently takes my hand and walks me to a chair.

A few minutes later, the invigorating aroma of ginger tea wakes me up.

'Brooke Bond Red Label—The Taste of Togetherness,' Samir offers me a cup and sits beside me sipping his.

The warm liquid soothes my aching head a bit. Just like we had sat together at the Goa beach in silent togetherness, I could sit here for ages, sipping Brooke Bond, for a taste of his togetherness.

'It's funny that we always meet at an engagement,' I blabber, to distract my mind from dwelling any further on the taste or togetherness.

'Well, technically, this was a birthday party, which you were trying to make into an engagement,' he clarifies.

'I wasn't. Your girlfriend was!'

'And you foiled her plans?'

'How so? What did I do?' My integrity at stake, I am sort of indignant now. I agree the thought of ruining Sonia's proposal did cross my mind, but I don't want credit for a crime I didn't commit.

'Who designed all those treasure hunt clues based on our Goa encounter? Two-lipped flower is Tulip, Hindu Mythology FWB is Radhe-Shyam, Dried-petal-mixture is Potpourri.' His eyes stare at me mischievously.

I guess unintentionally, I might have dropped some hints. Okay, maybe lots of hints. But that still doesn't explain how I made him reject Sonia. It's not like he loves me or anything. Does he?

'How exactly did I break the engagement?' I question, looking at him expectantly.

'Look, I will be honest here. I was planning to meet you next week in Delhi. I had no idea you were here. I was really intrigued by those clues and then I saw you dancing at the tree house. I didn't know what to do. Okay!'

So he got confused. Maybe he felt a resurgence of attraction towards me. Does that mean he loves me?

'What did you tell Sonia?' I ask up front. I really need to know if he admitted his feelings for me to Sonia. She sure as hell is blaming me.

'I was honest with her. I told her I love her, but I just wasn't sure this was it.'

How typical of Samir! I am sharing a together-moment with you, so obviously I love you, but why complicate it with marriage? Hello? I am the one getting blamed for treason, while he walks away smugly with an honest label.

'What about me? What did you tell Sonia about me?' I demand seriously. Funny that I still have a faint hope that he might love me. A hope that is blinding me to the financial crisis I am in.

'Nothing, there isn't much to say really. We just had a one-night stand long time back, right?'

I have known all along that I meant nothing to him, yet it hurts when he dismisses me so casually. I blink away the moisture brimming in my eyes, and then lean forward, to tease him 'I wonder whatever led Sonia to believe that you and I are sizzling together like fish and chips. Huh?'

Sometimes, fake laughter is all you need to wipe tears.

'Obviously, she asked me if you were the reason for breakup and I said maybe.' He laughs too, clearly unable to see my hurt.

He really cares for no one but himself. Not for me. Not for Sonia.

'Why can't you admit that you were just using Sonia,' I angrily blurt out my thoughts.

'Look, my feelings are very pure in a relationship. I am not lying to anyone. The girl knows that we are both in it for fun. We spend more time and get to know more. I like to learn and grow with every relationship. I don't have to be bound to them all.' He says all this calmly, without raising his voice.

I find it incredible how he thinks of a relationship as an extra-curricular activity—a play, learn and grow opportunity. How could I even think this man was worth my love? I raise my chin, cross my arms and pin him with a cold glare. Unknowingly, I am still playing power games with him.

'Well, your co-education with Sonia has caused me a huge monetary loss.' My tone is sarcastic.

'I think you ought to be a little more grateful considering I saved your life,' he replies, undisturbed by my accusation.

'I thought I saved everyone's life?' I retort with an exasperated frown, my hands raised in a WTF gesture.

'I used you as an excuse to break the engagement. So technically I saved the lives. Although you get the credit for it,' he gloats.

What credit? Credit my foot! It's all bad credit. I mumble to myself when the image of a precious heart-shaped ring looms in front of my eyes. Shucks! The RING. Suddenly I feel hair prickling at the back of my neck. I can hear bankruptcy knocking on my door. Forget bankruptcy. I will soon be in jail.

'Do you have the ring?' I ask, panicking, my heart pounding loudly like the school recess bell.

'No, I don't. But really, you are planning to sell a symbol

of love to recover your money? How cheap!'

I stand up and stamp hard on the floor. 'I paid for the ring. It's bloody charged on my card,' I yell.

'No way! Really?' He bursts out laughing.

The ferry is swaying again. I sit down on the bench facing away from him. No point wasting your anger on someone who doesn't have angry emoticons to respond with.

'How much?' He asks in a matter-of-fact way.

'Twenty-five lakhs,' I mumble.

'Holy shit! You must be rich to lend this kind of money to your clients.'

I guess he can't stop mocking.

'If you were not afraid to commit, it would have been all fine.'

'Fine and dead,' he elaborates.

He has a point. Whatever. I am feeling scared, stupid, angry, hurt and confused all at once. Scared because I am in deep shit; stupid because I got into it myself; angry because it's his shit; hurt because he is not kissing me; confused because I don't know what face to make. I end up showing him my I-think-you-are-an-arrogant-jerk face and he smiles conceitedly.

'You, of all girls surely get it? You said you prefer to forget a random hookup like an unknown cafe in a narrow lane where you enjoy a nice coffee on a vacation but you couldn't care to remember its name or street. Why double standards now?'

I am definitely not his kind who has sex like its coffee. But he thinks I am because I had lied to save my pride. Why should I try and change his views now? How does it matter anyway? I turn away and sulk silently. He gets up, goes down the steps and disappears. I can hear the sound of the ferry's engine, as it cuts across the water now. I hope we get off soon. Tired and hungry I want to go home, curl up in my bed and sleep off this nightmare.

A little while later, I also head down. I don't see her climbing up the stairs until I hear her scorn.

'Oh my! I finally have the honour of meeting the girl who has had both my husband and my ex-boyfriend,' Radhika sneers.

The same Radhika at whose wedding I had added cut-lime pieces in mason jars, rose petals in green ice candy and played hooky with Samir. She is a close friend and co-worker of Sonia's—I had seen Radhika with her husband Deepak on the island. I am surprised she knows who I am. Or, maybe, ever since I fell out of the tree house, everyone now knows who I am. I won't be surprised if someone recorded my fall and it's a viral video on WhatsApp right now.

'Wonder what the guys see in you?' she says scrutinizing me.

I feel naked and vulnerable under her condescending gaze. I want to say something smart and intelligent but my mind is blank. I just look down at my feet, examining the chipped green nail polish.

'Ah... looks like you need repair,' she says following my gaze and then walks away haughtily.

Okay. Even if I am the bad girl who broke the engagement, but that actually saved your life. Maybe you can pay me a few lakhs as a reward. That way I can pay for my repairs and my debt too. A damn smart idea but Radhika is already gone. I go down to wash my face and pee.

A few hours later, the ferry finally docks at an elevated junkyard by the coast. We get into a state bus, which is waiting to transfer us all to the Phuket City Centre. The streets are barren, except for uprooted trees and upturned cars. All the locals have run up to the hills for fear of aftershocks. As we drive past the coastline, an innocent child shouts in joy when he sees a dolphin swept inland. He doesn't know that the world of singing whales and lazing sea lions has turned into a graveyard for marine and human life. His mother turns his head away as we pass by a beach littered with dead fish and sea turtles alongside human bodies. I get the same feeling I get in a planetarium—of being a minuscule particle in this large universe. This is too gruesome a reality for anyone to handle. And the realization that it could have been me, makes it even more real. Families huddle, cry and hug each other. I watch Pyare hold NetGen and console her as she convulses in shock.

I have no one's shoulder to rest my head on. I want to call Ma but my phone is dead. Everyone's phone is out of charge. I finally find a pay phone in the city centre and call home. I am overjoyed to hear Mom's loving voice. I choke with tears. She kisses me on the phone and tells me how worried they were about me when they saw the horrifying pictures of Phi Phi Island on TV.

Wait…how does she know I was at Phi Phi? I was supposed to be in Ooty. Just then Didi takes the phone from Ma and blasts me. She tells me how irresponsible I am and that I need to grow up. Ma saw the magic-tree-house-at-Phi-Phi picture I posted yesterday on FB in my inebriated state. That they have been trying to reach me since morning but couldn't get through. That papa had an attack when he heard about the Tsunami and is admitted at the hospital right now, struggling for his life.

Ma takes the phone back from Didi and says, '*Beta, Vir ko leke hospital aa ja bas.* Only your marriage can save Papa now.' I hear her muffled sobs as the line disconnects. I slump down in the phone booth and cry my heart out. No one bothers to stop by and ask. Death is the flavour of the day and tearful eyes the latest rage.

Bad Boyfriend, Good Friend

I don't want Papa to see me teary-eyed and sad. So I apply bright red lipstick, slip on the green shoe covers and walk into the ICU wearing a cheerful smile that fades at the sight of the clean, sterile and lifeless room.

The ICU feels a lot like a prison. Unavoidable. Scary. Cold. Just like a prisoner, a patient can't leave the place without the doctor's permission. Family can only visit during regulated hours. You stop being someone's husband, dad or brother. You become a mere number in a game of Housie. A game where the caller-in-charge-of-your-future is always lurking around with numbered coins in a bag, waiting to announce the next number to free from the shackles.

FYI, I have never been to prison before—also this is my first time in an ICU. Although, prison might as well turn out be my next stop. But we will worry about credit card payment and prison later, I remind myself. One battle at a time.

I avoid looking at other beds and walk straight to the bed number 174. Ignoring the soft clinking sound of the Tambola coins echoing in my mind, I reapply a bright smile and pull aside the pale-green cloth hung in front of bed 174. Papa is resting, with his head slightly raised, on the bed. Draped in the loose hospital gown, wires in and out of his arms, he looks like a part of the machinery surrounding him. A contrasting image rushes to my mind. It's a faint memory from decades ago of a man in control—an authoritative figure, responsible for the well-being of the entire family. He smiles faintly as he opens his eyes and sees me. I remove the plastic wrap from the papaya bowl by his bedside and feed him. We don't talk much. He doesn't have much energy. I leave as soon he closes his eyes for a nap. As I walk out, I blink away the tears from my eyes.

Outside in the waiting hall, I see Ma talking to Samir. An unshaven yet dashing Samir who has accompanied me straight from the airport. Ma is wearing a crisp, cotton saree and a fresh bindi, just like she always does for her tea date with Papa. I am surprised at how well she is holding herself. In fact, it was her quick thinking that has saved Papa's life. I don't want Ma or Samir to see me vulnerable. So I sit down on an empty chair and pretend to be busy with my phone.

'Where do you work, beta?' I hear Ma speaking to Samir. She is sitting on a chair across from me. She hasn't noticed me yet. The subtle smile of approval on her face means that she likes Samir.

'Aunty ji, I run my own business. I am an entrepreneur.' Samir says confidently, sitting next to her.

Ouch. Ma doesn't think very highly of entrepreneurs. For her, entrepreneur, self-employed, laid-off and jobless are all synonyms for no-steady-income.

'But your FB profile says you are in consulting?' Ma asks puzzled.

Oh no, she is confusing him for Vir. Of course, she had found out that I have a boyfriend from Vir's FB activity. She had called me up to find all his details. And she had been very happy to know he was an MBA and a consultant. Before I can butt in and clarify, Samir replies smoothly, without bothering to ask whose FB profile mom is referring to, 'Aunty ji, I left my job. Now I do wedding photography.'

An entrepreneur who is a photographer? Ma is rather shocked at the demotion. She has perhaps already told the *ladeez* in her kitty that her daughter is dating a highflying MBA consultant. But I know Mom—always optimistic.

'*Chalo theek hai,*' she says. 'Following passion is the new fashion these days. Don't mind my asking beta, but how much do you make?'

Okay, now she is getting personal and a tad bit embarrassing. I have to inform Ma that he is not my boyfriend Vir. I look up and my eyes lock with Samir's. He gives me an I-got-this blink, and signals me to relax.

He looks back at my Mom, and replies, 'Aunty ji, it's a young start-up with three offices and twenty-five employees. Right now we are making only about a crore a month, but we hope to double by end of this year.'

No kidding! A crore a month? My Mom is seriously thinking she should take photography lessons now. I am thinking I should ask him to pay off my debt, especially since the ring was for him. It's his problem, even if he didn't want it.

'Beta, I am an uber-cool mom,' Mom informs Samir, beaming proudly with a seven-figure smile. 'I married Meha's dad by just looking at his biodata and a passport size photo. But marketing brochure dekh ke who marries nowadays? I know kids today want free sample. *Ab sample to tumne kar hi liya hai,*' she says, casting a meaningful glance in my direction.

'*Facebook friends bhi tum ho, to shaadi mein der kyon, Vir?*' She asks him directly.

I don't know where to look, so I look further inside my phone. My mother has just given Samir, who she thinks is Vir, a go-ahead to have an intimate relationship with me. I understand she is really modern, but she has also asked him to marry me, while we are in a hospital waiting room! Now she knows I am listening in to their conversation. How desperate and humiliating is that? As I look for an invisibility cloak to hide myself, the reason for mom's weird behaviour suddenly dawns on me. It's all because of that prophecy—'*ek ladke ke saath sambhog will solve bitiya's problems*'. It's obvious that she believes I got stuck in the Tsunami because water is supposed to bring me ill luck. But I am alive because Vir was with me when it happened. So now she wants me to marry him so I can stay safe forever. Tough luck! I also want to marry him, but he's a cold fish.

'Aunty ji, smile na, please. You are looking like Madhubala. Let me click a picture,' Samir changes the topic. Ma, delighted at the compliment, poses coyly. And then she leaves with a spring in her step, for her tea date with bed number 174.

Samir may not be a good boyfriend, but he is definitely a good friend. I am thinking of how to thank him for all his help. Just then, Di arrives, who went home to look after the kids. She engulfs me in a bear hug—scolding, crying, and showering me with sisterly love all at once. Before I can disengage fully from her embrace, Samir smiles and leaves.

Next morning, I take a detour through Starbucks to shake off the Blue Cloud, who has been sitting glued to me ever since I heard about Papa. There's also the Deep Purple Nerve, who keeps popping up, making me rather jumpy. I wanted to go to the hospital, but Ma said to come during the evening visiting hours. So I reach my office and start to count the money, trying to find peace in the humdrum of life.

I am proud of the way I had figured the estimates and planning for Sonia's proposal. But now there is this big tumour of twenty-five lakhs that is making us ill. How am I ever going to collect so many zeroes? I know my parents don't have much savings. I definitely have none. I can ask Didi and Jijaji for a loan, although they have also just bought a new house. Even if I get some weddings to design, I can at best save about a lakh a month. Even then it seems like I will be paying off my debt for the next two and a half years. Math sucks! Suddenly, the Enchanted Land atop The Faraway Tree has switched to the-land-of-living-on-minimum-wages.

I put my feet up, look out the window and consider my options. If only I could reach out to Sonia. I am ready to fall on her freshly manicured feet, kiss her Jimmy Choo shoes and ask for forgiveness. Plus the money for the ring. She must have realized, like I did, that my falling down and breaking her engagement has indeed saved all our lives. If her mood is good, I can even ask for a life-saving reward. Not much, say about ₹50,000—just enough for a Maldives trip. Business is anyway closing. I might as well go on a vacation. The minute I think of Sonia, I find her staring back at me. It's like I have a direct line with God, ever since my short stay in heaven. Standing with nine thin, underwear models, all wearing the new 'Body' line of Veronica Secret lingerie collection, Sonia looks chilly hot.

'How do you like the ad copy?' The creative assistant asks me, as he lowers the ad copy so the models are now huddled around his crotch area.

'Ooh la la ooh la la…tu hai meri fantasy' sings the office boy, his eyes darting from bra to bra as he holds out the tray with tea cups for us.

I take my ginger tea and stare at 'The Perfect Body' written boldly over the horizontal row of panties.

For some reason, I don't like the ad. It seems to suggest that these women, including Sonia, have a perfect body while I don't. It may be true but who wants to hear the fat truth, that too from a lingerie ad? Besides, the world would be so monotonous if all the leaves of a tree were arranged in a symmetry and if all the clouds had the same shape. I honestly tell the cute ass that I find the ad to be too perfect. He should change either the models or the message to make it more real. But he laughs it off. Both the creative ass and the office boy leave my desk, huddling the perfect bodies.

I am wondering what Samir will think of Sonia's perfect body plastered in public, when I see a mail from him materialize in my inbox. I have wanted to call him since yesterday to ask his thoughts on my mom's suggestion, but I haven't been able to gather the courage to do so.

'Hey Senorita, it was nice meeting your mom yesterday.'

He has me at Senorita.

'Wanted to let you know that I am leaving tonight for London for some urgent work.'

Okay. Is this email like a work-related am-away-from-my-desk communication, or a public Facebook style status update, or honey-I-will-be-late-for-dinner kind of personal message?

'I can understand that you must be really stressed. Let me know if I can help in anyway.'

Oh yes. If stress could burn calories, I would have a 'Perfect Body' like Sonia right now. But somehow just thinking aloud with your mail is making me feel good. How about you move in with me till Papa gets better? Anyway I am alone these days. Also, can you please persuade your ex-girlfriend to pay for the ring?

'I called Sonia, you know, to apologize. She listened but when I asked her about the ring and your payment, she hung up.'

I should be feeling disappointed right now because Sonia has refused to pay, but instead I feel a warm, fuzzy sensation envelope me. He called Sonia for me. He was thinking about me. He cares.

'I can lend some money, if you need. Not much, say about five lakhs. The credit card companies can really fleece you with interest on any outstanding payment.'

Interest! I never understood that chapter well. But my loyal friend, excel, tells me that even a three per cent interest on twenty-five lakh rupees will be seventy thousand. So, even in my best-case scenario of saving a lakh a month, I will be paying back just the interest. The original amount will remain unpaid. It's like trying to fill a swimming pool with a bucket of water every day and realizing that all the water is getting evaporated, leaving the pool as empty as before. I was hugely mistaken. I am in the land of lifelong imprisonment.

'Hey listen. I have some good news for you.'

I can certainly use some 'good news'. My stock is depleted. I am a little skeptical of 'good news' because it often comes in a combo with a 'bad news'.

'You probably already know about the wedding carnival happening in October in Delhi. It's a huge event.'

Yes, I do. It's the biggest in Asia and its entry fee is fifty thousand bucks. And I have no money. And Tying a Knot is as good as closed. So I guess, a wedding carnival is not much use to me unless I am getting married myself, which, in fact, my mom was trying to arrange with you, yesterday. Why is my life in such a mess?

'I just learnt about an online reality show being done by some matrimonial websites prior to the carnival. It's called *Live-In: An Evil or Evolution.*'

Why exactly is he telling me this? He can't possibly be thinking of living-in with me for this reality show? I couldn't. I mean, Ma will be OK, but Papa will never agree. Hello stupid, you can't agree. You can't allow him to hurt you again.

'The winner of this reality show will get a cash prize of ten lakh rupees, besides a waiver of the entry fee.'

Ten lakhs! Now we are talking. How do I enrol?

'Five couples will be living in. They will post on social media, tweet, instagram, etc. The show goes on for a month or so. The most popular couple will win ten lakhs. There are some other prizes too. Here is the link, you can find out more.'

I open the link in another window. It looks very interesting. But it seems like the entry to the reality show is by invitation only.

'I have an invite for the show. I can recommend your name if you want to participate with your boyfriend Vir.'

Hmm... That's an idea. This could be my light at the end of this dark, stinking, scary, tunnel. An online, social reality show sounds perfect for a virtual couple.

'Btw, an advice for old-time sake, I find your BF rather artificial. Even when you post about your dad's sickness, he likes it.'

That's true. Facebook likes become awkward on sad posts. And I know my BF is not real, he is artificial. But imagine love advice coming from someone who has just stood up his girlfriend at Phi Phi island on a proposal worth one crore.

'Anyway, hope to see you on Friday, 11am @Chaayos, Galleria. I have some projects, on which we can work together on. TC Sam.'

I type a mail thanking Samir and confirming the meeting. But I don't want him to think I have nothing better to do than read and reread his mail. So I leave it in the drafts folder to send it later.

I poke Vir on FB to ask him about the reality show. He pokes me back instantly. It's amazing how he is always there for me. I wonder how many real people are working behind his virtual face or is it just some lines of code?

Me: I would like to start living-in with you, 'socially'.

Vir: What does that mean?

Me: It means we live-in together in the online, social world through our FB posts, tweets, instagram, etc.

Vir: Totally possible.

Me: Awesome! Can you…er…physically meet me?

Vir: I'm sorry. That option is unavailable.

Me: Ok, bye. TTYL.

What? It was worth a try. Maybe there is a real, nice guy behind the virtual face. Anyway, the reality show seems all sorted. Hopefully, if I can win this ten-lakh-cash prize, borrow five lakhs from Samir, another five from friends and family, I will be looking only at a five-lakh-outstanding payment. That seems manageable. I check my phone for any news from Mom. There is none, which is perhaps a good sign. Not much has changed from last month. I am still shutting shop. I still haven't got a boyfriend or source of Vitamin S. But, somehow, bigger problems have a way of putting life in perspective. As long as I can pay off my debt and Papa gets better, I think I will survive.

It's six in the evening. I just got back from the hospital. The neighbouring Sharma uncle hands me some bills. He looks even frailer than last time. I don't have the energy to ask him why. The house looks empty without Mansi. I try calling her but her phone is unreachable. She should be home in a week's time now. I can tell from her pictures on FB (yes, there is connectivity even on the Everest Base Camp route), that they reached the base camp yesterday and are now descending. It sure looks beautiful. And she is trekking with nine other men, all CXOs dealing with mid-life crisis. She looks happy. Poor men!

I put on some soft music and slump down on the beanbag. I don't even feel like switching on the lights. I am in big trouble. Not the money one. The boyfriend one. I wish I had made up an excuse when Mummy called to say Papa wants to meet Samir, who, by the way, is Vir for them. Hell, I had no idea why Papa wanted to meet Samir. All Mom told was that we can't stress Papa, so I promptly called Samsung Do Not Call and asked if he could come meet my Dad. No, Samir didn't refuse. Although now I wish he had. He showed up alright at 4 p.m., as promised. He came. He spoke sweetly. He conquered. All of them—Ma, Papa, Didi and even the little Diyu. And now Papa wants me to marry him. Listen, I want to marry him too. But he doesn't want to marry me or anyone for that matter. How do I tell my Dad that Samir is a free spirit like the wind? He doesn't like containment. And he is not Vir.

I can't tell Dad anything because the doctor says we can't let him get stressed. So if Dad wants it, I have to do it. I need to get Samir to walk a few steps together with me, under a shared umbrella, even if it is on a road with a dead end.

I just don't know how. Yet.

I sigh and hum along the lovely song from *PK* playing on my phone.

'Bin puchhe mera naam aur pataa
Rasmon ko rakh ke pare...
Chaar kadam bas chaar kadam
Chal do naa saath mere'

(Without asking my name or address, keeping the rituals
aside, just walk four steps with me.)

Fake Marriage

'J for Togetherness' says the poster at the quaint chai boutique that has opened in the Galleria market. It reminds me of the 'together' moments I had spent with Samir—moments of 'love' as he calls them. They are much like a box of chocolates. Delicious while they last, but gone before you know it and leaving behind weight that is hard to get rid of. Yet, here I am today, to ask him for another box of chocolates. To flirt, seduce and make him feel guilty enough so he that he will agree to be my fake fiancé.

It's 11.20 a.m. He is twenty-minutes late. I am wondering if I should text him. Just then, I see him at the door talking to a very pretty girl in a simple, knee length, floral print dress. I see her smile and flick her hair back. OMG! She is so flirting with him. I can see his hand on her shoulder. He is flirting back.

Its okay. I assure myself. You will do fine. Deep breathe. Be confident. And smile.

Several girls look up as he walks past their table in his slim-fit, grey chinos, a thin, stripe shirt, and designer glares. I smile as he comes and sits down with me. The familiar wild-rose fragrance drains away all my stress. Maybe I should just ask him for a bottle of his perfume.

'Sorry, I got delayed. Was finishing up some work,' he says sweetly.

I don't know whether the pretty, floral-print girl was working with him or she was the work herself. I shower him with a no-problem smile.

'You look nice...er....,' he fumbles as he gives me a once-over. 'It's been a while since I...er...saw you in a saree.'

Ah, so he remembers that I wore a saree that night. I was hoping he would. I have very carefully selected a purple, chiffon saree, with turquoise-blue border and matched it with a sweetheart neck, sleeveless blouse—especially for today.

'I had a business meeting in the morning, with a traditional family.' I give him my practiced excuse for wearing a gorgeous saree. So far it's all going as per my plan.

He orders two *cutting chai* and *bun maska* for both of us without looking at the menu and begins to tell me about a few upcoming weddings, where he thinks we can work together. One is in Paris and the other is in Maldives, both in September.

Maldives has me hooked. I eagerly nod to convey my interest in everything, but I am having a tough time maintaining eye contact or keeping the flutter of my heart at bay.

'Great. I will email you the details for both,' he concludes and then inquires about my dad.

'Papa is...um...better.'

'You seem worried. Is everything al right?' He asks, with a genuine concern in his voice.

'Actually, Dad wants me married,' my voice falls and I look at the tumbler of chai on the table.

'Ahh, and you are not ready yet!' He chuckles understandably. He takes a sip of his chai and reclines on his chair.

'I am ready,' I say with poise, looking him straight in the eye.

'With whom? Vir?'

'Yes. I think Vir is perfect for me,' I say to make him jealous. 'Anyway, I believe marriage is the only way to make love last. If you are afraid to commit, you are afraid to love.' This, accompanied by a dare-you-to-marry-if-you-can look.

'Ah. The same old, overrated love,' he shakes his head dismissively. 'I thought you were different. Don't you want to have some fun?'

Yes, I am different and stupid. That's why I allowed you to trample my heart under your feet. I feel like pulling his out and stamping on it right now. Instead I giggle, pretending to be amused by his question.

'I do want to have fun,' I say, with playfulness dancing in my eyes. 'But I won't pick up a guy, let's say you,' I lean closer to him and pause for the effect, 'to have sex with and then just leave.' And I pulled away from him, back straight, arms folded. This is where he is supposed to feel guilty and then agree to whatever I ask of him.

'For the record, you left me in Goa. With a note to never call you back. Even then I tried, but you had changed your number,' he replies curtly.

He had called. I didn't know this. I might have been in the flight at the time and then I changed my number after returning from Goa. But his number is still the same. And I never tried to call him back. Uh-oh, this is not how it's supposed to go. My agenda is not to establish who ditched. I am here to seize the nut, just like the squirrel in my office backyard.

'Let's forget the past, shall we?' I say endearingly, placing my hand over his on the table.

His eyes soften at the touch, but his body is rigid. I see him eyeing for a waiter to ask for the bill. I need to act fast.

'Samir, you know how unwell Papa is. And he wants me married ASAP, but Vir is caught up with work abroad and can't come right now.' The words rush out.

'Well, Vir needs to be here for the reality show anyway in two weeks. I thought you said you were participating,' he says, his voice devoid of any emotion.

'Huh? Why does Vir need to be here for the reality show?' I ask, completely baffled.

'How do you suppose you live-in together?'

'Online?'

He bursts out laughing. It dispels the tension hanging in the air. He explains why Vir needs to be present for the show. There will be weekly photo and video shoots of the participating couples. And friends and family will be polled too for their views.

Oops! I knew the online reality show was too good to be true. What am I supposed to do now? I was here to convince him to be my fake fiancé for Papa's sake but now I also need a partner for the reality show to win ten lakhs. Suddenly, I have an idea—an idea that can kill two birds with one stone. I order another round of chai to make him stay for a little longer.

'Samir, can you do something for me?' I ask with a degree of helplessness.

'What can I do for you, Senorita?' He teases, the sparkle back in his eyes and his mood livened up by laughing at my expense.

I need him to stay in this mood.

'First, I really want to thank you for being so nice to my Mom, even when she mistook you for Vir,' I say, smiling affectionately.

'I am always nice to women,' he banters.

'Actually, it's not Mom's fault. She hasn't met Vir.'

'I guessed as much.'

'Smart huh?'

'Was born that way,'

'I did try to tell my Mom that you weren't Vir, but you didn't let me.'

'What's in a name? I will continue to be handsome whatever you call me,' he says, an arrogant grin plastered across his face.

'Oh! And Ma really liked all the flattering things you told her. "Aunty ji, Meha looks like your sister. Aunty ji, you are like wine, improving with age."'

'I shall tell the truth, the whole truth and nothing but the truth,' he proclaims.

I laugh, amused by his drama and continue, 'And what did you tell Tanu Di? She is over the moon since she met you.'

'I just mentioned that my friend Radhika needs a website designed for her business and she could do it,' he explains.

Oh no! I hate that condescending Radhika. I don't think Tanu Di will be able to stand her either, I think to myself, but I don't say it aloud.

'How sweet of you to help Didi.'

'What is it that you want me to do, Senorita?' He asks, giving me a suspicious, naughty smile.

I ignore his question, because I am not done yet.

'And Vaishno Devi ka prasad! How did you think of that?' I ask genuinely astonished. This part had really clinched the deal for my Dad.

'Someone in the office gave it to me in the afternoon and I thought it might help your Dad in recovery. You know how sometimes they say that faith heals.'

Okay, his thought on my Dad's wellbeing is really touching. I take a gulp of water to swallow the emotions rising in my throat and then continue. 'Well, you shared so many positive moments with my family, that now they totally love you. And they want me to marry you. Who they think is Vir. But Vir is abroad. So I need your help.' I finally conclude my praise-o-logue.

'Whoa! Are you proposing to me?'

'No, humbly requesting that you own up your mistakes and help a poor girl.'

'Mistakes?'

'Ya. Pretending to be Vir and stealing my entire family's heart. That amounts to impersonation and theft.'

'Hmm. So, what's my punishment?' He asks, staring intently into my eyes.

'Well...um...we can enroll in the reality show, for now,' I say measuring each word carefully, as I try to accomplish both my tasks.

'I thought this was about your Dad?'

'It's also about your mistakes,' I reason.

'Senorita, I am sorry for my mistakes, but...'

'Well who dumped Sonia?' I say, getting aggressive.

'I wouldn't put it that way,' he says defensively.

'Who lost the ring?'

'If I had known it was charged on your card, believe me I would have been careful,' he sniggers lightly.

'But you were careless. And it has caused me a huge loss. So now you need to enroll in the reality show with me so I can get back my money and we can tell my Dad that we are living in and will marry later.' I lay out all my cards.

'Why?'

'Why what?'

'Why will we marry later?'

'Oh! Because your sister can't come for the wedding right

now,' I suggest casually. I had actually researched on FB that his elder sister, living in the States, is pregnant right now.

He nods, eyeing me suspiciously. I avoid direct eye contact, but from the corner of my eye, I see a soft, warm glow of happiness in his eyes. It is soon shrouded by a cloud of uncertainty and confusion. And then his face becomes opaque.

'What happens after the show?' He asks after a few seconds of silence.

'We break-up. Dad will be fine by then. So it's okay.'

'What about Vir? Won't he object?'

'It's all right. I can handle him,' I say nonchalantly.

'Sorry, but I can't do this,' he shakes his head, with a grim expression on his face.

Puhleez! So much effort for nothing. I am exhausted now. I have tried all the weapons in my armoury—seduction, flirting, daring, flattery, guilt-trap and pleading. Crestfallen, I slump into my chair, morosely studying the leftover maska bun.

'I can't pretend to be Vir anymore,' he says thoughtfully. 'If I do this, I've got to be me.'

What does he mean? I look up at him bewildered.

'I can fake love, but I can't fake myself,' he says with a cute smile.

Relieved that I have a partner for the reality show and a fake fiancé for my Dad, I jump up and give him a tight hug across the table.

As soon as I hug him, I realize that it was a bad idea. The wild-rose scent throws me off balance and the chai tumbler topples off the table, spilling the left over tea onto his trousers.

'I'm so sorry,' I say sheepishly.

'Ahh...If the stains come with a hug, then I guess *daag acche hain* right?' He banters playfully.

Oh my gosh! What have I walked into? Living with a hot, witty, head-turner whose fragrance alone makes my legs turn to jelly.

'Scared?' He asks, reading my anxiety.

I nod truthfully and ask, 'Are you?'

'A little actually,' he admits honestly. 'I have loved often, but I have never faked love.'

Yes, it's hard to fake love. However, for me, it will be harder to fake that I am faking.

'Looks like it's our destiny to be hum-suffers,' he chortles, pleased with his own pun, his eyes locked with mine.

My heart skips many beats. I don't care if he is faking the fondness in his eyes. I know I love him. I always have. And while, he can never be mine, I want to enjoy my box of chocolates for now. We will worry about heartaches later. After all, what are girlfriends for, if not to fix a broken heart?

I smile back at him and get ready to dance to the tune of 'Shudh desi, desi desi romance...kamine haye re...haye re crazy crazy vazy romance.'

Naked Encounter

'To or not to is the big question facing the youth today. The question is not about sex, it's about whether to marry.'

Samir is busy capturing his stream of thoughts on his phone, as he steps out of the bathroom with only a towel wrapped around his waist. Suddenly, after all these years, he feels the desire to write again. He feels alive. That was part of the reason he agreed to take part in the reality show with Meha. Like all his decisions, this too was an impulsive one.

'Why marry when you can tarry? Marriage is like having a house of your own. We all dream of it, but it's permanent and it locks you down. What's wrong with an open relationship like the two banks of a river? The two banks are always together, although they never really meet. Sometimes they come close and sometimes they move apart, but they stay side by side forever. Isn't that true love?'

Eyes closed, he is engrossed in analysing love from his protagonist's perspective, when he hears a woman's surprised squeal. He opens his eyes and finds himself staring at a beautiful, heart-shaped face, with gullible eyes, and full, but rather badly chapped lips. He sees that she has hastily wrapped a shawl over her seemingly naked body. Her shapely legs are left uncovered as the shawl ends much above her knees, leaving a lot to be seen.

'I am sorry,' he apologizes and looks away.

She is startled, but not perturbed. She turns her back to him, slides her dirty track pants up her legs and unwillingly pulls on her smelly t-shirt. She also hastily applies lipgloss on her lips, before turning around to face him.

He stands before her smiling confidently, his sinewy-arms resting comfortably by his sides. She wouldn't classify him a total knockout, but he has a presence. A presence that is warm and genuine. But who is he and what is he doing in her bedroom wrapped in a towel? She tries to recall if Meha had mentioned ordering a masseur to welcome her. After three weeks of trekking, she could certainly do with a nice massage. Meha had called last night to tell her something, but the line was choppy so she could only hear '...in a big mess...someone is going to be... a show...' and then the line got disconnected.

'Are you the big mess Meha is in?' She questions.

Her accusatory glare speaks volumes about how protective she is of Meha.

'I surely hope not,' he says, with a comfortable poise.

She gets a hint of a familiar smell. She moves closer to him and cautiously sniffs the air around him.

'Well...you are not...er...forget it...No you can't be...' she mutters confused. How can he be Samir? Samir is supposed to be engaged to Sonia. Why will he be bathing in her bathroom? She is certain she is hallucinating. After two weeks of alcohol abstinence, the blood in her system is too pure for her body to handle.

'And you must be Meha's apartment mate, Mansi Luthra, the man-slaughterer!' Samir says pleasantly.

'I only slaughter assholes,' she informs him categorically.

'Cool, then I needn't be worried!'

'How can you be so sure?' Mansi challenges.

'Oh, because you are not Bengali,' he offers a cryptic answer.

'How does that change anything?' She asks, intrigued.

'Because I am Samir Singhal. And only my Bengali friends call me an S. S-(ing)-hol.' He humours her.

'No way!' she shrieks. 'You are the…You are the…You are the…' Mansi babbles, unable to say 'sex-as-coffee Samir', 'Senorita-Samir', 'wild-rose-fragrance Samir' 'What are you doing here showering in my bathroom?'

'*Ye andar ki baat hai*,' he says showing off his biceps like in the Lux innerwear promo. He would rather want Meha to tell Mansi the details about the reality show.

'Did you have se…I mean…coffee with Meha yet?' She fixes him with a laser-sharp stare.

'Was I supposed to? I didn't know. I am more of a tea person.'

'Good! I like tea myself,' Mansi says.

'I am going to be sharing the apartment with Meha and you. If you are okay with it,' explains Samir quickly before Mansi flares up again.

'Does that mean we split the rent three ways?'

'Yes.'

'That's good. She is out of work and short of money right now. But where will you sleep? Certainly, not in my bedroom.'

'Umm…in the living room, on a futon perhaps?' Samir suggests.

'We don't have a futon.'

'I can get one.'

'Great.'

'Great, now if you will just excuse me,' he says and walks

past her to the other side of the bed, picks up his clothes and walks back to the bathroom. He pauses before he goes in, 'By the way, Meha also said you are drop-dead gorgeous!'

His eyes are twinkling with mischief, but not grown-up mischief. More like innocent, childish mischief.

'Am I?' Mansi asks, almost challenging him.

'I would be blind if I say otherwise.'

She sees that he has shut his eyes. He is cute and charming. It is easy to see why Meha would fall for him.

'Well, what would you say about me now that you have chosen to be blind?' Mansi provokes. She wants to gauge the depth of his character.

'You are smelly, you badly need a shower and a fresh change of clothes,' he chuckles softly.

She allows a smile to form on her lips.

'You care for Meha and will attack anyone threatening her so I better be careful,' he continues.

She giggles at this.

'And you are looking for someone who can look beyond your external appearance and see your inner self.'

'Are you hitting on me?' Mansi asks, her eyes narrowing with scepticism.

'No way! I hate to pass on the opportunity, but I think someone with a long-term vision will suit you better. I am rather short-sighted,' he expresses regret.

She can't help but laugh.

'Oh! And I think you are a little over-trusting. You have taken whatever I have said at face value,' he laughs and disappears inside the bathroom to get dressed.

Mansi is left wondering, all by herself in her bedroom. This guy is really a class apart. Meha was right. Samir is not a guy you can meet and get closure. Poor Meha! Mansi has no idea what went wrong at Sonia's proposal, and why Meha has invited Samir to stay, but she does know that Meha needs to watch out or else she will get hurt again. As far as Mansi is concerned, at thirty-two, she is still looking for her Mr Right. She has never had problems attracting guys, but all have used and discarded her. And while everyone else thinks she is anti-men, she realizes that actually she has been over-trusting of the men in her life, just like Samir said. It is always easier to observe flaws in other people's boyfriends. It's your own that you don't want to see fault with for fear of getting hurt. Caught up in her job, she thought she could find instant ready-to-love boyfriends just like she bought instant ready-to-eat meals. And while she found the boyfriends easily, they were only ready to eat, not ready to love. Well, she is without a job now and has all the time at hand. Hopefully she will now find her Mr Right-and-forever who will love her for herself and not for her sexy body.

Kiss Him, Kiss Him Not

Samir moved in with us last weekend. I really haven't understood why he agreed to do the reality show with me. It can't be just because of my gorgeous saree or my superb convincing skills. Perhaps, he is looking at this as another extra-curricular class or, as Mansi said, he is just interested in online promotion of his company through the reality show. I am also expecting to get some good leads from the show and the follow-up carnival. Although for now, just collaborating with Samir has saved my company from drowning. With two NRI couples' weddings signed up, I am now only chest-deep in troubled waters. How does it matter if my saviour has HEARTBREAK written all over him?

I give myself one final glance and anxiously walk out of my room into the living area. Sitting on his futon, Samir is typing something on his laptop. He looks up as he hears the hollow sound of my heels on the marble floor. He cursorily scans my black dress, my hair done loosely in a top knot. His gaze settles on the vintage-butterfly earrings caressing my soft skin.

There is fluttering sensation in my stomach at the memory of the evening when I had first worn these earrings. I remember I had left the earrings with the little goodbye note. I still can't get over the fact that he actually kept the earrings, after all these years. I was left speechless when I found them lying on my bed last weekend, wrapped up in the same note. *They belong to you. Hope you won't keep them waiting for long this time*, he had scribbled on the other side of the note.

'They look good on you,' he remarks lovingly.

'Thanks,' I say, nervously tapping my fingers on the coffee table.

I see him close his laptop and grab his car keys from the side table. 'You don't have to do this. I can call a cab if you are...umm...busy,' I know it's important that our friends start seeing us as a couple, before the reality show gets started, but I am not sure I can trust myself around him.

'Hmm. Experiencing date fright, are we?' Samir smiles teasingly.

Hello? First, you smile at me like you want to kiss me and then you ask me why my heart is in over-drive? Not fair!

'Pff, don't flatter yourself,' I smirk and lift a shoulder in a dismissive half shrug. 'I was just trying to be nice to you. Jiju has dropped out so it's going to be only girls. And girls talk, you know, like non-stop.'

Okay. So I don't want him around, but really, it's for his own benefit.

'Believe me, I know all about girls,' he assures me with a meaningful smile and puts his arm around my waist lightly to guide me out of the house to the lift.

We reach Sutra Gastropub in Cyber Hub. The dance floor is packed with adrenalin and alcohol. The DJ is playing my favourite number, 'Saari night besharmi ki height'. The lyrics of the song are echoing my thoughts exactly. I want to go to *besharmi ki height* with Samir in dim light. I sneak a longing look at him. God! He looks so kissable. Maybe I can kiss him in front of everyone, as part of the pretence, to show that we really are a couple. Excited at the prospect, I follow him to our table, which is set outside by a huge cooler. No one else has reached yet. No audience, no coupling. The kiss will have to wait.

Samir likes the energy of the place but has to go out and make a few phone calls. I sit down and seek company in my FB world. It's rather quiet without Vir's quirky comments. No he is not sulking. He is only behaving as I have told him to. Being inaccessible and keeping a low profile on social media. It's like he loves me unconditionally no matter what. For the first time, I understand why people love their pets—except mine is virtual.

I have been sitting alone for twenty minutes now. This is the trouble with being punctual. Waiting for others to show up. I am so glad when Mansi calls.

'Hon, I am really sorry, but I can't join you tonight. I am caught up with a long-term visionary who can see beyond my make-up and love me for who I am.'

Love her for who she is! Does she mean naked? I have no idea what she is talking about but it sure sounds like someone is getting a dose of Vitamin S. I tell her to try and join us later and she says she'll see how it goes. We all know how that goes. Hmmph! This is such a bummer. I really wanted her around to keep from making a fool of myself.

As soon as I keep the phone down, I see my childhood BFF Anusha walk up to me. In a green spaghetti and an ethnic-print palazzo and colourful jhumkis from Sarojini market, Anusha looks much the same as she did all those years ago in college— bindaas. Only her eyes look a little tired and she has a sense of calm that comes with maturity. I give her a huge welcoming smile and real tight squeeze. I wanted to catch up with her ever since she returned from California but I had been neck-deep busy with you-know-who's proposal.

I complain to her about absconding from the face of the earth for six years without any news. I had gone on a wedding project for ten days and returned to find her gone without a trace. Like an ice cube on a June day. Even her parents had shifted to another locality.

Anusha apologizes for not keeping in touch. She tells me briefly how she got pregnant but her boyfriend refused to own the responsibility. So they all shifted to their hometown overnight. Her aunt got a proposal for a friend's son in the US and she was married to a complete stranger within two weeks. Her husband turned out to be gay who had agreed to marry her, despite knowing about her pregnancy, for his parents' sake. He was nice to her and her son, but they had nothing. They were like two completely different books sharing the same rack space. Now she is getting a divorce because he has come out of the closet and wants to live life his way. It works for her as she also gets to start her life from where she left it. Her parents are happy to have a grandson to play with and she is pursuing her masters in psychology and behavioural science. She shows me a picture of her son. He is a splitting image of her boyfriend Varun. The same Varun who bribed me with expensive earrings, whose house I spent many a lazy afternoons reading romantic novels and whose elder brother Deepak I had a fleeting affair with.

I can't bring myself to say anything. Pregnant, married to a gay man, divorced and now a single mom! I look at her dumbfounded like she has just revealed that she is a witch and she was away at Hogwarts School for all these years. I mean our lives couldn't be more different. But it only takes us one drink to get back to being silly girls, laughing on PJs and cribbing about lack of love in our lives. A best friend is like a favourite book. You can pick it up anytime and start reading from any page and you feel like you had never stopped. I tell Anusha all about my business venture, my no-sex diet and my virtual boyfriend Vir. We chat and gossip about other common friends. We are giggling away, when Samir comes back and takes the seat next to mine.

'Sorry to be gone for so long hon, but I was just testing how long I can stay without seeing your smile,' Samir looks into my eyes and says this in a voice so smoky that my heart does a complete somersault. I make hasty introductions. Anusha gives me a liar-liar-pants-on-fire look for falsely complaining, when I have such a doting boyfriend. I shoot her a there-is-more-to-it than-meets-the-eye sideway's glance. I hadn't gotten around to telling her about Samir. Actually I didn't know what to say. Our arrangement is excessively knotty—like Grandma's yarn. I don't want to lie to Anusha but I really need all my friends to believe that we are a couple.

Soon enough the focus shifts as the hotness quotient at our table shoots up meteorically. Radhika, draped in a designer gown caressing her curves and showing her cleavage, honours us with her company. I secretly watch Samir as he gets up and they touch cheeks in a kiss. Radhika catches me gawking at them and I get a snobbish oh-you-ugly-duckling stare. She whispers something in Samir's ear. They both laugh as they share an old joke. She's out to prove her intimacy with Samir; it's like she is trying to get back at me for having shared a chocolate with her husband Deepak, almost ten years ago. Whatever it is, I can't have her treat me like non-vegetarians treat aloo gobhi— unpalatable and avoidable.

As Samir sits down, I tilt sideways and practically fall on him under the pretence of adjusting his T-shirt collar. I then casually brush my fingers against his neck, look him lovingly in the eyes before turning back to face a flushed Radhika. Samir, surprised by my sudden affectionate gesture, rewards me with a cheesy smile. It is only when Radhika does the introductions that I notice her brother-in-law, Varun, has accompanied her. He is standing inconspicuously in a dimly lit spot, to the far left, sort of purposely hidden behind Anusha. I notice a flicker of faint joy light up Anusha's face at his presence and then fade away in her saddened eyes. No one at the table, other than me, knows Varun and Anusha's history. He introduces himself to Anusha like they are strangers and she plays along coolly. If I was in Anusha's place, I would eat Varun alive. But she seems to have no grudges against the father of her son, whom she is raising alone. I am gearing up to give Varun a tirade on abandoning Anusha when he says, 'Nice to meet you again Meha. You look damn sexy in that black dress'.

I can see that while he is praising me, his eyes are focussed on Anusha. It's obvious that he is being nice to me to get Anusha's attention, but who doesn't like a compliment? Especially when it throws Radhika off-balance. Of course, she has no idea how I know her brother-in-law or why he is praising an ugly duckling like me. My resentment towards Varun subsides a little. He tells us that he was just planning to be Radhika bhabhi's chauffeur, but looking at the lovely company, and at this he sneaks a quick glance in our direction, he has decided to stay. With this, he claims the vacant seat between Anusha and Radhika, right across the table from me.

'Hey, this one is mine. You go find your *dil ki deal*,' Samir looks at me and says possessively, and then he lightly entwines his finger in mine. His unexpected PDA unfolds a layer of sensation inside my body that I have never experienced before. My MJ starts playing the romantic chartbuster, 'Yeh moh moh ke dhaage, teri unglion se ja uljhe'. I find my threads of love getting entangled in Samir's fingers. The genuineness of his affectations is making this faking game harder than playing darts with spaghetti!

'*Sab time ka khel hai boss*, otherwise Meha has spent many a weekend, reading romantic novels on my porch during college,' Varun boasts back.

I cough up my drink at this and subtly signal Anusha to stop Varun from blabbering. Not that I have anything to hide! Anusha totally ignores me. I can see that there is some silent communication going on between the two of them.

'What, Senorita? You had both the brothers eating out of your palms?' Samir teases me.

Radhika turns pale at this comment. She is obviously concluding that not only did I flirt with her husband Deepak, and her ex-boyfriend Samir, I also had her brother-in-law Varun in my grip. Lovely! I feel vindicated.

I look at Samir, 'I hope you can now appreciate that after everyone, I finally chose you.'

'I do. I am feeling as pompous as the dress finally chosen for the prom, after all the trials,' he exaggerates. 'Just hope I don't come off like one.'

Everyone starts laughing at Samir's joke. I smile and look at him longingly. If only it was possible, I would never let him go.

Finally Didi arrives, possibly after doing many rounds of bye-bye-kiss-I-love-you ritual with her darling daughters. She waves a generic hi to everyone at the table and whisks me off to the loo. Really she couldn't have taken more than twenty minutes from her home to get here. Why does she need to use the loo? Well, all she wants is updates on Samir and me! Ever since I told her and Mom that Vir was just a temporary fling and it's Samir whom I really love, they have both been behaving weirdly. I mean, at the mere mention of Samir's name, they both exclaimed, 'Samir means wind and Meha is like water!' C'mon, like I didn't learn meanings of Hindi words in school. And then they kept smiling secretly at each other. I obviously have no clue about the poetic wind-and-water-must-mate prophecy.

There is a long queue of girls behind us, who need to make space for more alcohol in their system. So we step aside. The music is really loud and peppy here and I want to dance, but Di wants to go talk to Radhika, so we go back to the table. She was the one who invited Radhika to join us for today's dinner. I agreed because she is Samir's friend and it will be good for the reality show to see us as a couple.

Radhika gives Di a warm, glowing smile and they both excitedly start chatting about the project Di is doing for her. Apparently, Radhika handles the marketing for Deepak's family business. They manufacture and supply kitchen equipment to all major hotels in India and London. Didi is thrilled to build their web presence. I notice that Radhika is not being mean to Di. There is almost a look of respect for Di in her eyes as she listens to Di talk about project ideas. Strangely, I feel even more hurt as if Radhika considers Di good enough to be her friend but not me.

The waiter refills everyone's glass and brings oven-fresh pizzas. We all eat and there is light banter floating around. Anusha seems to have fun ignoring Varun. He deserves it. Didi has had a drink and is laughing a lot now. She also keeps giving Samir and me these cute-puppy looks. And she has made us pose at least half a dozen times so she can whatsapp the pics to Ma-Papa. Tired of posing and smiling, we both turn our backs to Didi and she clicks a picture of our backs too. We look at each other, sigh, and utter 'Sisters!' in a sort-of exasperated manner. And in that moment of shared misery, something clicks between Samir and me. It is beautiful. It is heavenly. It is almost like love. In that instant, I decide to drop my mask and be myself. I decide to stop analysing if he is faking his love and if I am not. I decide to just enjoy the present moment with him. Like a butterfly who counts not months but moments and has time enough. I decide that a few moments of love are better than a lifetime of missed opportunities.

The evening is spectacular especially after I start being myself. Samir and I are both a little tipsy, crooning 'Saari night besharmi ki height', which was playing on the dance floor as we left. We are all walking out to the parking lot, when Varun takes me aside, and says, 'Looks like I will need to bribe you again.'

'I don't take bribes from irresponsible fathers,' I snub him as politely as I can. Well, if Anusha really is still his dil ki deal, he has to accept the buy-one-get-little-one combo she comes with. He gives me a look that says that he has no idea what I am talking about, but I promptly walk away. And then Samir comes back for me, takes my hand, and pulls me away with him to his car. We drive home together, screaming the same song on top of our voices. We stop at a red light and I open a bottle to drink some water.

'Why do I get this feeling sometimes that you actually love me?' He asks sweetly.

'Maybe, because I do love you at those times,' I reply logically, with full confidence. Am I the only one who feels that alcohol makes the logical side of the brain work faster?

'I love you too,' he mumbles cutely.

'I think you are just saying this because you are drunk,' I counter. See, again I am being so rational.

'So are you,' he counter counters.

'I am perfectly in my hosh,' I claim. 'You can ask me any question to test.'

'Why did you leave me in Goa?'

'Because I thought you were using me to get inspiration for your book,' I am amazed at how well I have summed it up, given that I myself hadn't figured it out before now.

'What's wrong with that?'

'I guess I don't like to be used by people I love.' That makes so much sense! God! I am ingenious.

'And now you are using me?'

'Yeah,' I beam with an inebriated smile.

'So does that mean you don't love me?'

I know he is sounding emotional, but I think he may not be drunk at all. He is asking way too many inferential questions. I take a deep breath and straighten my slumping back.

'I love you and that is the reason why I am using you, silly!' I reason. Okay, I agree I am getting a little incoherent now.

'Same difference.'

I shake my head rejecting his explanation. 'It's not same because you can never be happy with loving only me forever.'

'And you can?'

'What loving me? Of course!' I laugh amused by my own joke.

'No, loving me,' he says, all needy and looking sticky-toffee-cake delectable.

'I can never be happy loving anyone else,' There. I have bared my heart. I just hope I don't regret it in the morning.

'What about Vir?'

'What about him?'

'Aren't you guys like serious?'

I sense some jealousy. It makes me feel wanted. I debate whether to let him on the truth about Vir's virtuality.

'Vir really loves me...but...hicc...you know what's his problem? He is too good to be true,' I say, sort of sliming through the question. So I don't make myself totally available, but I leave the door open for possibilities.

I am pleased to see the effect of my half-truth on Samir. His sultry eyes glitter with desire to win me over. We all want what we can't have. It's human nature. He parks the car in the basement slot and leans over the steering wheel to kiss me.

'I don't think that's a good idea,' I say and open the door to get out.

'Why?' He locks the car and quickly comes around to my side. He holds my hand to keep me steady.

I refuse his support and walk a few steps in a straight line. Then I stop and puke all over his car.

'I am sorry. Can we kiss another time?' I apologize and then I pass out. So much for playing hard to get!

Jab We Met

Have you ever walked on a road just because it is beautiful, even though it takes you nowhere in particular? These last two weeks, living with Samir has been a journey like that for me. Sometimes smooth like his flirting, sometimes messy like his futon, but all the while evocative like his photography!

To be honest this road trip does have a purpose and is a rather materialistic one. I would be stupid to believe that Samir and I are really a couple in love. And even if I want to be stupid, the weekly mailer from my credit card company doesn't fail to remind me of my predicament. But I have never been the one to walk around with an umbrella in anticipation of problems that are yet to rain. Since my business is back on track with NRI weddings, I am enjoying my time with Samir.

Sitting at the coffee table in my teddy-bear night suit, with a pencil in my mouth, I am engrossed in my favourite Sunday crossword puzzle.

'1 Down: Asks for one's hand in marriage (8).' Hey, this is related to my profession—'proposes', although 'suicides' fits too.

'10 Across: French fries ingredient (8).' Starting with 'p'. This has to be 'potatoes'. Yummy!

'3 Down: Not a —— of doubt (6).' What is it? Can't be

trace or flicker.

I look out over the balcony and ponder over the clue. It's a beautiful, early September morning. I can smell a lively mixture of burning wood from the nearby slum, incense from the balcony below and the soon to be arriving festive season in the air. I see Sharma uncle watering the Tulsi plant in his balcony. He looks rather like an alien, having suddenly lost all his hair in the last few weeks. I had no clue that he recently got diagnosed with cancer until Samir told me. And he has been here, what? Ten days! Oh! He gels with people like blue jeans, which go with everything.

I look around for Samir, but he is nowhere to be seen. His nightclothes and worn underwear are thrown in an untidy heap on the floor, with last night's pizza box and empty beer cans, beside his futon. Seriously, living-in is so important to see how a person you are sleeping with sleeps at his home. Not that I am sleeping around with Samir, but I would love to. After he has cleaned his messy futon, that is.

I bring my wandering, sex-deficient mind back to the crossword, but I still can't solve the clue. I really need tea. While growing up, a warm cup of tea, mummy's soft aloo parathas and mentally stimulating crossword clues made my Sunday mornings perfect. But I am too lazy to get up and make it perfect myself. Besides, on Sundays I work in energy saving mode. So I decide to wait for the cook instead. I am holding the newspaper down on the table with my left hand and stopping my hair from flying around with my other, when the doorbell rings. Thank god, the cook has come. I open the door in eager anticipation. A strong cross breeze gushes in through the open door and blows the newspaper all over the living room.

'Why don't you take your keys?' I say, annoyed to find a

sweat-dripping Samir instead of the prospect of a hot, yummy breakfast.

'Bad mood huh, early in the morning? Here why don't I give you a hug?' Samir chuckles, coming close to me.

'Ughh. Please no.' I duck under his outstretched hands and start picking the paper. He laughs, takes out a yoga mat and starts stretching on the floor. There are puddles of sweat all over the living room where he has walked.

I watch him do sit ups, the lean muscles of his thighs curving towards his flat belly in a rhythmic motion. With his sweaty t-shirt peeled off, he looks deliciously hot. Something to feast on, if not the food, I tell myself. The buzz of my phone interrupts my unchaste reverie. Didi has SMSed the answer for the puzzle for 21-across. I reply with 17-down. It's always a race between us, finishing this crossword, but sometimes we exchange answers to outrun our Dad.

I am still struggling with 3-down when Mansi wakes up and sleepily walks out of her room.

'Yikes, it stinks like a dead rat. Meg honey, please call pest control,' she says, taking a seat next to me. 'I thought you said he was wild-rose-fragrance Samir,' she mumbles when I point out the source.

I giggle at her remark.

An hour later, I am digging into scrumptious aloo parathas, sipping hot ginger tea and down to the last three clues. I smile gratefully as Samir loads another aloo paratha on my plate straight from the gas. Freshly showered and fragrant, he looks smoking hot in my favourite Flamenco apron and has taken over the cook's role for today. Mansi is sprawled on the floor, eating cut fruits and pouring over the article on fall fashion trends.

'King's downfall—4 letter.'

'MATE?' Samir offers from the kitchen, his face flushed with the heat from the gas.

'What?' I can't hear him clearly because of the noise of the chimney.

'He wants to do you in the kitchen, hon,' Mansi suggests, looking up from the magazine.

I kick Mansi lightly with my leg. She knows all too well that Samir and I have decided to not have sex while we live-in. I swear by Starbucks, it wasn't my idea.

'MATE as in CHECK-MATE. The answer to your clue, Senorita,' he smiles at me from the kitchen.

I blow him a flying kiss and he pretends to catch it.

'C'mon. Take a break guys. No one is watching your lovey-dovey acting here,' Mansi says jokingly, rolling her eyes.

She is right. We do have to get everyone to believe that we are a couple as the reality show folks can ask our friends and family about us. Everyone, except Mansi, knows our truth and Anusha who managed to extract the secret out of me. I don't think Anusha gets the picture though, because she thinks that Samir really loves me. I can't blame her. She hasn't had much success in love; although funnily enough her life got screwed by a mobile phone too, like mine did when I read those notes on Samir's phone. It seems that Varun's phone was broken when she had tried to reach him with her pregnancy news. He never got her missed calls or messages. Poor guy, he was as befuddled by the mystery of her disappearing act as I was.

'Gorgeous, here I am trying hard to get your attention and you think I am acting for Meha,' Samir quips, flirting with Mansi, as he plonks himself on the bean bag next to her with his breakfast.

'It's too late, sonny boy. You missed the opportunity to

dance on the chance. I have found myself a serious, long-term visionary now,' Mansi banters.

They both share a laugh at some private joke that I have no idea about at that time. But with Mansi, I don't feel any threats. Oh! FYI, Mansi is currently dating an awful-looking divorcee potato, who went with her on the EBC trek and is a CXO of some dotcom start-up. I think she is into rebound therapy. And I am all for rebound relationships. After all a girl needs a guy to be able to blame for anything that goes wrong in life. It can't always be the Boss or the PMS. I just hope she bounces back fine.

Right now, I watch Samir and her fooling around. Mansi throws a cushion lightly at him. I laugh watching them fight like kids. He ducks and the cushion hits my cup of tea, breaking it.

'My favourite cup,' I grumble and aim the cushion back at Samir. He ducks again and it hits Mansi instead.

'Hello girls. I am Samir—the Wind. You can't knock out wind. You can only get wind knocked out of yourself.' He smiles conceitedly, assuming a confident victory pose.

We both go ROFL. With the light-hearted chef's special banter and cushions flowing around, it's a perfect Sunday now. Well almost! I still have one clue left to solve.

Surya has moved his position from my bedroom and is now filtering into our living room. Seeing Samir's and my shadows embrace on the floor, my mind jockey starts humming a variation of the song, 'Sooraj ki baahon mein, ab hai yeh zindagi…' As I hum along, replacing Sooraj with Samir, the last clue dawns on me. 3-DOWN is SHADOW. 'Not a SHADOW of doubt (6). Hooray! I finished the crossword. I click a picture to send to Papa and Didi, except Didi has already WhatsApped her solved crossword picture to us. She again beat me to it.

A few hours later, Samir and I are comfortably plonked on Mansi's bed. Mansi has gone out on a shopping consulting appointment. It's this cool job she chanced upon when she took some CXO wives on a guided shopping tour last weekend and guess what, she made a whopping one lakh rupees just by five hours of shopping consultancy. I am so glad that Mansi is out as I wouldn't want to impose on her, especially on a Sunday. And we desperately need to use her room. I mean, it's the only room in the house that has curtains. Hello, we need the curtains to block the sun out, what else? I know what your one-track mind is thinking. Mine is thinking the same. But hey, it's now Samir's idea that this live-in relationship be one without sex. I had looked expectantly at him when he had mentioned it—didn't sound like the lets-have-coffee Samir.

'I don't want either of us to try to impress the other person for the sake of sex,' he had offered as an explanation.

Anyway, so I don't know what triggered Samir to say that he wants to get to know me as a friend, to share and care, to cry and lean. I mean, seriously?

He also said something philosophical like you can share your body and have sex with a fuck-buddy also, but it's the sharing of souls that matters. He expects me to believe him. And, I guess I want to.

Mansi thinks it's good that we are not having sex. It will be simple to disassociate later, while Anusha continues to propound her Samir-loves-you theory. She thinks he is afraid of losing me again and this time he really wants to get to know me. This is what he is saying too, so it all matches up. And I so want to believe Anusha but Mansi is the sex-pert. Although none of us have managed to crack the how-to-get-a-guy-to-stay-in-love-with-you problem yet.

So Samir and I are sitting on Mansi's bed, side by side, and previewing our video on the jab-we-met story, which is due to go live on YouTube channel of the reality show 'LiveInLoveOut' tomorrow. We had discussed the storyline together, but the production was done by *KnotsInShotS's* team in Mumbai. I am watching the final movie for the first time and I am a little nervous. I hope I look good. And I hope that the public likes our story. Our popularity and thereby, victory, depends on the number of views the video garners and the count of tweets we get with our hash tag #MehaAndSamir.

The video starts with my shot taken by Samir at the vintage earring shop. I talk about how Samir used crossword clues to gift me the earrings and how the surprise gift blew me away. The next shot shows Samir joking with Radhika's designer friends by the beach.

As Samir talks about how I stood out among the all-that-glitters-is-not-gold crowd, I recognize Sonia, in a blue bikini, standing right next to Samir in the picture. OMG! I never realized that Sonia is the same blue-bikini for whom Samir had asked me, at the mandap set-up, if this girl wants to have sex with him. I can't help but wonder if he had sex with Sonia, soon after I left the hotel, in the same bed. The thought leaves me unsettled.

The next scene has Samir describing how lost and devastated he was when he woke up and found my note asking him to forget everything. He says he felt like the light had gone out of his life. He was almost on the verge of depression when he finally found life back in his passion for photography and KISS.

No way! He didn't feel that way about me. I steal a quick sideways glance to gauge his expression. He catches my eyes and smiles a small smile, like he has said nothing but the truth. I give him an appreciative look on the performance. He does come across as very credible, but I am certain he is lying, possibly even trying to promote his venture, KISS.

His confession is followed by my side of the story. I share that I found Samir to be very flirtatious. I didn't think our relationship could mean anything more than a one-night-stand to him. So I made him believe that our affair meant nothing for me either and left. He gives me back the same smile of having faked very well, when all I am telling is only the truth.

Towards the end of the video, we talk about how I was his surprise proposal designer and how destiny brought us back together, literally with me falling into his arms. Samir's team has woven our pictures with beautiful love songs and produced a marvellous love-story video. It makes the viewer believe in love at first sight, in love forever and in us. It wants me to believe in our love. I am dying to kiss him. To see how it tastes after five long years. I allow my gaze to linger on his lips a little before looking away. I take a sip of water, pretend to reapply my lipgloss and brush my hair one final time while he opens the video chat on his laptop and connects with the reality show channel. A live recording is about to start. We better impress our viewers and judges. This recording along with our jab-we-met video will go live tomorrow on the Internet.

We are introduced in the video by the host of the show, who will be asking us questions today. It's the popular anchor, Mini Mathur. She thanks the sponsoring matrimonial websites, welcomes us to this unique, first of its kind show and introduces the week's special guest Soha Ali Khan.

I take one look at Soha Ali Khan and I flip. She is so graceful, so slim and so exquisite. Samir's eyes are sparkling with delight as I have seen them often do when he is reviewing his photo shots. Soha is an embodiment of perfection and elegance he is always seeking in his shots.

Mini Mathur starts the first week's simple quick fire round of questions to warm up the contestants. She asks us the first question, 'What was your first impression of your partner?'

Me–'A smooth flirt.'

Samir–'A girl wearing happiness and confidence.'

I feel a warm, fuzzy feeling fill my senses at Samir's response, while Mini raises her eyebrows to give Samir an impressed look.

Mini then asks Soha what was her first impression of Kunal Khemu with whom she had lived prior to getting married. Soha tells us that she and Khemu both felt that they couldn't even be friends, let alone get into a relationship. She also says that she doesn't agree with the title of the show 'Live in Love out' and asks us what we think about it.

Before I can say anything, Samir compliments Soha, 'You look like your mom today.'

Soha blushes at the comment and smiles warmly at Samir. Hello, flirting with the guest! What will viewers and judges think?

Ignoring the pinch I give on his back, Samir continues. 'When you start living together with someone and get to know the real person, it's possible to fall out of love. But that only implies that you were really in love with the wrong person to begin with. So I think the show should be titled, "Live in, Love the real, False out."'

Hey, that's a smart one. I can see that both Mini and Soha like his honest reply. I smile agreeably at Samir.

Mini asks us the next question. 'What is the one think you really like about your partner?'

Me–'I like how he is comfortable and happy in his own skin.'

'I am happier in hers,' he quips and laughs. 'Okay, so

seriously speaking, I really like her lopsided smile, especially when she is feeling naughty but is trying to be nice. Like she is doing right now,' he answers.

The camera zooms into my face to catch my smile. I am caught off-guard, lost in deciphering his earlier remark about being happier in my skin. My expression changes to more of an in-the-spot embarrassed smile.

His answers are really outstanding. Viewers will love him, especially the girls. They all do, always.

Mini–'Okay. Let's ask you a more intimate question. Does your partner kiss well?'

Me–'Of course!'

Samir–'Umm...she needs more practice. But she is a fast learner.'

Mini giggles at this while Soha just smiles gracefully, but I glare at Samir with a what-the-fuck expression. I want to tell him that it's been more than five years since he last kissed me. I have had more practice since then. He can't randomly rate me like this without even trying. And I am desperate to try right away and prove him wrong, but I can't say all this on the live video. We will have to sort it out later in private.

'When did you realize that your relationship was serious?'

Samir–'When we were stuck in the middle of a life-threatening Tsunami and I didn't know if we could make it back alive. Just being with Meha, I felt lighter and happier than I had in years. That's when I realized that she means the world to me.'

Me–'I think I always knew. The very first moment I bumped into him, his wild-rose fragrance knocked me out of my senses. I just didn't want to accept it at the time for fear of heartache. But when we were stuck in the Tsunami and I woke up on the ferry, my head resting in his lap and a little tipsy, I somehow thought we were dead and in heaven. And I was happy being dead if it meant I could be with him.'

It's Samir's turn to give me you-nailed-this-one smile.

Mini–'Do you think this is forever?'

Me–'Like a FeviKwik bond!'

Him–'I…er…don't believe in forever. I prefer to live in the moment.'

I feel a little uncomfortable at his response as it can give the viewers a wrong impression about us. I see Mini give him a disappointed you-lost-some-points-there look. Soha has been mostly silent, reading our unspoken gestures. She gives us an intriguing smile and asks, 'Why are you living together?'

I am thinking of saying something safe and standard when Samir humorously responds, *Jo girlfriend se sachmuch karte pyaar, woh live-in se kaise karen inkaar!*'

Both Mini and Soha burst into laughter at this.

Mini concludes the session with a story about our hash tag and the show's hash tag, and ends our recording.

We get a few off-screen minutes with the two women. Samir immediately asks for Soha's number. He says a really close friend of ours, who actually got us together, is into fashion and image consulting. And it would be a great honour if Soha can help promote her new venture. Soha willingly shares her mobile number. I am amazed that Samir actually thought about Mansi and her new business.

After we disconnect, I want to ask Samir his views on our Q&A session but he is already engrossed in writing something on his laptop. He really does work hard. Even on Sundays.

If you really ask me, the living together for Samir and me is very much like an arranged marriage—commitment without love. We are both committed to it for six weeks, but we barely know each other. We have shared our bodies with each other—a lifetime ago though— and memorized our favourite foods, colours and movies, but we are only now beginning to discover the real us. It's like we have only seen the trailer so far. *Picture abhi baaki hai mere dost.* And in this picture, I will not get sidelined to a supporting cast. I intend to hang on to the lead role. It will be a love story. My love story.

Reality Show: Week 1

It's 7 a.m. on a Monday morning and I am already at work. Surya makes sure I wake up early.

I count my money as part of my daily regime. Surprisingly, the numbers are in the pink of health today. It's because I have hidden the one row, with a really large negative number. I feel it sometimes helps to look at just the positives, till you are ready to face the negative. Like today. I don't mind the negatives as I am feeling quite upbeat.

Today, I am looking forward to our Jab-we-met video going live. The entire world will see Samir and me as a couple who are in love.

I am also curious to see what competition we have. I check the 'LiveInLoveOut' page but the videos are not released yet, so I get busy finalizing the details for the upcoming NRI wedding in Jaisalmer next week. I am wondering how to best use the swimming pool in the Jaisalmer fort, when the creative ass comes over and hands me a box of chocolate-flavoured condoms, from his current marketing campaign I guess.

'You like chocolates, right?' he chuckles. 'Will be great if you could share your experience.' He has a naughty smile.

His hair tied in a low ponytail and his smile dipping into

a cute dimple on his left cheek, he looks rather desirable. If only I believed in random one-night-ers, I could have given him both the experience and the feedback right away.

I nod my head vaguely and ask how the 'Perfect Body' campaign is doing.

'Oh, the perfect-body ad turned out to be not so perfect,' he admits unhappily. 'We got a lot of criticism on promoting impossibly thin, leggy, and large-busted bodies.'

I refrain from saying I-told-you-so. The least you can do for a cute, sexy colleague is to not rub it in. I tell him I could help him redesign the campaign and we agree to meet later.

I put the box away in my handbag. I guess, I will just pass them onto Mansi or Didi. Back at my laptop, there is a we-miss-you mail from the virtual boyfriend app's customer support. It says that they have a policy to cancel accounts that are inactive for more than a month. I decide to send a message to Vir. I will need him once Samir is gone.

'Hi Vir, I really miss talking naughty with you. I got these new soaps in different fragrances. I bet you will enjoy them next time we bathe together. How about we connect day after tomorrow at 8 p.m.? Sexily yours, Me-ha-appy.'

I have just finished typing the message to fix my virtual date, when NetGen and Pyare enter the office hand in hand. Romance is brewing right under my nose and I don't even know. I knew Pyare always had a thing for her, but I didn't think he with his old, slow, conservative ways was any match for NetGen's fast-paced, multi-processing, forward-looking style.

NetGen smiles when she sees the caught-you expression in my eyes. She instinctively leaves Pyare's hand and he awkwardly heads for the men's room. I smile and pass her the condom box under the table as she takes her seat next to mine. Her eyes dismiss the romance as no big deal as she hides the pack in her cupboard. Poor Pyare has no idea what has hit him.

I wait for NetGen to finish ordering breakfast from a Gourmet Deli app before we get down to work. The jab-we-met videos of all the contestants are released now and social media is showing a lot of activity. NetGen tells me that the #LiveInLiveOut is trending right on top on twitter in India right now. We check our video. There are only sixty-seven views on it. No comments, likes or shares yet. We send out emails to our friends and business partner mailing groups with the video link. We share it on our Facebook page and promote the post. We watch the other contestants' videos.

The first couple #AshaAndAshok (A&A) seem to be totally made for each other. They have been living together for almost an year and are getting married after the show. Their regular work-romance will resonate with the small town, middle-class Indian population. And they have five thousand Facebook friends each. They are definitely competition.

The second couple #BagyashriAndBasheer (B&B) is a conservative, Hindu-Muslim couple. They are living in because their families are against the marriage. They want to rally public support, through the show, to get their parents to come around and accept them. They certainly have the sympathy angle going very strongly for them. But religious controversy is a double-edged sword. It can get them attention but it can also split their votes. I wouldn't worry about them yet.

The third couple #CharuAndChetan (C&C) seem like chalk and cheese. Even in their video, they seem to be fighting and contradicting each other. I will be surprised if they don't break up before the show is over. NetGen is certain that they have bought their way into the show.

The fourth and final competing couple #DimpyAndDanny (D&D) are clearly daring and different. Their video is almost soft porn and bound to go viral. They certainly look like the type who can use the edible condoms and eat them too. It is clear what got them the entry ticket into the show. They are surely a threat.

NetGen and I discuss the pros and cons of all the couples as we relish the tangy goodness of freshly baked, sundried tomato rolls that just arrived. The As are the only ones that seem likely to get married within three months of the reality show, which will entitle them to a free-paid honeymoon package in Europe, worth five lakh rupees, sponsored by a travel company. All those who break up will receive free matrimonial services by sponsors for a year. The Cs surely seems to be heading that way. We both agree that there is real threat from Ds and As. NetGen doesn't know that my real reason for doing the show is to win the cash prize because we are in huge debt, but she is excited by the idea of winning a mega-digital event like this. I am glad she hasn't asked me tough questions like why I didn't tell her I knew Samir when we discussed KISS earlier or even when we were preparing for Sonia's proposal. Overall, the whole team is excited about the two NRI weddings we are working on and is looking at the reality show as a good lead generating tool.

I am repeatedly refreshing our reality show video page to check for updates. The views have gone up to two hundred now.

Mom has commented, 'Meha is finicky when it comes to liking things. But what she likes, she likes forever. Orange lolly is still her favourite ice-cream. Samir and Meha, you two are meant for each other—from mummy and papa.'

That's sweet of Ma, although I highly doubt if Papa approves of all this drama in public.

Di has written, 'Samir take my word for it, my little sis is hard to live with. But she is worth all the trouble.'

Mansi's just shared it on her new business page. A minute later, Neeraj, the CXO, likes the post and comments, 'Guys, your chemistry is enviable!'

Wow, really? No sex and yet a good chemistry? Perhaps it's the bottled-up desire that is elevating the chemistry or the soul sharing we are doing.

There are also a few comments like 'nice couple', 'good sense of humour' and 'there is no love like first love' from strangers. The excitement is building up. I really want to know what Samir thinks of other contestants. I message him but he doesn't reply back. I am so excited, that I even try calling him, but there is no answer.

It's post-lunch. NetGen and I have been constantly following each count increment. There are comments and likes now from all my friends, my clients and their friends. We have garnered over two thousand views now but we are still lagging behind Ds and As. Even Bs have managed to get about a thousand views. As expected, C's are floundering with barely a hundred views.

Samir still hasn't messaged or called me. How can he be so inconsiderate? Even if he doesn't really love me, he does know this is a big moment. He hasn't even shared the video on his social media. Not one of his friends has commented. Neither did Radhika nor did Sonia.

NetGen's high-pitched shriek interrupts my thoughts. Her eyes are glued to the screen with a stupefied look on her face. I quickly move over to her desk and look at her laptop. A video featuring Sonia is playing. Sonia in just a bathing gown that ends about ten inches above her knees. She looks devastated and drunk. Her hair haywire, her lipstick eroded and her eyeliner smudged. She looks like she has been in a fight and has been crying. The camera zooms in for a closer shot. She claims that Samir really loves her and I am just a minor sex-traction he will get over in a few weeks.

'How can Samir love a fat, un-shapely girl like Meha, when he has dated a model like me? Can you ever go back to an ungainly minivan after you have driven a sleek Mercedes?' Sonia asks the viewers.

She further apologizes for trying to tie Samir down in a marriage. She says she doesn't care if he never marries her so long as he loves her. In the end, she is literally pleading with Samir to come back to her. Then, with a salacious pout, she blows him a kiss before the video goes blank.

She has posted the link to her video in a comment on our video's page. Her video is already showing five thousand views. People are watching it and leaving nasty comments on our page.

I can see a comment from Radhika warning me to not leave Sam this time. Funny that Radhika hasn't sided with Sonia. In fact, she almost seems to be approving of Samir and me in her own snobbish way.

My ex-boss, Sarika, has also found out about us and added a vile comment, 'Meha is a thief. She stole Sonia's project from us and now she has stolen her lover too. She used to work with me earlier and I always knew she was jealous of my success. But I didn't think she could stoop so low. Imagine your wedding designer having sex with your fiancé! Meha should be disqualified from reality show on moral grounds.'

Fuck Sarika! She has the guts to lecture me on morality.

There is also a comment from Samir's sister, 'Sonia and Samir were so much in love. I was really hoping they would get married.'

168 Let's Have Coffee

I don't believe one bit that Samir really loves Sonia but I am feeling humiliated by this public slandering. Ashamed and shaken, I am unable to look away from the video and face anyone. From the corner of my eye though, I can see that NetGen looks flabbergasted by Sonia's accusations. She is not personally mortified but she is worried about the implications of the video on our brand.

I try to call Samir. He still doesn't take my call. Frustrated, I leave office holding back my tears. I just keep walking, without any idea of where I am going. First Ma calls and then Didi, but I take neither of their calls. What can I tell them? That Sonia is possibly right. That this is all fake. But then why does it hurt so much? I call Mansi but her number is unreachable, so I call Anusha. Thankfully, she answers my call immediately but asks me to hold. I can hear little kids shouting and crying in background. I guess she is with her son in a play area. I hear her asking Varun to keep an eye on her son as she walks away to a quieter spot. I know Varun is trying hard to win over Anusha once again.

'Why are you crying Meha?' Anusha asks in a calm, gentle voice, as she comes back on line.

Anusha hasn't seen Sonia's video so I fill her with the details in between the sobs.

'Are you worried that the video will harm your chances of winning the show?'

'A bit.'

'You think Samir will leave you and go to her?'

I nod my head and wiping the tears on my sleeve, I say, 'Maybe.'

'Silly girl! You are crying because she called you fat,' Anusha states, being able to peek into my innermost thoughts.

'Mm-hmm.'

'Meha, you shouldn't doubt yourself just because of somebody else's definition of pretty and perfect. May be Samir prefers an all-weather SUV over a high maintenance car.'

Talking to Anusha makes me see things in perspective. I am smart, witty and creative. And I am anything but a sex-traction, I reassure myself. So, when Samir finally calls me an hour later, I am sitting in Starbucks, sipping Frappuccino and feeling much better. I pick up the phone but say nothing. Sensing my silent protest, he tells me he was directing a long-distance video shoot in Singapore and hence he was couldn't talk to me earlier.

I still keep silent. I don't know how to break the news of my public defamation without bursting into tears.

'Sonia called me before going live with the video,' he says.

Oh! So not only has he seen the video, he knew about it even before it went public.

'You didn't stop her?' I am appalled at his lack of concern.

'How? By going and having sex with her?' Samir replies sharply.

What is he blabbering? And why is he so curt and cold? I am the one who is getting blamed by strangers online.

'Sonia called me while in the bath tub at a hotel and asked me to meet her. She said she will post the video live if I didn't reach her in thirty minutes.'

'Is she in town?' I ask apprehensively.

'She is in Delhi, for an ad shoot,' he replies.

'I am glad you didn't go,' I say softly, calming down. I can't imagine the stuff she would have put online had Samir gone to meet her. Not to mention, what all she would have done with him.

'I couldn't. I was caught up with work.'

'You mean you would have otherwise gone…and had…er…?' I ask getting all agitated again.

'Well, if you can schedule a sex date with Vir so can I, right?' Samir taunts.

Oh no! I look at my messages history. I accidentally sent the message I had typed for Vir to Samir. I can't tell him that Vir is just some lines of code in a computer system. He'll think I am totally worthless. And a liar. He is rather touchy about lies, even the harmless ones.

'Listen Samir, it's not what you think it is,' I try to explain guiltily. 'Vir is not even in town. I was just…er…it was just sexting.'

I am almost on the verge of tears again. The anxiety of reality show, the humiliation from Sonia's video and the tension of being so close to Samir and yet so far is getting to me.

'Calm down, Senorita,' Samir says, sensing my discomfort. 'I was just pulling your leg. Really your private life is none of my business.'

I almost feel a tinge of dismay hearing this. I really want Samir to make my private life his business. But I am relieved that he is not creating a big fuss over Vir.

'Listen, I am sorry about Sonia's video. Don't believe a word of it, okay?'

'So you don't think I have huge butts?' I ask childishly.

'Of course you have huge butts! And they make you B-U-T-full,' he jests.

I know he is joking, but I like jokes that imply that I am beautiful. Feeling happier, I ask him how I should explain the video to my Mom.

'You are telling me? Sonia gifted my mom a diamond pendant few weeks back and had promised her a diamond string necklace for the wedding. Apparently, she had my Mom and sister in confidence for the wedding proposal,' he reveals.

'Fuck.' I swear.

'Who?' He asks laughing naughtily.

'You!'

'Come over then.'

'Where?' I ask playing along.

'In my office.'

'I would have, except we have decided to abstain. Remember?'

'Remind me again. Whose idea was that?'

'All yours baby,' I say flirtingly.

'Oh fuck me for the fucking idea,' Samir says and we both crack up.

Laughing with him dissipates all my tension. Not to mention the message from NetGen saying that #MehaAndSamir is, in fact, in top trends because Sonia's video has gone viral. Everyone in the country wants to sympathize with a sexy, semi-naked model. As a by-product, they are also watching our video and leaving comments, which are mostly distasteful, but some decent too. End of week one, Ds are ranked one, we are tied at the second position with As and Bs and Cs are fourth and fifth respectively. I feel this is pretty good, given the shaky start we had. As part of the show's requirement, every participant has to share a new discovery about his or her partner from the first week of the #LiveInLoveOut reality show. We purposefully keep ours non-mushy and regular day-to-day stuff.

Samir–'She buys way more stuff than she ever wears. I think she should do a charity sale so I can get some more cupboard space :) Also, can anyone help me understand why we need a bedcover on top of a bed sheet every day?'

Meha–'He makes amazing aloo parathas, but cleaning the

kitchen after he cooks is a task. And he doesn't always smell rosy. He sweats and stinks like a pig after a workout. But he makes me laugh when I am down and he likes me the way I am.'

Week one of the reality show ends. It doesn't get me the attention I wanted from the world, but it gets me attention alright. I am happy that Samir and I have become more comfortable with each other's distinct ways. I feel almost as close to him as I do to Mansi. I guess becoming a friend is the first step to life-long relationship.

Reality Show: Week 2

It's the second week of the reality show. We are sitting in Starbucks discussing the final designs for the Jaisalmer wedding next week.

I have been enjoying the attention I am getting from Samir. I like it when he likes my posts, when he retweets my tweets and when he forwards me non-veg jokes. I also enjoy working together with him and that bit of the enjoyment is far more real and satisfying. Like just now when I told him that I intend to transform the swimming pool in the Jaisalmer fort into a hookah lounge, with deep blue tables matching the floor tile pattern, the praise in his eyes was genuine. And it made me happier than any praise from anyone else.

Sipping on my favourite Frappuccino, I show him the elephant motifs being custom printed on tents, when a chubby woman in her mid-twenties walks upto me. She thanks me for making her proud of her body and asks for my autograph. I am taken by surprise. I was aware that Sonia's video calling me fat had made me the voice of all busty and butt-sy women in the online world, but I had no idea I was recognizable-in-a-crowd famous. I think it's my role as the new, brand ambassador for Veronica Secret 'Body' line bras that has made me this popular.

Excited, I give the autograph, acknowledge Samir's approving smile and try to continue the discussion on the elephant motifs. But soon I find myself surrounded by more girls seeking selfies and relationship advice.

'I don't like it that my boyfriend keeps telling me to lose weight,' says a girl with smoky, captivating eyes and a charming smile.

'You're not exactly fat,' sighs another, with boobs the size of pumpkins. 'I can't even see the next step when climbing down a stair. I fell over my last boyfriend and almost crushed him.'

'Can the Veronica bra help me get a boyfriend too?' A pretty face asks.

I don't know what to tell these girls. When Veronica bra had taken my recommendation to launch an entirely new ad campaign, featuring women with all body shapes and sizes, it had sounded all important to be their advisor but I had no idea of the impact it could have on real people's emotions. Samir is watching me with curiosity. I want to say something meaningful. I think about the campaign's new tag line 'Be yourself—everyone else is taken.' I tell them what I believe in, that relationships may start on the basis of physical attraction, but that alone cannot sustain them. We need to feel beautiful inside to look beautiful. If a certain bra, cosmetic or dress makes you feel better about yourself, go for it. But the only person you need to look good to is yourself. The idea seems to connect with my audience. More people come over and start listening and I start enjoying my mini-celebrity status.

After a while, I look for Samir to ensure that he is not feeling neglected. He is surrounded by women too! Only his admirers happen to be the sexy-by-the-book dames. Suddenly I find myself feeling not so beautiful. All my advice goes out of the door. These girls already have the oomph. What more can they possibly need? I get my answer as I overhear a size-zero girl, asking for gyan on how to hitch a boyfriend who can look beyond her body into her soul. I realize that all women irrespective of their body shape and size are really looking for the thing called love. I want to hear how Samir, a strong non-believer of love, responds to this.

'Girls, men aren't like women,' Samir says, leaning back on to the sofa, his arms outstretched. 'A woman seeks emotional understanding, while a man is looking for fertile soil to spread his genes.'

I have to admit, he is certainly being truthful. And very often, girls are okay with just open honesty, especially when it comes from someone as dashing as him. He tells them the best they can hope to get is a guy who will make the bed after finishing his business in it.

Well, that's certainly more than what he does. I mean, he never makes his bed. It's another thing that we are not doing any bed business anyway. Although he does cook aloo parathas. I feel he is being really good at being friend-without-benefits. I know we all think men only want benefits, but I think men can be great friends with or without benefits as long as we girls don't go all needy and possessive.

'Can I call you sometime when I need advice?' I hear one of the girls ask.

'What's your number?' I see it's the hep girl in uber-short shorts asking.

'Are you open to, you know, affairs on the side?' A fair, dimpled one eagerly inquires.

I see Samir laughing, a hand on one girl's shoulder. Instinctively I feel jealous and needy and possessive. All of which are the wrong things to feel. I literally pull Samir away insisting that we need to leave. He tries to tell me that it's raining outside but I drag him out without waiting for him to exchange numbers.

As we step out in the open, I find it is indeed pouring— completely offseason. We both make a dash for his car, which is parked further away. Suddenly the smell of fresh, wet earth transports me to my childhood. And I slow down. I am a schoolgirl, enjoying the rain in our backyard. I listen to the sound of the raindrops on the paved surface. I jump in the puddles to splash the water around. I try to catch the raindrops in my mouth. I dance merrily to the tune of 'Mere khwaabon mein jo aaye' from DDLJ that my MJ has picked for the moment from my school days.

When we finally reach home half an hour later, both soaked to the skin and cold. As we walk past Mansi's closed door, I can tell that she is inside with the CXO. These days, they spend a lot of time together. Indoors, fully clothed and talking. I know, because I have barged into her room a couple times, accidentally out of habit and found them doing nothing. My latest theory on this is that he is a shrink. Samir disagrees. Anyway, the relevant bit at the moment is that Mansi's bathroom is inaccessible So Samir and I both head to my room. While I fetch dry clothes from my cupboard, he takes off his shirt. I look hesitantly at him, keenly aware that my pale-blue cotton kurta is clinging to my bare skin. I feel a sweet tension building in the room. He holds the bathroom door open for me. When I come out, I find that he has changed into fresh shorts, but he is still without a shirt. A shiver runs down my spine looking at his half-naked and devastatingly handsome frame.

'Still feeling cold?' He asks caringly.

I vaguely shake my head in a nod, but my heart has begun to beat so fast that everything is becoming a blur. I think I am about to fall when he steps forward and holds my arms. His slight touch ignites my body. Warmth spreads like wildfire and fills me with liquid-ecstasy. He gingerly swipes a lock of wet hair stuck to my cheek. His fingers graze my lips, gingerly move across my cheek, and tuck the hair behind my ear. I want to kiss him, but I wait for him to make the first move. He slowly closes the distance between our bodies and places his soft, wet lips on my cheek, his hands now holding me in a loving embrace. I gently link my arms around his neck and listen to his heartbeat in tandem with mine. One moment he is looking into my eyes and the next, we are in this hungry, incredibly passionate, unrestrained kiss. His tongue invades my mouth, urgently exploring every crevice. Mad with longing, I reciprocate, the storm of my desire feeding his hunger. I am about to lose myself within him, when he stops. His heart still racing faster than a rollercoaster, he moves away.

'I know you need to practise kissing. And I can help. But I won't be able to stop at just the lips. *Yeh dil maange more,*' he says, his eyes glinting with raw lust.

Why is he saying all this? I step closer and wrap my arms around him. He looks down at me, with a forced smile on his lips, and says, 'I know you are in a relationship with Vir and you don't like sex-on-the-side and I don't want to lose what we have, so I better stop while I can.' And he loosens out of my grip leaving me cold and hungry.

I want to fall back in his arms. I want to tell him the truth about Vir, but I have a reality show to win. I can't risk Samir getting angry about an innocuous virtual lie and walking out of the show. I love him, but I love staying out of jail even more.

And for that I need money. I say nothing.

'I'll make hot chocolate for us. You go find a movie to watch together,' he says, tickling me on the side of my waist.

I laugh faintly, my body still tense from the encounter. I guess I will have to settle for a hot chocolate and a movie.

Sitting cross-legged on his futon, unbothered by the mess on the floor, I sip hot chocolate and dig into crumbling hazelnut cookies. Samir is sitting right beside, his hand hanging loosely over my shoulder, watching my all-time favourite movie *Zindagi Naa Milegi Dobara* and cracking jokes. The moment has passed and I am back to being content with being friends with him. I am absorbed in the emotional drama when I hear Samir sniffle. I look at him nonplussed as the tears flow down his cheeks. Between the two of us, if you were to ask, I would say that he is the practical one while I am more sensitive. For instance, I will be guilty and heartbroken for days for having spoiled my green sandals in the rain today. But he will just order a new pair of shoes online, probably the exact same one.

'Are you crying?' I ask, surprised.

'Don't you dare tell anyone about this,' he warns me.

'God promise,' I pinch the front of my neck with my forefinger and thumb.

He takes my hand, threading his fingers through mine, gives me a be-there-for-me-forever friendly smile and we continue to watch the movie.

Sharing secrets with a friend is like letting them read an unpublished chapter of your story. It surely gives them the power to hurt you, but it also acts as a bridge connecting your story to theirs. I feel a certain joy at sharing a part of him. Knowing his little secret makes me feel far closer to him than physical intimacy with his body. I like this connection in our stories. I don't know what hopes and dreams my heart is weaving, but I find myself humming 'Ude, khule aasaman mein khwaabon ke parindey...Oho, ab toh, jo bhi ho so ho' from the movie we are watching, for rest of the day. It seems like my dreams have found wings and I don't care what happens next.

In the middle of the week, we are expected to share this week's special moment. Samir posts a picture of me dancing in the unexpected rain outside Starbucks. 'Spontaneous and carefree—like when I first met her,' he says.

I post a picture of him surrounded by his latest girlfriends— the aunties in the complex who all dress up for their weekly cyber class with him. It's hilarious to see that they may have lost their teeth, but they still love the candy. I title it 'Surrounded by women—like when I first met him.'

End of week two, Ds are still at the top of the charts, despite being criticized by the self-proclaimed preservers of India's tradition. There is an entire controversy on Ds' page about doing-it-openly to doing-it-secretly.

While they are our competitors, Samir supports their stand in the controversy. 'It's not like the world doesn't know how we have crossed a billion mark,' he quips.

I may not approve of Samir's polygamous lifestyle, but I tend to agree that sex shouldn't be treated like a second-class citizen. With the ancient Hindu text *Kamasutra* being recognized widely as the seminal work on sex and internationally acclaimed erotic sculptures of Khajuraho temples, aren't we Indians supposed to be torchbearers when it comes to sexual knowledge? Why are we then told to think of sex as a shady business? Seriously, I almost grew up believing sex to be a shameful act like swearing or stealing.

Anyway, for us, there really is no sex to show or hide. Yet, we have managed to stay at the second position with the 'Be yourself' bra campaign and the support from Samir's senior girlfriends and their girlfriends. As are trailing behind us now but only by a small number of votes. Bs are fourth having gained momentum with the festival of Eid around the corner while Cs are still coming last, serving more to amuse the viewers than garner their votes.

I am happy with our second position right now. I don't know how we will beat the Ds, but I am certain that it will take more than porn to win this show. Ma is also on top of the world. Not only because I sent her a free 'Perfect Body' bra but also because her kitty friends find Samir a very charismatic son-in-law. Dad is recovering. Business is looking up. Even our Facebook page has reached 39,990 likes and only needs ten more FB likes to get to a round figure, like myself. But for the steep fall from Samir's heart, expected at the end of the reality show, life has never been better.

I go to the old squirrel post on my Facebook page and scroll down to the last comment from Samir suggesting the sweet person to ask for another treat and reply, 'I am glad I asked for another treat.'

Reality Show: Week 3

We are in an old, rustic Jaisalmer palace-hotel located on the outskirts of the city, having arrived here late last night. I am standing on top of a tall tower, still catching my breath, after climbing up five flights of stairs to get the network. This is the only place in the entire palace where there is any network signal. And it so happens that this week's reality show activity is all about tweeting the differences between you and your partner and gaining twitter followers. With even NetGen having accompanied us here for the wedding, staying connected to the online world is going to be breathless and tiring.

'Last-minute packing done. Rushing to catch the flight. A little planning never hurts. Driving fast can #MehaAndSamir #LiveInLoveOut.' I send my first tweet of the 'spot the differences' week, highlighting Samir's lack of planning which made us almost miss our flight.

I am eager to see what Samir says about me. I know he left the room really early to capture the first rays of the rising sun bathe the yellow, mudstone walls of the Sonar Quila. I don't think he is back yet. I wonder when he will find the time and the signal to tweet. As my phone syncs, I am surprised to see that Samir already managed to tweet an hour ago.

'My mess clutters her mind. Well, her vacant bed is blanking my mind and driving me crazy! #SpotTheDifference #LiveInLoveOut #MehaAndSamir.'

I smile, amused.

The day goes by in a blur. Sitting on a charpoy, its legs adorned in *rani*-colour satin, I admire the little white tents embellishing the barren land behind the palace. After hours of labouring in the piercing desert heat, I am satisfied with the way the mehendi venue resonates with the sandy starkness. Parched, I guzzle down half a bottle of cold water and pour the rest on my burning skin.

I watch NetGen arrange the clay lanterns amidst rose petals, along the pathway. Pyare is standing nearby talking to the parrot reader. I notice Pyare squeezing NetGen's hands, every few minutes, as they start to twitch in the absence of social media. I was actually worried that she would go berserk without the keep-alive beeps of her devices, but she hasn't once made the dash to the tower top. Pyare's affectionate gesture is keeping her calm but making me long for the warmth of Samir's friendly hug.

I am sure Samir is somewhere around in the hotel itself, but it's been so busy that I haven't had a chance to talk to him all day. I did see him with a flock of who-else-but-pretty-girls at breakfast and tried to catch his attention, but he was busy reading their palms. Incorrigible flirt! I wonder why I took the trouble to find a parrot reader. I am sure he would have readily done the honours.

I wonder if Samir has tweeted again about me. I eagerly head to the top of the sandstone tower and wait for my phone to sync. He hasn't tweeted again! I want to know what he is thinking. Is he tired? Is he missing me? I was hoping to hold on to a piece of him through his words. I try calling him but his phone is unreachable. Well, there is no way I am climbing up the tower again today. Some more exercising like this and I will lose my membership in the B-U-T-fulls club.

The next day, I manage to catch Samir's attention on several occasions. I give him all kinds of stares, loving, busy and angry, but he royally ignores every single one of them. Hurt, I wait till its evening before I climb up the tower to tweet. I want him to wait for my tweet like I waited for his. I am shocked when I realize that he hasn't tweeted till now. Not only am I desperate to talk to him, I am now worried that we will lose our rank in the show.

Irked by his non-responsiveness, I tweet, 'Poor communication skills. Can't differentiate between an angry silence, a serene silence, a busy silence and a lonely silence.'

Another day passes. We have now been together in this beautiful palace, sharing the same room and working on the same wedding, for more than three days and he has barely said a word to me. Everyone is praising the decor and appreciating my team's efforts, but no, he can't even spare a loving smile. I know it's a hectic schedule, but I am certain that he is avoiding me on purpose. Last evening, during mehendi, when I was called by the bride's mom, he was standing right there talking to an old lady. He saw me approach and turned his back to me. Why he is doing this? Maybe he doesn't want anyone here to find out that we are supposedly a couple. Maybe he wants to be able to flirt with the girls freely. As I stand atop the tower, all by myself on a romantic starry night, I read his tweets from yesterday and today, both together.

'Jumps to conclusions, often wrong. There are better ways to exercise e.g. asking. Rule of life—KISS (Keep It Simple Senorita).

'I said ask, but please not at bedtime. Men also need beauty sleep.'

The first tweet is in response to my comment on his poor communication skills. He obviously thinks I am over-reading his responses or lack of them. The second tweet is because I did ask, like he has suggested, except I woke him up in the middle of the night to do so. Well, if he avoids me all day, and he is busy typing God-knows-what till midnight, when am I supposed to talk? Besides, what does he mean by saying better ways to exercise? Does he think I need to exercise? And boy, he does like to use the acronym KISS for everything.

I feel like launching a palace-wide hunt, extracting him from whichever girl's embrace he is in and giving him a long hard kiss. But I know I can't, because I have no idea where to start and I am too tired. If only everything was as simple as he seems to make it sound. Feeling helpless and annoyed by his implication that I am seeing problems where there are none, I tweet back: 'Has no feelings. Sees life in moments. In still pictures. Can't see the complete story behind the pictures.'

Already feeling low, my heart further sinks, when I find a mail in my inbox updating us on the mid-week reality show stats. Apparently, As have taken a strong lead this week with their army of social media friends, retweeting their tweets. Ds seem to have taken a hit, as this week requires more words than action. Most astonishing is Cs sudden rise to third position with their newly found love. Since media always likes new news, they are all over Cs loving tweets. With limited connectivity, an un-cooperative Samir, and a busy workweek, we are left behind in the race. Crestfallen, I wish for the week to get over so we can return to being a living-in-separate-room but loving couple rather than sleeping-in-same-room but not talking strangers.

Next day, as I am soaking in the early morning tranquillity, with a cup of green tea, I see Samir returning from a run. Forgetting all our differences and happy because the wedding is about to get over, I ask him if I can borrow his razor because I have forgotten mine. He actually refuses. Can you believe it? I mean we are in this god forsaken, deserted fort. There is no parlour in a hundred-kilometre radius. My underarms need work, as I have to wear a halter-neck blouse for the evening function. And he refuses to share a razor. He can kiss me, exchange saliva with me, but he can't allow the blade that grazes his stubble trim my silkier and softer...um...well stubble. How fussy can someone be?

So obviously I run up the sandstone tower immediately to tweet, 'Has sharing problems and commitment issues. Sometimes selfish.'

When I check later he has responded, 'Sharing a bed doesn't mean I have to share everything. I have an identity that is me. And a razor that is mine. And I like it that way.'

There's another tweet, 'Unsure of what she wants. Confused and insecure.'

I can understand why he thinks I am confused. Earlier today, he took the initiative to organize a trip to the sand dunes because he knew that I really wanted to go. But then, I got all jealous and angry when he showed up in the jeep with all those bimbos. So obviously I didn't go with them. And I couldn't tell him that what I really wanted was to be with him alone.

Why is it so hard for him to see that I really love him? I trudge down the stone stairs, feeling sad, cold and hungry. I bet he has had dinner at the dunes without me. It's the first time in my life that I haven't enjoyed planning a wedding. And that says something.

I am glad when the dreadful week is finally over and we are on our flight home. NetGen and I are discussing the blog post to cover the wedding. Samir comes over to our row and asks NetGen if she could exchange seats with him. He sits down next to me, takes my hand and gives it a tight squeeze. I try to pull my hand away, but he keeps holding on to it tightly.

'So what kind of silence is this?' He asks jokingly.

I keep quiet in an angry-sad-confused-lonely silence.

'I am sorry, I hurt you,' he says with a sheepish smile, his eyes searching mine for forgiveness.

Okay, so this is the weirdest thing with Martians. They think that relationships are like an on-off switch. I haven't the faintest idea why he was so unfriendly with me for last six days and now he expects me to give him an all-ok-smile, just because he is saying sorry. Not happening!

'My mom, she was there at the wedding,' he says softly when I continue to ignore him.

I turn to stare at him, shocked.

'Family friend. Remember?'

I vaguely recollect him telling me this, weeks ago at Chaayos. Well, he could have reminded me. And he could have introduced me to his mom. After all, the next week of reality show is a family week. Surely she knows about us and the show.

'She is not overly fond of you, you see. I avoided you so she doesn't find out that you are around. Believe me, you don't want to feature in her *"usne mere bete pe jadu tona kar diya hai"* melodramatic soap.'

Ouch! I squirm as I picture myself in the role of a sweet, innocent, helpless girl being viciously rebuked by a hideous, cunning to-be mother-in-law.

He looks in my eyes and apologizes for the bad things he

tweeted about me. 'Every time I sat down to tweet, I would think about you and I would see this huge expanse of soft, fluffy white clouds that I so love. And then I had to focus on a little black dot of your negatives and blow it up into a sinister blob.'

It was very mean of him to not share the damn razor, which by the way I anyway used behind his back, but I have to admit, his confession is seriously romantic. I look at him, molten and gooey with forgiveness and love. I don't tell him that whatever I tweeted about him was mostly true. It's not important. What is important is that I continue to love him despite all those tweets. I think that this week was not meant to test our love for each other, but to see how we can cope with our differences. Love doesn't need to be perfect; it only needs to be true.

'By the way, next time you sneakily use my razor, just leave it on the slab. Don't lay it out neatly on a towel to dry. It gives you away,' he says, his face serious but his eyes smiling. And then he gets up and goes back to his seat.

End of week three, I know we are doomed, having fallen to the fourth rank, but somehow I am not as upset. I feel a strange joyous cloud hovering over me. My MJ is telling me, 'Haule haule ho jayega pyaar chal yaar, haule haule ho jayega pyaar.'

Reality Show: Week 4

The fourth week starts on a really good note. We get a message from the show's host, informing us that the As who were at the top of the chart last week have been disqualified. Apparently, a scrub of their online chats revealed that they are already married in court and have enrolled in the realty show to earn a free honeymoon. Samir claims he always knew they were married because the guy would agree with everything the girl said and that kind of democratic agreement happens only after marriage. I am largely thrilled that we have one less couple to beat, although this week being a family week, our performance really depends on how our parents behave. For once, I wish I had not been a difficult teenager.

Before we know it, it's already the middle of the week and our parents' comments are about to be released. Sitting at our coffee table, I watch the boys playing cricket in field outside. I am really edgy. I suck hard on the straw to sip the last drop of Frappuccino that Samir got for me on his way back from work. He has really been very sweet to me. That is worrying me even more. It's making me wonder what he is trying to make up for. I do hope his parents have sent their views, because he never got me to talk to them. He simply said he has it under control.

The door bell rings. It must be Samir. He had gone to check on Sharma uncle who is not keeping very well. Samir never remembers to take his keys. I am used to it now. I open the door willingly. We stand at the door, just looking at each other, while our eyes make love with our souls, oblivious of the cross-ventilation that is causing the loose papers lying on his futon to fly all over. Finally he breaks eye contact.

'Let's see how our parents have rated us, shall we?' he says, walking in. I nod and follow him hypnotically.

First, we read my mom's comment. 'My parents thought I was too bold to step out of the kitchen and do a job. I feel the kids today are bold to bring their personal lives out of the bedroom into the social media. Parents are always cautious and change is never easy. I would have been ok with anyone Meha chose for herself and Samir just happens to be truly the prince charming every mom wishes for her daughter.'

'Wow, that's a straight ten on ten. What did you bribe your mom with?' Samir asks me teasingly.

'Nothing,' I dismiss his question. It's not my mom that I was worried about. I had full faith in Samir's charm. I am just not sure how well it works on men, especially potential father-in-laws. Samir had a conversation with my parents on the phone yesterday. When I asked him how it went, he just said fine.

I move on to my Dad's comments with mixed emotions. 'I like the boy but I don't approve of the modern ways. If he has already read the book, how do I know he will ever buy it?'

Hmm...Not bad. Not bad at all, knowing my dad. It's not all nice but definitely very like a cautious-and-grudging-father-of-the-bride. I think the judges will give him a seven on ten. Samir must have really impressed Dad yesterday, as he did not out rightly reject him.

'What did you promise my Dad, a pilgrimage to Mansarovar?' I look at Samir admiringly.

'I told him I will marry you, if that's what you want,' he says with a playful grin. 'I thought that was safe enough. He only wants you married, whether the card says Vir or Samir doesn't bother him. I am relying on you now Senorita, to marry Vir once the show is over. Don't make me a liar in your father's eyes.'

I look at him bewildered. 'What if I don't want to marry Vir anymore?' I ask, searching his eyes for an answer.

A faint smile tugs at his lips as his eyes sparkle warmly with love. The love I had seen in those eyes all those years ago. My heart misses a beat. Should I tell him the truth about Vir? While I am debating, he has moved on to his Dad's comment.

His Dad has posted, 'I am okay with whatever my son wants.'

Well, now I know where Samir's concise communication skills come from, especially when trying to evade a situation. So, his father's comment is probably a five on ten. Its okay I guess. Last one is his mom's. Her post is the longest of all the parents and the most, shall we say, scandalous.

I am sorry to say this, but Samir, you have hugely disappointed me. After all these years of hardships, in raising you all by myself, this is how you reward your Mom. By denying her the simple pleasures of a diamond necklace and a soni bahu. But it's not all your fault. I know you are scared of commitment because your asshole of a father left me when you were so young. But you are not your Dad. Remember the favourite doll that you always played with when you were a little boy. Beta, that baby doll is Sonia. I have couriered baba Shankardev ka amulet at your office address. Please wear it. I am sure it will free you from that chudail Meha's kala jadu.

'Your parents are divorced?' I ask, hugely shaken.

'It's okay. They are not dead,' he jokes.

'This isn't a time for jokes, Samir. Why didn't you tell me?' I am so worried about what my parents are thinking right now as they read all this.

'It wouldn't have changed a thing. Dad is least bothered. He has posted exactly the SMS I sent him. And Mom would have said what she wanted to. No one can change her mind, least of all you,' Samir says coolly, totally unaffected by his family drama unfolding in public.

'Look at the bright side. I think my Mom's drama will add spice to our story,' he adds thoughtfully.

Spicy drama it is for sure, and Sonia's vile video did work in our favour, but I am finding it all too hard to digest. And I can see people calling me an evil witch on the Internet.

'Listen, I don't think Ds are really a competition,' Samir says confidently. 'I mean people may enjoy their *"petikot me dhamaka"* and *"balam pichkari"* stunts but think about it, there is no way all those matrimonial companies can openly endorse porn. With As out, we only really need to worry about Cs. I think we need something that captures the public's and judges' imagination alike. And what can be better than a *"saas-bahu"* drama? It's mainstream, it's entertaining, and we Indians are a sucker for it.'

He does have a point. And to be truthful, I don't care about how anyone thinks about us as long as they are thinking of us as a couple. I like this feeling of us being united against everyone else. It makes me feel like I am one with him, as if we belong together. We don't have much time to debate and analyse as it's time for the online, live video chat with Mini Mathur. Sadly, there is no celebrity joining us today. Although I have heard that they are planning a mega star-studded finale.

I fix my hair, adjust my bra straps and fix my lipstick. We have both coordinated our outfits reflecting the harmony in our relationship, especially after last week's name-calling. I am in a bottle green, short-sleeved, crossover-neck-top paired with mid-rise, boot-cut jeans, while he is in matching tee and jeans.

'Ooh, that was quite an unexpected unfolding of your family story out there, Samir,' Mini says as soon as she fills in the laptop screen. Wearing a bright, orange, strappy dress, with a bust enhancing, kundan embroidery belt, she looks glam. Least bothered with what really happens to us, she is only interested in keeping the show's ratings high.

'Anyway, so while we will only know the judges and janta's verdict by the end of the week, I have news to share with you. This time about the couple that is standing between you and the victory cup,' she says building the suspense.

I have my fingers crossed, hoping Cs are out as well. They seemed fishy to me right from the start. My heart is beating so hard, I can barely hear the video Mini is showing us. The video shows the judges discussing the Cs. The judges have just learnt that Cs were in love with different people, who are now a couple. They had entered the contest to break their ex's coupling and win them back and have been only pretending to be together to make their exes jealous. But now they somehow seem to be head over heels in love with each other.

'It's ditto like that awesome Meg Ryan's movie, *Addicted to Love*,' I blurt out frantically. I ask Mini if the judges think that Cs should be disqualified for deception, but she informs me that judges rather like the 'meant-for-each-other' twist in their story. It has given them a differentiating factor.

I lower my head in dismay, when Samir who has been looking down my blouse all this while, suddenly exclaims, 'You've got a tattoo, there?' He points to the butterfly, inked right above my heart, peeking out my low neckline.

I flush in embarrassment, while Mini is regarding us with a sceptical stare. Oh God, I know what she is thinking. She is wondering why Samir doesn't know about my tattoo.

'I...er...got it done just yesterday. For you,' I say, in as sultry as voice I can feign on the spot. 'I was going to surprise you with it tonight.'

Samir gives me a girl-you-have-got-your-wits-about-you look and then adds, 'Now we both have a butterfly tattoo, don't we.' And he rolls his T-shirt sleeve up to show the butterfly on his upper left arm to Mini.

I have of course seen him shirtless before, but Mini goes all, 'Aww, how sweet. You two are so tattoo-ally in love.'

Soon enough, Mini wishes us luck, reminds every one of our hash tag and signs off. I turn to Samir to finally tell him about Vir's virtuality and get him out of our way, but Samir is engrossed in reading a message on his phone. In fact, he seems to be bursting with an explosion of happiness inside him and then he leaves the house hurriedly like a gust of wind.

By the time he gets back, I am almost asleep. He kisses me on my forehead, says he loves me and says something about his dream having come true. A dream he has been chasing for very long. I smile back in my sleep. I am too sleepy to tell him about Vir, but I soon will. It doesn't matter now. I know he loves me and I have never stopped loving him. My MJ has a lullaby ready, 'Tum hi ho...Meri aashiqui ab tum hi ho'.

When the week's results come, Samir's hunch is proven right. His mom's *saas-bahu* drama and our tattoo news works as our revival capsule. We are able to marginally defeat Cs and come out first at the end of week four.

Reality Show: Week 5

I am totally, madly and truly in love with Samir and I think he is in love with me too. I float through week five as if no trouble is so important that it can't be ignored and I can even live in the dungeons if he is with me. Well, maybe not dungeons.

I look at my laptop's blank screen and smile. This week we are supposed to tell the world why we want to spend our lives with our chosen partner.

I write, *'Love is a journey of shared moments—movie with caramel popcorn, bike ride to Manesar, walking in the woods at dusk, dinner at a dhaba, followed by dot, dot, dot in a barn. I could get used to this.'*

Samir has posted a romantic poem for me.

She is fun, she is witty,
She is creative, she is pretty,
She is a clean freak; she is sometimes a pain,
She has a lovely smile, in kissing she still needs to train,
She drives me crazy, she makes me jive,
She is everything I want, she makes me alive.

I can't believe Anusha was right all along about Samir's feelings for me. I am very happy that she also has finally found happiness with Varun. I guess sometimes God takes time to fix the grammatical errors he makes in our stories, but he does fix them eventually. While my love life was on a chapter break and my start-up was facing a big question mark—but now they have both been infused with fresh pages to continue their adventure.

End of week five, we are a little behind Ds, but a little ahead of Cs and clearly on our way to victory. Bs seem to have disappeared off the net, no one knows where.

Reality Show: Week 6

'Meha, will you live-in with me forever...er...I mean, will you marry me?' Samir asks, down on one knee.

'Why do you suddenly want to marry me?' She asks with an air of superiority.

'Because you make me happy like no one else.' He sounds honest. 'And I have had a fair share of else,' he chuckles, but then becomes serious again as he finds her measuring gaze watching him.

'How do you know one day you won't get bored of me? What if you find someone whom you start "preferring" more than me?' She argues.

'I don't know,' he says helplessly. 'But if I do, I will be honest with you. I won't go sneaking behind your back.'

'I think you are all set then,' she says and gets back to her designs. Samir hovers around restlessly in her room.

'Do you think it's a good idea to propose to her in front of the judges during the finale?' He asks Mansi, standing over her shoulder, watching her perfect the designs.

Mansi turns to look up at his face. She wants to help Samir. After all, it is because of Samir that Soha Ali Khan has agreed to be the showstopper for her fashion show. Besides, this will make her BFF Meha truly happy. But she has loads of loose ends to wrap up. And Samir is over thinking the proposal.

'Samir, we have been rehearsing for almost an hour,' she says, trying to hide her exasperation. He is immediately apologetic. Mansi softens her voice and says, 'Meha loves grandeur. She loves style. Believe me, she will love this.'

He knows Mansi will not say something just because he wants to hear it. He likes her no-nonsense honesty. But he is still unsure.

'But what if...what about Vir?' Samir asks hesitantly.

'You know what, let me tell you a little secret. I think Meha wouldn't mind this one breach of BFF-secrecy pact,' she says impatiently.

'What the F?' Samir exclaims as Mansi reveals Vir's virtual reality to him. So there never was a boyfriend. Meha conned him into living in so she could save her own ass! Her lovely ass. Normally, he doesn't like being taken for a ride, but this one has been rewarding. It could have been even more rewarding had he known there was no Vir. And while he wasn't really worried about Vir, it feels good to have him out of the picture. He walks out of the room doing a celebratory jig. He is on his way to meet his Meha.

It's about six in the evening. I am sitting on Samir's futon, amongst his mess, waiting for him. The clutter doesn't annoy me anymore. It actually makes me feel loved. It holds memories of the moments Samir and I have shared in the last six weeks. I pick up his fountain pen with which he wrote the beautiful poem about me last week, on a pale brown textured paper, burnt at the edges to create an old parchment effect. There is a crumpled Starbucks receipt from a month ago when we got wet in the rain. I can still taste his wet lips claiming mine. A solved Sunday crossword bookmarks a page in the picture book that Rhea had lovingly offered him because she has outgrown it. I love the way he is become a part of me and my family. I pick up the T-shirt he had worn the night before to inhale his wild-rose fragrance.

I haven't seen him since the morning and am eagerly waiting for him to take me in his arms. He was supposed to join me for Anusha and Varun's court marriage in the afternoon, but at the last minute he messaged that an emergency had come up and he would meet me at home later. To while away time, I look at the pictures from the wedding, although it wasn't exactly a wedding, if you ask me. It was a rather small affair. Actually, it wasn't even an affair. It was more like a case hearing with the judge. Varun's elder brother, Deepak and I were the witnesses. Deepak looked handsome as ever. He excitedly told me that he and Radhika are expecting a baby. And he was very grateful to Tanu Di for having finally knocked some sense into Rad's head. Huh? Now doesn't Di always manage to do that? He offered everyone fine Lindt chocolates after the ceremony and I greedily took two. He gave me a knowing smile and then we parted.

It's almost dinner time. I am hungry but I want to have dinner with Samir. Rather I want to have him for dinner. I am mindlessly leafing through odd pictures he has taken, when a certain letter lying amidst the pictures catches my attention. It is a note from Neworld Publishers. I hesitantly pick it up and start reading.

Dear Samir Singhal,

As discussed I'm happy to make an offer on your book Let's Have Coffee (working title). The book reads well. I especially like the online reality show twist.

I'd like to offer a Hardback royalty of 10 per cent and e-book rights for 25 per cent. This offer is for all languages rights.

Do let me know if the offer is acceptable to you. If there are any queries, please feel free to call/e-mail me.

Look forward to your response,

Regards,
Chief Commissioning Editor
Neworld Publishers

I feel the firm ground beneath me turn to a slippery slide. My whole world comes down around me, like an unauthorized colony being demolished on court orders.

It was always the book, back then and now.

'The book was his reason to do the reality show, his long-held dream that has come true. He never cared much for you,' my mind taunts. 'And why should he? Who likes a bouquet of rough and sturdy sunflowers that are easy maintenance? It's always the aromatic, slender, soft roses that people love.'

'But I have seen love in his eyes for me,' my heart fights back meekly, drowning in my tears.

'Ha ha. Don't you get it? He likes a variety of flowers in his bouquet, you silly girl,' my mind mocks.

I have no idea for how long I keep sitting on his futon, among his things, my heart crying for him and my mind reprimanding him. I am so lost in my grief that I don't hear the bell ringing the first few times. I trudge slowly to the front door, my eyes puffy and my hair a mess. I open the door and he is there. But he is not alone. He is holding an unconscious, and still gorgeous, Sonia in his arms. I say nothing. I just run inside my room and bolt it from inside. And then I cry my heart out.

I am not sure if he can hear my wailing, but he doesn't come running after me like I want him to, like he would if he loved me. It's only much later that I hear a knock on the door. He calls out my name and requests me to open the door. I walk to the door, unbolt it and go back to my spot on the bed. He walks in and puts his arms lovingly around me. I am sobbing uncontrollably now. It's unbearable to have him so close, to feel his caressing touch, to breathe his breath and know it is all a sham. He tries to hold my hands, but I push him away.

He sits at the opposite end of the bed and starts telling me how Sonia was in town for a shoot. She wanted to meet him but since he couldn't go, she tried to kill herself by cutting her wrist. Her assistant found her, managed to stop her and then called him. The doctor who had also been summoned told him to watch over her as she was emotionally fragile and vulnerable. He couldn't leave her alone in the hotel, so he brought her here.

My anger numbs a little on hearing about Sonia's shocking suicide attempt. I didn't know Sonia loved him so much that she would give up her life for him. Does she not realize that Samir doesn't feel the same for her? Is Samir still giving her mixed signals by continuing to stay in touch with her? Perhaps somewhere in his heart he still cares for Sonia.

I tell him I saw the letter of acceptance from his book publisher. 'Why did you keep it from me?' I challenge him. It's easier to debate facts rather than feelings.

'I had my reason, like you had yours to keep Vir alive,' he replies coldly, his tone becoming defensive.

I don't know how and when he found out about Vir, but I doubt he really cares. I think he is unhappy because I caught him red-handed using me for his book.

'I was going to tell you about Vir at the event this week,' I explain.

'I was also going to tell you something at the event this week,' he says wistfully.

'Have you been using our live-in experience for your book?' I ask point-blank. This is no time to play games.

'Of course,' he says casually.

'So none of it meant anything to you?' I ask, the anger at having been wronged rising again.

'How do you conclude that?' He is now getting annoyed for no reason.

I try to keep my rising anger in check. I just want to make sure I get all the answers and leave nothing to misinterpretation like last time.

'You don't believe in love forever, right?' I continue my line of interrogation.

'I don't know,' he says uncomfortably.

But I know that he treats every relationship as a learning experience. 'So I was just a creative-writing experiential class for you?' I comment cynically.

'Meha, do you even realize that you are talking rubbish?' He is trying to sound calm, but I can see he is irritated, and I am reaching my break point.

'Why do you still hang out with Radhika and Sonia and all your other ex-girlfriends?' I ask one last question. I am desperately looking for a straw to hang on to. I am hoping he will to deny my accusations. I am waiting for him to say he loves me.

'Because *har ek friend zaroori hota hai,* Meha.'

It hurts. But I know it's over.

'We are very different Samir,' I say devoid of all emotions. 'Loving is like sharing an umbrella for you, while for me it's much more intimate and much more meaningful.'

'You are right Meha. We are very different,' he says, with an edge to his voice. 'You find it hard to believe that someone can actually love you. You have trust issues. Without trust, no relationship can last, as you so like to say, forever.'

He says this and stomps out of my bedroom. I hear his phone ring on the way out. He picks it up. It's Sharma aunty. I only overhear 'fallen down, ambulance' as he talks in the corridor and then he is out of the house without any explanation.

I cry some more as that's about the only thing I feel like doing. After a while, I wash my face, apply some lipstick, and pat some powder to hide the red blotch around my nose and go to see Sonia. She looks like a sleeping beauty, even in this frail state. There is a bandage on her left wrist. I hold her fingers gingerly. She doesn't wake up. I look down at her pale hand. I see a ring on her engagement finger, with two diamond studded S's, facing each other to form a heart. I literally fall off the bed in shock. She doesn't hear the loud thud. She is heavily sedated. I carefully slip the ring out from her slightly swollen finger and turn it around to confirm the jeweller's mark. It's the same ring. Sonia has had it all this time and I have been paying all my meagre savings towards the interest accruing on my card. Did Samir know? Forgetting our hurtful break-up just moments ago, I dial his number. But he doesn't take my call. He never takes my call. I disconnect angrily.

I can call Anusha. She will hear me out even in the middle of her honeymoon, but it feels mean. And Mansi is on a flight to Mumbai for work. I couldn't have chosen a worse time to get my heart broken. It's depressing to wallow alone in my misery. Emotionally exhausted, I fall asleep, clutching the ring tightly in my fist.

It's already half past eight when I wake up, not because of Surya, since I finally got the curtains up just last week. What a waste. There is a note on the coffee table from Samir that he is taking Sonia back to the hotel.

I walk to the jewellery shop. The owner tries to tell me that he cannot return jewellery items like this after two months. And I burst out crying. I don't intend do. But it's like all the piled up stress and sorrow that is finally spilling over. The shop owner gets scared. There are a lot of potential buyers in his shop. It's festival season. He quickly orders a Campa for me and credits the full amount to my bank account. I walk out of the shop, with a major burden off my chest, but my heart still feels saddled with grief and I can't stop crying. My ever faithful MJ tunes up 'Kabira' from *Yeh Jaawani Hai Deewani*, replacing it with Samir's name. The lyrics seem to be written especially for me, imploring a lover, free spirited like a wind-storm, who has selfishly forgotten his old love, imploring him to return.

'Samir…aaa…maan ja
Kaisi teri khudgarzi,
Tujhe preet purani bisri…
Mast maula, mast kalandar,
Tu hawa kaa ek bavandar…'

I don't care to win the reality show any more but I don't want the world or Samir to know how heartbroken I am. So I post my last comment of the reality show, '*True love stays with you forever.*'

Samir posts nothing.

Sharma Uncle passed away two days back, on the night of our breakup. Samir has been busy with his funeral and other ceremonies. Their son has come from abroad, but he knows nothing of the local places. So Samir has been making all the arrangements. I go visit them for a little while, but I can't bring myself to see Aunty or even Samir. I stay mostly by myself. He comes home very late at night, sleeps and leaves early in mornings. It's back to the way we started, like strangers.

The reality show ends. Ranbir and Kareena make a guest appearance at the finale event, but we don't attend it. Judges announce the results. As expected, we would have won it, if not for the finale event yesterday which we never attended. So C's win the popular-couple award.

Back to Square One

When you get into a fight with a live-in boyfriend, you can't just walk away and play who-calls-first-to-apologize. I so wish Samir and I were still living together. Not only would it save me the anxiety of checking my phone every five minutes, but also because I still seem to love him with every broken piece of my heart.

It's been crazy busy arranging the standees, posters, brochures, etc., for the biggest Indian wedding carnival starting tomorrow. I sit at a coffee shop to take a break and browse through an app trying to find the few things I want to buy from among the billion items on sale. With my credit limit back to healthy, I can now finally experience the unmatched joy of impulsive and often unnecessary, discount shopping. I ought to be thrilled, but I find myself incapable of feeling anything these days.

I pick up the phone as soon as it rings, but it's not him.

'You took my ring?' Sonia straightaway launches an attack.

'I just took the ring I had paid for,' I reply caustically.

'And you think money can make it yours? It can make Samir yours?' She challenges me loudly, too loudly.

It dawns on me what that the ring meant to her. It was a memory of their times together. Like those butterfly earrings are to me. She was clinging on to it even when she tried to take her life. Perhaps she does really love Samir. I can feel her pain. I know what it feels like to be one of Samir's EXperiences, to reach EXpiry and see him EXit from your life. I have been there twice.

'Sonia, I am sorry,' I try to tell her that I never wanted to hurt her.

'Don't be,' she says indifferently, her voice losing the malice. 'It was never mine. Not the ring. Not Samir's heart. I am actually glad it's over. I wish I had listened to Radhika all those years ago when she told me that Samir is madly in love with a plain Jane. Anyway, I am leaving for Spain to erase my scars.'

I can't believe what Sonia is saying. Samir was in love with a plain Jane, as in me? Radhika must have misunderstood our romance at her wedding. She probably didn't know that Samir was only interested in me for his book. I might have been his muse for the book, but I am definitely not the one his heart beats for.

As if I don't already have enough problems to deal with, I see Sarika marching towards me. I had seen the Dreams Wedding Limited banner earlier so I knew they had a really big stall. I just wasn't particularly hoping to run into her.

'Aha...I see that you're still afloat, huh?' she remarks haughtily.

'No thanks to you,' I reply curtly.

'Hmm, still ill-mannered and arrogant! So, how does it feel to use someone's boyfriend for your benefits?' Sarika says with derision. She has some nerve blaming me.

'Of all people you should know the feeling, Sarika. I can't deny I learnt all about benefits and business from you,' I respond, enjoying her unease.

She makes a disgusting face and leaves. It feels good to get back.

ᛞ

It's a cool Sunday morning. October has brought with it the crisp air of festivities. I am sitting at the coffee table looking out over the balcony. Sharma Aunty is watering the Tulsi plant in the balcony. A maid is gossiping on her phone in the balcony below, while the twin brats she watches are asleep. A neglected crossword sheet stares back at me from the table. My mind is busy cajoling my bruised heart to focus on '5 Down' but my heart is longing for a perfect Sunday. The maid gives me hot ginger tea with an aloo paratha, but it still doesn't make my Sunday perfect. There is no light-hearted banter, no stinky smell and no Samir.

It's been a week since he walked out from the apartment. He later sent someone from his office to collect his stuff. Believe me, I am trying hard to forget and I may have succeeded if only everything in the house wouldn't keep reminding me of him. Even the aloo paratha reminds me of him. I take a sip of tea and let it soothe my soul.

Mansi joins me at the table, takes one bite from my plate, looks at her oily fingers and says, 'Yikes! Where is Samir? I like his parathas. This cook's love is in the oil!'

Mansi and I haven't synced in a while. First she was away for work and then I was working late at nights for the carnival, so she has no idea that Samir has left the apartment and me.

I don't want to tell Mansi about our break-up. I haven't told anyone. I am thinking if I keep shut about it, it will somehow disappear.

'He has gone to the US to meet his nephew. His sister just

had a baby,' I relay the information I was given by his colleague, Payal when she met me at the carnival yesterday. It's Samir I had been longing to run into, but I get Payal instead and she crushed all my hopes.

'So how did the finale event go?' Mansi asks, sipping an awful looking extract of carrot, gooseberry and beetroot.

'We lost,' I casually shrug my shoulders.

Mansi seems lost. She is not listening to me.

'Didn't Samir tell you anything?' she asks.

I give her a vague questioning look, wondering if she knows about whatever Samir said to me. I don't offer any information, but I tell her about my encounter with Sarika and we both laugh about it.

The weeks pass by. I immerse myself in work. Thankfully, there is plenty of it. Gods are back in action and there are lots of auspicious dates for people to get married. I am thinking of consulting a pandit myself to find a good moment to message Samir since Facebook tells me that he is back in town. There's an FB picture of him holding his nephew, looking adorable with a baby in his arms.

Another imperfect Sunday is here. It's almost noon. Mansi left for a shopping appointment in the morning but I am still in my night suit. Papa and Didi finished their crossword long back. I haven't even looked at it.

I have been whiling away my time trying various score-your-love-compatibility games with our names to determine if Samir loves me. They aren't helping. I am wondering if I should go bathe when the doorbell rings. For a moment, I perk up at the sound, thinking its Samir. He never takes his keys. I excitedly open the door and find Sharma Aunty instead, in a crisp, light green cotton saree. I can see that she is trying to hold it together though she is broken from inside. Like me. I invite her in.

'Beta, this is Samir's poetry book. Please give it to him.' Aunty hands me a small, red-jacketed notebook.

I had seen it lying on the futon earlier but never knew Samir wrote poetry in it.

'Your Uncle had lot of fun sharing his poetry with Samir. I have no idea how he did it, but Samir always brightened up the darkest of his days,' Aunty says softly, her throat choked with tears.

I don't know what to say to someone who has just lost a life-partner of fifty years. I offer to make her some tea.

'He is really unique, that boy,' Aunty says, a little composed as she sips her tea. 'It's hard to find such unselfish kinds today.'

I say nothing. I don't want to tarnish Samir's image in her mind. He really was very kind to them. He was a very helpful friend to me too. He is just not the life-long companion variety.

'You are a very lucky girl,' Aunty smiles at me lovingly as she finishes the tea. 'Samir often said to your uncle that he wants to grow old with you, like the two of us. Bless you both, beta,' she says and gets up slowly to leave.

I don't know what he told Uncle about us. It could have been a part of faking for the reality show. I randomly flip through his poetry book. It feels good to hold a part of him in my arms. Some old poems are very dark. The recent ones are livelier. The last one is about a girl he loves. I read it again and again and cry. I wonder if he could have meant it for me. I want to believe he does. I replay the argument in my head again, as I have already done umpteen times. Perhaps I was too quick to judge. But I did ask him everything so clearly. I am re-evaluating each of his answers when Mansi barges into the house.

'You broke up with Samir?' she asks, clearly miffed, 'and you didn't tell me?!'

'I didn't break up. He did. And I didn't tell because I didn't want to dwell on the past. You only keep telling me to move ahead,' I reply indignantly.

'He couldn't have,' she says, disbelieving me. 'What did you do?'

'What do you mean what did I do? I offered myself on a platter and he chose to write a book instead on our story,' I say sulkily. She is supposed to side with me. Why is she defending him?

'Do you know he was going to propose to you at the finale event?' Mansi says.

I give her a don't-fuck-with-me look.

'Oh Meg! He made me practise so many times, it's not funny. I even told him about Vir and he was okay with it.'

I stare wide-eyed at Mansi with a doleful expression on my face. So Sharma Aunty was telling the truth. Samir did want to grow old with me. He even wrote that poem for me. I start crying.

'Listen, I know I have always told you that men only want sex,' Mansi talks to me like a mature adult. 'I still believe that. But if I had to bet on one asshole, it would be S. S-(ing)-hol.'

I laugh feeling lighter and happier than I have in weeks.

'By the way, I am moving in with Neeraj today,' Mansi mentions offhandedly. 'We intend to live-in like you guys and test our love.'

And then seeing the ghastly look on my face, she says, 'I had no idea you had broken up with Samir. Okay, I can wait till you call Samir.'

I call immediately but his phone is switched off. I call Payal to check and she reminds me that Samir Sir has already left for Maldives. But of course, most of my team is also leaving tonight for Maldives for the wedding. I want to go too. But I don't have a ticket or a visa. And I can't risk Papa getting another heart attack because I visited a water body purer than any river in India, but unfortunately outside the holy supervision of the Indian Gods. There is only one person who can help me now. I call Didi, while Mansi goes to her room to pack.

'I need your help'.

'You babysit Diyu for four hours next weekend,' Di bargains upfront.

'Why four? Last time it was three!' I argue. She is taking unfair advantage of my desperation.

'Bye. Talk to you later,' she is about to disconnect when I agree grudgingly, 'Ok, whatever.'

'So how much money do you want to borrow?' she asks.

How does she know I want money? Well I guess I am always short on money.

'It's not only money. I also need you to convince Ma-Papa for something,' I say, sheepishly.

'Hey, you aren't pregnant before marriage, are you?' She is amused. 'I'm afraid it's going to be twelve hours of babysitting for that!'

'Hell with babysitting, Di. I need to go to the Maldives. Tonight.'

'Oh, but you were anyway supposed to go there with Samir right, for work?' She sounds baffled.

I recount the entire story in short.

'Whoa! You decided to forgo Maldives because you had a fight with Samir?'

I try to tell her that it was more than a fight. It was a MAJOR fight, but she ignores me completely, like she always does. 'Mehu baby you must really love this guy to forgo Maldives for him.'

Thank god, she gets the conclusion right, although her derivation is a bit screwed.

'I will do the bookings. Consider this as a wedding gift from my side. But the babysitting hours are still required.'

'What about Ma-Papa?' I ask.

And then she reveals the entire prophecy to me, enjoying each and every one of my gasps and OMGs. 'So as long as you are with Samir, you are good.'

'But Di, you don't believe in all this prophecy bakwaas, do you?' I ask.

'Prophecy is only someone's thought. A thought by itself is nothing, Meha; your belief makes it true or false. Believing is like feeding oxygen to a thought. So believe in your love and go get Samir.'

Wow. Di is smart. I thank her profusely and promise to notify her as soon as I get hold of Samir and extract a kiss.

My MJ tunes to 'Muskurane ki wajah tum ho, gungunane ki wajah tum ho...' as I board the flight the next day to Male, Maldives.

Be My Nothing

Decorated in bubblegum pink and deep peach, the wedding venue is delectable. A colour palette so yummy, I could eat it! The fragrant and fresh, pineapple-flower vases, clustering around the tall transparent centrepiece on each table, compliment the lively colours. They were NetGen's idea. The team is busy getting the place ready for the lunch. I know I ought to meet them, but first things first. I need to confess my love and for that I need some liquid courage. I head to the bar set in a glass pagoda, surrounded by palm trees. I take a sip of the Sangria and look around.

My heart misses a beat as I spot Samir in a light-blue, open shirt and white shorts. He is standing farther away from the bar counter facing the beach, holding his camera in his hands, his back towards me. In a few moments, he turns around and starts walking towards the bar, looking down at his phone. I quickly gulp down the whole glass.

'Shining in the sand and sun like a pearl upon the ocean, come and feel me...oh feel me,' crooning the song that always lands me in his arms, I purposely collide with the crisp linen shirt. His eyes sparkle with happiness briefly as they meet mine before they become dark and dull.

'Sorry, I hope I didn't hurt you,' I apologize.

'You couldn't have,' he says gruffly, his body rigid at our contact.

'What do you mean?'

'Can't break what is already broken, can you?' he answers cryptically, as he bends down to pick up his fallen sunshades.

Ouch. He looks like someone put him into a blender and hit the whip button. I bite my lips in regret. He is hurt. Very hurt. But it was not all my fault. He could have given me some signs of his plans to propose to me. And he shouldn't have kept the book a secret. And it's not like I haven't suffered enough.

'Brokenhearted! That makes two of us.'

'Really? You look all shiny and bright.'

Not fair. Just because I managed to schedule a facial at the last minute, before the flight and I look all polished, doesn't make my heart any less bruised. He has no idea how much I have cried in last two weeks. Except for the pain in his eyes, Samir looks fit and fine too. His sinewy arms tanned, possibly by being out in the ocean for the yacht shoot yesterday. His face is taut. His lips are soft and...

'So do you still love me...er...your ex-live-in-girlfriend?' I ask, trying to focus.

'Love is a co-experienced positive emotion. Without reciprocation, it can't go very far just like a bicycle with one punctured tyre,' he says with a wry smile. 'What about you? Do you still love your ex-live-in-boyfriend?'

'That's why I am here. You see, the guy who broke my heart, my ex-live-in-boyfriend, he is the wedding photographer here,' I whisper secretively.

'Aha! Him I've met. He's a good guy,' Samir says, a little more relaxed now that he knows I am here for him. 'He told me his girlfriend dropped him like third-period French?'

'See, that's the thing. He has got it all wrong. I didn't leave him,' I defend my position.

'Well you call a guy an opportunist, insensitive and promiscuous and you still expect him to stick around?' Samir snaps angrily. 'If you want a loyal dog, you better look in a pet store.'

I didn't exactly call him those names. I think he is overreacting. Maybe it's the heat getting to him. Winning him back seems harder than putting toothpaste back in the tube.

'Hey, is your ex-live-in-girlfriend the one who is planning this wedding? I thought I saw you two steal an intimate, we-go-far-back-in-time look a while back?'

'Yup, she's the one,' he admits.

'What a coincidence!' I exclaim. 'Isn't it amazing that we must meet like this at a wedding planned by our EXes? Would you care for some cool beer, so we can further EXplore our connection?'

'Umm…I've actually got to be going,' he says indecisively. Why is he being so stubborn?

'Just so you know, I am the most B-U-T-full chick available at this wedding. You won't get buttier company'.

His face softens at our shared joke. There is almost a hint of smile trying to reach his eyes. He leans forward a bit. I think he is going to kiss me and I desperately want him too. Oh no, he is looking away. He is still angry. I need a change of tactics here. Mansi always said that men are like cats. Chase them and they run away. Ignore them and they come running to you.

So as I quickly spot NetGen in the distance, I say, 'Sorry. I got to go. Duty is calling. Maybe we can meet at the beach later in the evening if you have time.'

I turn to leave. I am almost worried I've made a mistake when a vague 'ok-see-ya' reaches my ears. I raise my hand in thumbs up casually to let him know I heard him and walk away.

I confidently sashay by the table where NetGen is intimately chatting with a tall firang. Hey, something is amiss. My signature—freshly-cut lime pieces are missing in the transparent mason jar on the table. Your team can only do so much. The final personal touch at any wedding has to be yours. I am glad I am here. I message the team to get it fixed and then walk over to the beautiful pier jutting into the clear blue ocean, where the wedding mandap is going to be set up for tomorrow. The chairs will be decorated with alternating pink and peach-knotted bows. The mandap itself will have peach curtains, lined with fresh pink and green flowers on the four corner poles and a thick string of matching flowers all around the top edges. With low seating and a huge brass hawan kund, it will be the most beautiful mandap I have ever done. Though it's hard to concentrate on anything when your heart is pining to be in your lover's arms, thankfully my work is very exciting. And it keeps me on my flat heels till the sun decides to call it a day.

I quickly shower and get into my most comfortable clothes. No clinging bottoms. No plunging neckline. I am playing it uber cool.

I find Samir seated at the open restaurant by the beach, in casual light brown dungarees and a plain dark brown, round neck tee.

'Look who is here!' he says feigning surprise at running into me. 'We do have a special EXtra connect!' he jokes light-heartedly.

There is nothing more joyful than seeing the smile on a face you love. As I take the seat opposite him, the sea breeze blows my hair all over. I tie it back with a scarf. For a few minutes, we just sit in shared silence. Looking at the last rays of the sun disappear in the vastness of the ocean. Watching the restless waves travel for miles only to shower their love on the shore and become one with it and then start the journey all over again. It is like when you love someone, you have to offer it up constantly—to cherish the other person. Just being together cannot make a relationship last forever, it takes endless moments of love to make it forever.

'Samir,' I am unwilling to break the lovely silence, but I need to say it before it's too late.

'Ya,' he says softly.

I try to read his face. He seems calm, but his eyes look forlorn.

'I am sorry for doubting you,' I apologize.

'I am sorry too Meha. I never attended the finale event. I know we would have won,' he says genuinely.

Oh! Of course, he doesn't know about the ring and he is feeling responsible for having me lose the cash prize. It serves him right for not taking my calls! But I want to tell him now. So I tell him the whole story. He is not at all surprised to hear that Sonia is off to Spainier pastures. It seems he always knew that Sonia's love for him was only skin-deep. He also never felt 'the-same-love' for her. Knowing that what he feels for me is special makes me feel, well, special. I feel all the pieces of my heart joining back together, and I am beaming with an unbearable happiness.

'So, are you seeing someone?' I ask after two bottles of beer are down.

'Only you!' he says, intently gazing into his eyes. 'Are you in love with anyone?'

'I think so,' I admit at last.

'And you think it will last forever?' he asks, the longing evident in his eyes now.

'Someone very close to me once told me that love is rather over-rated and nothing lasts forever,' I say, looking straight into his honest eyes.

'So will you be my nothing?' I propose. Just like that. No ring. No fancy outfit. No candles. It's just him and me by the beach where it all started.

'Be My Nothing. That's a nice line. Let me write it down,' he says beaming with happiness and opens his phone to jot it down in his notes.

'Hey!' I say, mildly complaining and get up to grab his phone.

He swiftly slides the phone down his back pocket and grabs hold of me instead and then he starts to sing the Senorita song from *Zindagi Naa Milegi Dobara*.

'Na main samjha, Na main jaana, jo bhi tumne mujhse kaha hai Senorita. Magar phir bhi, na jane kyun, mujhe sun ke acha laga hai Senorita.'

My mind tells me he is really out of tune, but my heart has never heard anything more melodious. I don't know who makes the first move, but we start dancing, and our lips are locked together for a long time.

I wake up in the morning, safely ensconced in Samir's arms, blissfully unaware of the torrential downpour, which has now become a trademark at beach weddings that are designed by me and shot by Samir. This is the third one in a row, after Goa, Phi Phi and now Maldives. I look out from our balcony to find the pier completely submerged under water with no sign of the mandap.

What follows is a flurry of action, a whole new floating mandap at the hotel lobby and a whole lot of unplanned fun.

Let's Have Coffee

Six months later

I can tell that Samir is lost in his thoughts. He hasn't noticed that I am wearing the vintage butterfly earrings especially for today's occasion.

'Feeling nervous?' I ask him.

'A little.'

'You will be fine,' I assure him, giving his hands a tight squeeze.

'Want a drink?' I ask as a waiter passes by with wine glasses.

He doesn't. I guess he would rather retain his logical prowess so he can impress them. I would too for something so important in my life, although I find alcohol sharpens my logical brain cells.

'What if they hate me and rip me apart?' he asks, really concerned.

'Of course they will rip you apart. It's their job,' I reply coolly. It's so much easier to stay calm when it's someone else's neck on the line.

'You are not helping,' he says, slightly irritated.

'What do you want me to do? Lie?' I ask laughing.

'No, please, never,' he is earnest.

I smile lovingly at him. Not lying to each other is a pact we made six months ago as we embarked on our journey together as a couple in a LTR—committed, long-term relationship. And to my credit, I haven't lied since then. I tell him about all my online purchases. I tell him when I don't like a picture he has clicked. He is okay with all of those.

'I will love you, no matter what,' I say tenderly and plant a gentle kiss on his lips.

Immediately his tense muscles relax and a faint smile forms on his lips.

'How about a quickie?' he asks, his eyes brightening up at the prospect.

'Now?' I am surprised by his suggestion.

I see some people at the snack counter outside and hear many more talking excitedly in the adjoining hall. We are in a convention centre at Epicentre, Gurgaon, for Samir's book launch. There are over fifty people gathered in the hall including my parents and Di. Some journalists have already arrived. Everyone is enjoying wine and cheese at the moment, but the event is about to commence. We are just waiting for the chief guest. Besides, I am wearing a new georgette dress, which I don't want to get all crumpled. I didn't exactly plan for sex.

'It always helps me relax and ease the tension,' he says to convince me.

I know it does. And he is looking rather hot, his hair all scrunched up in a freestyle look and his eyes rather pensive and dreamy.

'Where?' I ask, considering the option but not completely convinced yet.

'Loo?'

'There is only one each for men and women here. Can't

keep it occupied,' I reason.

'We could go to the store room. I know the receptionist has a key,' he says.

'Why am I not surprised? You have done it before in the store room here,' I speak my mind out loud. It comes with the no-lying contract.

He just shrugs his shoulders vaguely.

'With the receptionist?' I ask unbelievably and then decide I don't want to know his answer. Past is past, I try to remind myself. It's immaterial.

'Please Senorita, we only have ten minutes before I get called on the stage,' he says desperately.

'Oh! Sam, you know I prefer foreplay and I can't do it under stress,' I resist, although I am beginning to feel excited by the idea.

'What if I tell you that your left nipple is pressing hard against the fabric of your blouse,' he says, holding me tightly around the waist.

I feel a shiver run down my spine as his cold fingers find their way on my back, having slipped under my blouse. I can feel his hardness rub against my skirt, his back to the guests.

'Sam, Ma is looking this way,' I panic and try to pull away from him, but he holds me tight, his hand having found way to the front and now freely fondling my breasts.

'She can see nothing,' he reassures.

I peek over his shoulders and realize he is right. We are standing in one corner, secluded from everyone, and I am completely hidden behind his body. I am glad that no one can see what Samir is doing, but the idea of being seen by someone in the public heightens my desire immediately.

'Meet me by the stairs. I will get the keys to the store room and see you in five,' he says, withdrawing his hands abruptly and leaving me standing by myself, craving for more.

Highly aroused, I rush out of the hall to the other side, avoiding Tanu Di, Mansi and a whole lot of folks from Samir's office whom I know. I am about to exit the hall, when Sharma Aunty stops me and asks about Samir. I know she has flown especially for his book launch from New York, where she now spends most of her time with her son, and she wants Samir's help in getting Uncle's poetry book published, but she will have to wait. I promise Aunty to send Samir her way as soon as I find him. And finish having sex with him.

We both reach the stairs together and climb up two steps at a time, his hand locked in mine, the desire driving us mad now. We quickly dash to the storeroom on the second floor, unlock it and shut it behind us. I am rushing out of my dress as he unzips his pants. His eager hands are all over me. I am wet. His lips have found mine. He is on fire and I am only too willing to burn along with him. Five minutes later he wipes the sweat from his forehead, tucks his shirt back in, gives me a peck on the cheek and marches out smiling gaily.

'See you at the launch,' he shouts back, already climbing down the stairs with a certain spring in his step.

'See you,' I say softly, glowing with happiness. I slowly inhale the musty smell of the storeroom mixed with his wild rose fragrance, as I fish around for my clothes.

When I reach the convention room after having fixed my hair and makeup a few minutes later, I find Samir near the stage surrounded by eager girls some of who are journalists. As I walk by, I hear a sexy looking reporter ask him how he likes his coffee. He pauses for a second, his eyes dancing mischievously and replies in a tone so seductive that it can make any woman go weak in her knees, 'Without sugar, except when I have it with my girlfriend.'

I hear a collective sigh of disappointment from the girls and it fills me with utmost joy. I walk over to where Tanu Di is standing, busy giving advice on pre-natal classes to Radhika who is now in her third trimester. I am still not overly fond of Radhika, who manages to look sexy and gorgeous even with her bump. Radhika is also not as warm to me as she is towards Di, but ever since Samir and I announced our relationship officially on Facebook, she has stopped casting those ugly-duckling stares. Anusha, who is now Radhika's sister-in-law, tells me that Radhika only disliked me because she thought I caused Samir grief and she really cares for Samir. I have begun to trust Anusha's judgement, but I can never stop being jealous of Radhika for having had an affair with Samir. I guess it's the same for Radhika.

I give a warm hug to Di and compliment Radhika on her pregnancy glow. Di inquires where I was hiding all this while. I ignore the question and instead ask her about the latest website she is designing. She is only too happy to talk about it having finally found her feet in web consulting. Not only has the work brought back a purpose in her life, she is also re-discovering a renewed love in her marriage, and the advantages of an unmarried younger sister.

'Hey Mehu, can you babysit the girls next weekend? Your jiju and I are planning to get away for a night,' Di asks in an extra sweet voice.

'What's in it for me Di?' I reply smartly. You, see, she has exploited my needs so many times that I have finally learnt not to give free favours anymore.

We get involved reminding each other of the various favours from the past and who owes whom more. As we are busy settling scores, Radhika excuses herself to go to the loo. Ten minutes later when Mansi joins us, Di has reminded me of five more instances for which I owe her. It's not fair that she has such good memory. Mansi can tell from my bewildered expression that I am losing the battle with Di.

A waiter passes by and both Mansi and I help ourselves to a drink. I also pick a small piece of the delicious, herb cheese.

'Hey, you seem to have lost weight honey. Looks like Samir is not feeding you aloo parathas anymore,' Mansi chuckles light-heartedly.

I smile. Mansi knows how to cheer me up anytime. Samir is feeding me parathas all right. It must be all the Vitamin S that he feeds me too, that's causing the weight loss. I ask Mansi about her life and how things are going with the CXO. She tells me that she is really happy with Neeraj except he is scared of re-marrying as he just got out of a nasty divorce. I think Neeraj is insecure about having a designer girlfriend like Mansi just like I could never believe that Samir could be mine, for real, forever. I should have a chat with him.

Since Mansi has become a very high flying, celebrity fashion consultant and she doesn't live with us anymore, I don't get to meet her as often. So I ask her to come over with her CXO one of these Sundays for Samir's aloo parathas. She misses our Sunday fun and is keen to come. I doubt she will, but I don't hold it against her. I don't need to meet her every weekend to prove our closeness. I know she is always there for me when I need her—like she has made the effort today to ensure that Soha Ali Khan comes as the chief guest for Samir's book launch. It's so apt that Soha should launch this book. I remember how Soha had told me in the first week of the reality show itself that Samir was totally into me. I find myself glowing a little more in his love and wonder how I landed up being the luckiest person in this world. And then I tell myself that sometimes love doesn't have to be perfect, it only needs to be true. And then I drink some more wine.

The energy and excitement around me announces that Soha Ali Khan has arrived. Mansi excuses herself to go welcome her. Dressed in a flowing red gown with a front cut above the knees, Soha takes everyone's breath away. I watch Samir joke with her on the stage as he hands her a copy of his book. Soha holds up the book cover of *Let's Have Coffee*, Samir's first novel, for everyone to see. The room is buzzing with sounds of shutters and phone cameras. Everyone applauds as Samir calls me over to the stage and introduces me as his inspiration behind the book. I blush at the honour and then soon get away from the limelight. This is his moment and I want to enjoy it from a distance. I take a seat in a corner and listen with rapt attention as Samir reads out a few passages from the book.

'I woke up that morning to find her gone. I had so wanted to tell her that I love her. I rushed to the lobby but she had checked out. I called her number, it was switched off. Then I found this note under my phone. It said not to come after her. I still tried. I sent her an FB request. I tried calling her a few times but in no vain. I hadn't realized it at the time but I had fallen in love with her. I kept moving from one relationship to another, all the time looking for her. Sometimes the girl had her laugh. Sometimes she had her humour. But none were her. It's only when she fell from the sky in my arms six months ago that I realized I didn't want to look for anyone anymore. I realized I loved her.'

I figure a lot of reporters will soon be looking to hear my side of the story and while it would be nice to see my name in print, I would rather my personal life stays private. I know you are thinking about the reality show, but that was only a game. Even though my feelings for Sam were real even then, now, my relationship with Samir is too important for me to have it analysed in media.

I take refuge in the digital world. I respond to an NRI client whose wedding I am planning in Greece next month. I like a post by Pyare. He is standing amidst his freshly delivered cow babies having gone back to full time organic farming. He never said anything to anyone but he calls me every now and then and indirectly enquires about NetGen. I tell him the latest on her boyfriend scene—last month it was a real-world chef from a five-star hotel, the month before it was an upcoming guitarist, and previous to that was an online gamer like herself. She is really on an experiential spree. I know, Pyare still loves her. Something tells me theirs will be a story much like ours, five years from now.

I spot Ma carrying twenty copies of the book, one each for each one of her kitty friends, to get them signed by Samir. Papa is standing in a corner, lost in his own world. He wasn't very supportive of our continued living in without marriage so Samir and I gave him the green signal, but he hasn't said anything about us getting married lately. I guess he is just waiting for an auspicious date. Of course, there is no way for me to know the real reason behind his matured silence. Even Mom and Di don't have a clue about the latest prediction by Chugh uncle that while I need to mate with wind to stay safe, I can never be married to Samir. That marriage with Samir will calm my stars, but it will create havoc for Samir eventually causing his death. I don't know why Papa hasn't shared the prophecy with anyone. He likes Samir even more since Samir took him for the Mansarovar yatra in a helicopter.

Whenever Papa will deem it necessary to tell me about the prophecy, I am sure I will tell him that the prophecy needs my belief to become real and I only believe in loving Samir till the end.

Please wish us luck, so our love can develop like wine, slowly, tastefully forever over years, even if we end up like the two butterflies following each other with no binding of marriage and yet together forever.

Acknowledgements

I am truly grateful to be able to publish my third novel. Both my previous novels were, to some extent, based on incidents from my life. This is my first novel that is largely fictional. For those who have read my first two novels, my favourite character Tanu continues to exist as the protagonist's elder sister.

Few years ago, I recall reading a newspaper article on Invisible Boyfriend app. I wondered how I would behave if random hookups and sex were so accessible and acceptable when I was in my twenties. Is my belief in love outdated and overrated? Why do people get (and stay) married? I asked my social media friends for book ideas and while most of them wanted me to write a book on midlife crisis, I chose to untangle love and relationships in today's digital world.

I couldn't have written this book without talking to real people from the current generation. Foremost, I would like to thank my neighbour Ritu Lall's niece, Devika Narain, who is a rocking wedding planner. She told me all the interesting stories behind a wedding and allowed me a peek into her personal world. I am also thankful to Payal, Varun, Deepika, Joyita, and many more who openly shared their life stories and enlightened me.

I also want to thank my BFF, Sonal Bansal, the one person

who keeps me sane. It was while I was telling her how having sex has become as casual as having coffee that the book's title took shape.

Shivani Kapoor, for her encouraging smile and readiness for beer (or chai) meetups while I iterated various ideas for the book. It was her enthusiasm for the plot that helped me see it through.

My girl's trip gang—Shalini Jain, Pooja Goyal, Puja Gupta, Priyanka Aggarwal—and especially Shilpa Malik for her unknowing (and possibly unwilling) inspiration for the protagonist Meha's sense of humour. Thanks girls, for always being there and helping me shape my story.

I would like to thank Ritu Uberoy, my co-founder at RivoKids, who understood my desire to write (yet again) and let me off the moral hook as I divided my time between our e-venture and the book.

I would like to express gratitude to my friend and bestseller author Nirupama Subramaniyan. As always, she read my manuscript and gave me valuable feedback. I also thank Anita Vasudeva for her critical feedback on the characters and storyline. I know I can always count on you.

I would also like to thank my WhatsApp group Crazy Core—Sujatha and Pawan Kumar, Nisha and Bhupi Singh, Kamal and Amarinder Dhaliwal—for ensuring that I stay crazy.

The entire Rupa Publications team—Kapish Mehra for reading my synopsis and immediately liking it; the Managing Editor, Elina Majumdar, for having the confidence in my book and its youth appeal and my Editor-in-Charge, Sunayna Saraswat, for her careful edits and thoughtful comments.

My late dad (RIP), mom, bhai, bhabhi and sister, for supporting me always and my mother-in-law who brightens my life with her positivity.

My one and only husband, Alok for keeping love alive in my life.

Most importantly, my daughters, Smiti and Muskaan, who helped my character get the 'whateva' attitude, came up with funny analogies, helped me get out of the mess in every chapter, and even wrote part of the prologue. I hope one day the three of us will co-author a successful novel.

www.ingramcontent.com/pod-product-compliance
Lightning Source LLC
Chambersburg PA
CBHW022141060526
44654CB00043B/616